Joel

The Craigdon Family Dynasty

Book Two

CHRIS TAYLOR

LCT Productions Pty Ltd
18364 Kamilaroi Highway, Narrabri NSW 2390

ISBN. 978-1-925119-76-3 (Paperback)

Joel is a work of fiction. Names, characters, places, brands, media and incidents either are the product of the author's imagination or are used fictitiously. Any resemblance to actual persons, living or dead, events, or locales, is entirely coincidental.

Published in the United States of America.

Books by Chris Taylor

THE MUNRO FAMILY SERIES

The Profiler
The Investigator
The Predator
The Betrayal
The Deception
The Negotiator
The Christmas Vigil
The Ransom
The Defendant
The Shooting
The Maker
(Available in Audio)

THE SYDNEY HARBOUR HOSPITAL SERIES

The Perfect Husband
The Body Thief
The Baby Snatchers
The Final Bullet
The Debt Collector
The Lab Test
The Stolen Identity
The Cliff-top Killer
The Likeable Fraudster

THE SYDNEY LEGAL SERIES

An Accidental Murderer
At the Hand of Her Father
A Woman Scorned
Lies and Deception
Ordinary Evil
The Ties That Bind
The Perfect Crime
A Toxic Inheritance
Malicious Love

THE CRAIGDON FAMILY SERIES
Callum
Joel
Isabella
Nicholas
Sophia
Flynn
Noah
Logan
Elizabeth

THE BARRINGTON FAMILY SERIES
Broken Lives
Broken Promises
Broken Bonds
Broken Spirits
Broken Vows
Broken Minds
Broken Dreams
Broken Hearts
Broken Homes

Chris Taylor writing as
BELLA CHRISTIAN

THIS IS WHERE IT ENDS SERIES
(in order)
Jessie's Story
Ryan's Story
Holly's Story
Sarah's Story
Veronica's Story

Get a FREE book when you sign up for Chris Taylor's
newsletter at: www.christaylorauthor.com.au

Love Audiobooks? Check out Chris Taylor Books on audio on Audible.com, Amazon.com and Apple Books.

Join Chris Taylor's Facebook reader group/fan page and be among the first to receive news of book releases, read and review books prior to release and other amazing offers. Join Now at: www.facebook.com/groups/1758023621144744/

Find out more about all of Chris Taylor's books, by visiting her website at: www.christaylorauthor.com.au

Dedication

This book is dedicated to Detective Superintendent Michael Kilfoyle (ret) for his endless enthusiasm and patience with me and my ceaseless questions in my quest to make my stories realistic and credible and the very best they can be.

And as always, to my husband, Linden. My best friend, my soul mate. I love you to the moon and back.

Acknowledgments

As usual, no book comes into being without a lot of help and support by my friends and family. A world of thanks must go to my wonderful editor, Pat Thomas. Thank you for everything that you do to make my stories even more amazing than I could ever dare to dream. To former Detective Superintendent Michael Kilfoyle, thank you for lending my story credibility. Any mistakes are wholly my own.

To Mary and all of the team at Miblart, thank you for the fantastic book cover. To my sister, Nicole Guihot and to my friends, Ally Thomson and Sue Ricardo, thank you for your excellent editorial comments, proof reading skills and suggestions. I hope you like the final result.

To Amy Atwell, Kirby and the dedicated team at Author EMS who are so much more than book formatters. Amy, once again, thank you for your magic.

To the fantastic writer organizations such as Romance Writers of Australia, Romance Writers of America and Romance Writers of New Zealand for all the help, support and encouragement they offer new and aspiring writers, including me.

To my readers, thank you for your support and love for my stories. Your encouragement and enjoyment make this journey all worthwhile.

And lastly, to my friends and family, especially my husband and children. Thank you for putting up with late dinners and even later conversations as I've emerged day after day from the sometimes scary but always enthralling world I've created on my computer.

Chapter One

The throbbing tempo of the music was so loud in the densely populated nightclub it reverberated through Joel Craigdon's chest and actually hurt his ears. Not that he minded. After the week he'd endured, the pounding beat from the state-of-the-art speakers in Sydney's illustrious Ivy Bar was a welcome distraction. He'd barely been home a week from his three-month European vacation, courtesy of a ten million dollar inheritance windfall, but as far as work went, it felt like he'd never left.

Already he was knee-deep in a fraud investigation that involved McClintock Properties, a high profile company that also happened to be his late father's fiercest competitor. When it came to business, McClintock had a reputation for being ruthless. It seemed someone in their ranks also had a penchant for theft. As a senior detective with the New South Wales Fraud Squad, Joel had been given the job of determining who was behind the large-scale transactions that were leaving McClintock accounts and being diverted offshore.

But it was Friday night in the city and he was hell-bent on doing his best to forget about work for a few hours and have a good time. Already he had a buzz on. The drinks had been flowing freely between him and his mates. They were work colleagues and by tacit agreement they were all there to let their hair down.

"Wan' another beer, James?" Joel shouted above the din. He lifted his empty glass toward Detective James Shepherd who'd been making out drunkenly with his wife. Sally-Ann looked at Joel and smiled.

"Thank you, Joel, but I think my husband's had enough," she replied.

James pulled a face, but then broke into a lopsided grin. He drew his wife close and planted another kiss on her mouth. "I think she's right." James winked at Joel. "We're going to get out of here." With that, James took Sally-Ann by the hand.

"Nice beard, by the way," Sally-Ann murmured as she pecked Joel on the cheek. "It suits you. Very European. Very chic."

Her husband merely rolled his eyes and turned away. With Sally-Ann in tow, James pushed his way through the crowd, headed for the exit.

Joel looked after them, feeling wistful. James was blissfully married to the woman of his dreams, Sally-Ann, a Chinese-Australian. She was one of the rising stars at the reputable law firm, Sydney Legal. Joel had been working with James in homicide when he and Sally-Ann met and fell in love. Though their road to domestic bliss had come with challenges, Joel had never seen his friend looking so happy. Too bad Joel hadn't found the same thing with Mary-Jane. They'd sure tried hard and long enough to make it happen.

Joel grimaced. It was Friday night and the Ivy Bar was packed with revelers. Determined to shake off his gloomy thoughts, he gazed around the club. Beautiful twenty-somethings, both guys and girls, were dancing to the throb of the music. Eyes closed, arms in the air, a press of bodies, heated flesh. Others were gathered near the bar. Conversation and laughter was competing with the din of the music. The general vibe was electric and tinged with a hint of desperation. It was as if the partygoers were determined to have the best time of their lives…or collapse in a sweaty, drunken heap, while trying.

Determined to recapture his party mood, Joel shouldered his way back to the bar and deposited his empty glass on the counter. He caught the eye of the buff barman and ordered another. With his arm casually propped against the bar, he turned to survey the crowd.

There was a rowdy group of young women screaming the words to the song being played by the DJ. One of the group wore a white veil. *A bachelorette party…*

A bit beyond them were a couple with their tongues down each other's throats, pressed together, hips gyrating, oblivious to the fact they were in public. Or perhaps they didn't care…

Joel's gaze drifted toward the place where tables and chairs were set up for those patrons who chose to sit. The lighting there was much brighter. His gaze landed on a stunning blond who sat at a table of dark-suited men. Their ties had been loosened, top buttons undone, and much laughter was being shared. The blond smiled occasionally, but it was clear she wasn't absorbed in the conversation. Joel wondered which man she was with.

She sat closest to one about Joel's age who looked like he could have just stepped off the set of a fashion shoot. Though it was late on a Friday night, the man didn't have a hair out of place. He looked vaguely familiar, but the beers Joel had consumed over the past few hours befuddled his mind and he couldn't place him.

As if becoming aware of his scrutiny, the blond woman looked up and saw him. Their gazes locked. It was like something out of a sappy movie. Joel's heart pounded. His body instinctively hardened. She had the bluest eyes he'd ever seen. Her long hair fell in soft waves over one shoulder. Her lips were full and red. The beguiling almond shape of her eyes was emphasized with black eyeliner. The thick lashes were dark with mascara. And then she lifted a single arched eyebrow in silent inquiry and he almost turned around to make sure no one was behind him…

Maintaining his cool, he calmly raised his glass in salute. Her eyes gleamed with amusement. She smiled, displaying perfect white teeth. She was every bit as glamorous as the man she sat beside. And then her companion bent his head and said something to her. She put her hand on his arm and nodded. The gesture was casual, familiar.

Jealousy stabbed Joel in the gut. He turned back toward the bar and drowned his disappointment in another drink. He might be known as a playboy among his circle of friends, but he drew the line at moving in on another man's woman.

Sheridan McClintock plastered a smile on her face and pretended she was enjoying herself. The conversation around the table had turned to football and she could barely suppress a groan. What was it about seemingly intelligent men who could almost come to fisticuffs over who would win the premiership? Watching football bored her to tears. It was even worse being forced to sit around with her brother and his mates and listen to the pros and cons of each team, hear about the players who were injured and out for the season and others who were on report… *Who cares?*

Zane glanced at her. Bending close so she could hear him, he asked, "Having fun?"

It was all Sheridan could do not to roll her eyes. It wasn't her brother's fault. Zane had only been trying to cheer her up by inviting her along. After dumping her cheating boyfriend six months earlier, it seemed she still hadn't regained her former spirit. Zane said he was concerned for her. He urged her to get out, have fun.

"You're only twenty-seven, Sheridan. Hardly ancient.

You're better off without that dickhead, anyway. I couldn't stand him from the start."

"His name is Dwight and he wasn't always a dickhead," she protested. "And you didn't think so, either. After all, you were the one who hired him. We wouldn't have crossed paths if you hadn't."

Zane growled. "So it's my fault, is it? I didn't tell you to fall for him. Or for the asshole to break your heart."

Sheridan compressed her lips and sighed. At the time she'd discovered Dwight cheating she'd been furious and upset; now that she'd had time to come to terms with the demise of her relationship, she wasn't at all sure he'd broken her heart.

"Come out with me and the guys," Zane had urged. "We're going to the Ivy Bar. Come and have some fun."

And so she'd pulled on a slinky black designer dress and matching black high heels. She'd carefully applied her makeup and put the straightener through her hair. To her annoyance, it still held a bit of a wave, but it was the best she could do. At least it wasn't curly, like it usually was.

She'd left for one of Sydney's most popular nightspots feeling good, determined to enjoy herself. And for a while, she had. She'd known her brother's friends for a long time. They knew each other so well, they were almost family. A steady stream of drinks flowed along with the laughter, but now the conversation had turned to football.

Feeling eyes upon her, Sheridan looked up toward the bar. Her gaze locked on the sexiest guy she'd ever seen. With hair so dark it was almost black and a neat black beard that caught the overhead lights, he seemed like something out of a dream. *Or a fantasy…*

Her heart skipped a beat and then pounded like she'd just run a marathon. He stared at her, his clear blue eyes full of invitation. And then his gaze dipped lower, over her breasts and lower still before returning to her face. There wasn't much of her he could see because of her position at the table, but everywhere his gaze had touched now tingled with awareness. Shocked at her boldness, she tilted her head and looked straight back at him, raising a single eyebrow as if daring him to come over.

And then Zane leaned toward her once again, a slight frown marring his expression. "We can leave, if you like."

She rested her hand on his forearm, grateful for his concern. "No, don't be silly. I'm a big girl. You're not responsible for me having a good time. In fact, I might go and get a drink."

"I can do that," Zane offered. "What would you like?"

"It's okay. I want to look over the cocktail menu," she lied. "Have fun with the boys. Don't worry about me. I'll be fine."

With that, she scooted out of her chair and collected her evening bag. After slinging it over her shoulder she gave the men at her table a jaunty wave. Without thinking about what she was doing, she made her way over to where the handsome stranger sat with his back to the room.

A whiff of expensive cologne drifted toward her and she was beset with a flurry of nerves. She'd never been the kind of girl who propositioned strangers. Hell, she'd never propositioned anyone, not even Dwight. He'd pursued her for more than a year before she gave in and went out to dinner with him.

And here she was, mulling over how to flirt openly with this stranger.

What the hell am I thinking? Am I crazy? Maybe I should just get out of here before he sees me…

And then he turned and smiled at her and all thoughts of leaving disappeared. He was even better looking up close. His eyes were more cobalt than blue. His skin was tanned and healthy. His teeth gleamed white against the blackness of his beard. Her heart beat so fast she thought it might leap right out of her chest.

"Hi, I'm Joel," he said.

His voice was deep, confident, sexy. It matched his physical presence. He had an air of authority about him that was instantly appealing. So different from Dwight who'd been almost groveling in his approach. At the beginning it had been flattering, but after a while, it had become downright irritating. The man in front of her didn't look like he'd grovel for anything.

She looked down at the hand he extended toward her and took it. "Sh-Sharon," she stammered, not at all sure why she'd given a fake name.

His expression didn't reveal he had the slightest inkling of her deception. Instead, he said, "It's nice to meet you, Sharon. Can I buy you a drink?"

Recovering her aplomb, she took the empty seat beside him and pulled herself up to the bar.

"I'll have a vodka and tonic with a slice of lime, please."

He smiled in acknowledgement. "One vodka and tonic with a slice of lime it is," he murmured, his eyes alight with amusement. With that, he signaled the barman.

Sheridan watched the confident way he gave her order and then asked for another beer. He was a man used to taking control. She liked that. It was refreshing to spend time with someone who appeared confident in who he was and what he stood for.

"Are you sure your boyfriend won't mind you talking to me?"

The question was asked in a lazy tone, but Sheridan caught the watchfulness in Joel's gaze. He must have seen her with Zane. She laughed and waved her hand, dismissing his concern.

"Oh, he's not my boyfriend. That's just my brother and his friends. They let me tag along." Realizing how pathetic that sounded, she pulled a face. "I'm sorry. I sound like a loser.

Like a single, twenty-seven-year-old woman who relies on her brother for a night out. Ugh!" And then realizing just how much she'd spilled about herself, embarrassment heated her cheeks.

"I-I'm sorry," she stammered. "I really should just shut my mouth. I mean, who tells a complete stranger something so personal? Jeez. I wouldn't blame you for checking this place for an escape route. In fact, the exit's right over there." She pointed through the crowd. "Quick, go while I'm not looking." She deliberately turned her back on him and silently wished the floor would open up and swallow her.

He threw back his head in a full-throated laugh. It was deep and rich and husky and sent shivers of desire pebbling across her skin. Beneath her dress, her nipples puckered. When he reached out and gently turned her around to face him, heat seared the bare skin of her upper arm where he touched her.

Ignoring her body's traitorous reaction, she kept her embarrassed gaze fixed on his shiny black boots. "Oh, great. Now you're laughing at me," she mumbled. "My humiliation is complete."

His laughter subsided. Out of the corner of her eye, she saw him reach toward her again. A long finger put gentle pressure on her chin and tilted her head up to face him. His cobalt eyes held lingering amusement, but it also held something else. Her breath caught as her brain registered what it was.

Desire.

She couldn't look away if she'd tried. Her heart thumped. Her mouth went dry. Her tongue darted out to wet her lips and his gaze zeroed in on her mouth. In fascination, she watched as his eyes darkened.

"God, you're erotic."

The words came out in a husky whisper. They wrapped

around her, cocooning her in a sexual haze of attraction. She'd grown up knowing she was beautiful. Plenty of men had told her so. But no one had called her *erotic*. The very word was so…sexy. And so completely did not describe her usual self.

Though she was pleased with the good genes she'd been blessed with, she'd never used her looks to get her way. To do so seemed demeaning. Besides, she'd done nothing to achieve those good looks. She was far more interested in being judged on her wit and intelligence. Those she'd worked hard on.

But to have a man so gorgeous he could have stepped off a movie set calling her erotic… It was the sexiest thing she'd ever heard.

She made a slight movement toward him and her lips parted of their own volition. She heard his indrawn breath a moment before he kissed her. Shocked and excited by his forwardness, she took a few seconds to respond. He tasted of beer and spearmint toothpaste. It was an unusual combination… Almost exotic.

A voice in her head admonished her for being so easy, but another one, just as insistent, urged her to take life by the hand. She was done with feeling despondent and discontent. It had been nearly six months since she'd tossed Dwight over. It was like Zane had said. It was time for her to let down her hair and have fun and Joel seemed the perfect choice for that.

What could it hurt to have a night of passion with a stranger? She'd been told it was the perfect way to get over a failed relationship. She'd never had a one night stand, but plenty of people had. There was something more than appealing about losing yourself in the arms of a stranger who found you so completely, desperately desirable…

With that thought in mind, she threw caution to the wind and relaxed into Joel's hard embrace. As one, they stood and came together. He pulled her in close. Her hands came up to rest on his shoulders. Thick muscles bunched beneath her fingers. He was tall and broad and muscular. In heels, she stood at six feet. He towered over her.

The kiss went on forever. They barely noticed when the bartender returned with their drinks. A few breathless moments later, Joel drew back from her slightly, his gaze dark and wild with need.

"Come home with me," he said, his voice husky and deep.

Sheridan nodded, once again shocked by her response and her behavior. She glanced over to where Zane sat engrossed in conversation with his friends. She'd text him later and tell him she'd gone home. No need to bother him now.

Joel took her by the hand and they wended their way through the crowd. As they neared the exit, Sheridan was filled with excitement and anticipation…and a sufficient degree of nerves.

They climbed into the back of a cab and after he gave the driver directions, he took her in his arms again. Instantly she was caught up in the heat of his kiss. Before she knew it, the cab pulled over to the curb outside a block of posh harborside apartments.

"We're here," he said simply. Giving her another lingering kiss, he leaned forward and paid the fare.

Chapter Two

Joel's cock was so hard he was in physical pain. Though he sampled his fair share of beautiful women while he'd gallivanted across Europe, it had been a few weeks since he'd had sex. His balls were heavy and tight and with every flick of Sharon's tongue, he thought he'd shatter to pieces. And what an embarrassment that would be…

After indulging in another bout of heated petting in the lift on the way up to his fifth-floor apartment, he fumbled with the key in the lock. They stumbled into the entryway still wrapped in each other's arms. She was obviously far worldlier than her passionate but rather inexpert kisses seemed to indicate. He wasn't sure what had cinched it for her, but from the moment she'd told him she was single, he'd wanted her for himself.

Not for forever, of course. As his ex-girlfriend MJ had found out, he wasn't the marrying kind. But for right now, he burned for Sharon in a way he'd never experienced before. And for that very reason he needed to slow things down, give her a chance to change her mind. He might be rock-hard and desperate to be inside her, but he was still a gentleman.

Breaking off yet another scorching kiss, he pulled off his jacket and tossed it over the back of the couch. He loosened his tie and it soon went the same way. Sharon balanced her hand on the back of his couch and tugged off her stilettos.

"How the hell do you walk in those?" he quipped, grinning.

She shrugged, as if the idea of not being able to walk in them hadn't occurred to her.

"Would you like a drink?" he asked and went over to the bar he'd had installed within weeks of buying the place.

She nodded. He smiled.

"Let me guess, a vodka and tonic with a slice of lime. Did I get that right?"

She grinned. "You have a good memory."

He poured her drink and collected a beer from the fridge and moved closer to her. "I'm good at lots of things."

Her eyes flared wide and her lips parted on a silent intake of air. Blood thundered through his veins and once again centered in his groin. In an effort to distract himself, he handed her the glass.

She murmured her thanks and glanced down at it. Then that single eyebrow arched. "No lime?"

"Sorry." He shrugged, completely unapologetic. "I'm fresh out of lime."

She merely smiled and with her gaze still locked on his, brought the glass up to her mouth. He watched her sip and then swallow and all the time he wanted her. As if she was fully aware of the power she had over him, she lowered the glass and then, with the tip of her tongue, slowly traced the outline of her full lips.

Without taking his eyes off her, Joel set his beer down and reached for her glass. He disposed of it in the same way he'd rid himself of his drink. With heart thumping, he drew her toward him. His shirtfront brushed her dress and just like that, his control snapped and he pulled her in hard against him. He fused his mouth to hers and the passion lying dormant immediately ignited again. She wrapped her arms around his neck and came up fully against him. His cock throbbed.

He cupped her ass and angled her hips so that she was flush against his erection. He swallowed her gasp. *She felt so good…*

In a flurry of movement, he tugged down her zipper and she stepped out of her dress. She reached for the buttons on his shirt and took way too long to release them. Impatient, he brushed her fingers aside and made short work of the task. His boots and pants and socks and underwear followed in quick succession.

He stood before her, naked and burning with need…and she was still in her underwear.

"You have too many clothes on," he muttered. "How about I help you with that?"

She stood still, her gaze on his as he reached around and undid the clasp on her bra. The black lace dropped to the floor. And then she stepped out of the scrap of fabric that masqueraded as matching panties.

He took his time and looked his fill. Even without the heels, she was tall, with slender hips and thighs. But she was also curvy in the places that mattered. Joel was unable to stand there a moment longer without touching her. With a muttered oath, he swung her into his arms and carried her down the hallway to his bedroom.

Sheridan's head spun with desire. She'd found Joel more than striking in his suit and tie. He was even more impressive naked. With his strong arms around her, he carried her effortlessly into his bedroom and deposited her on the biggest bed she'd ever seen. The drapes had yet to be drawn and she could see the twinkling lights of watercraft on the harbor. She didn't know who Joel was or what he did for a living, but it was obvious whatever it was paid well. And then he followed her down on the bed and the view became the last thing on her mind.

They lay on their sides facing each other, exploring. His body was hard and toned and muscular. Sheridan flicked his small nipples with her fingernails. They instantly puckered into tight little nubs. Her hand moved lower, scraping over the well-defined muscles that created a washboard across his stomach. When her finger dipped into the shallow indentation of his belly button he sucked in a breath.

Not to be outdone, he lifted one of her breasts to his mouth and suckled. The exquisite sensations that rocked through her left her breathless. His erection was a heated, hard length pressing into her stomach. She squirmed against him, desperate for the feeling of him deep inside her. He lifted his head from her breast and captured her lips in another searing kiss.

He was a most excellent kisser. She'd never realized until then that not all men were created equal when it came to kissing. His full lips were soft and sensuous, in contrast to the tickling sensation of his beard. With their lips still joined, he rolled with her until she was on her back.

Breaking off the kiss, he returned his attention to her nipples and took each in turn in his hot mouth. She moaned and lifted her hips in silent, desperate need.

"Please," she urged.

But he was having none of that. Inching his way across her ribs he kissed his way over her stomach. At the same time, his hand delved into the heat between her legs. His finger stroked her slit before finding her opening and slipping inside.

"You're so wet," he murmured huskily.

She moved against his hand, urging him on. He slipped a second finger inside her and she gasped. He moved up to take her mouth in another sweltering kiss. All the time, his fingers worked their magic inside her.

"Please," she begged again, mindless with need.

His answering smile was lazy, unconcerned, but desire glittered like diamonds in the depths of his blue eyes.

"Please what?" he asked in that husky voice that was driving her even wilder.

"I want you… I want you inside me."

His fingers pressed even deeper into her moist heat. "Are you sure?"

"Yes!" She lifted her hips and ground herself against his hand.

He chuckled, but she saw the strain around his mouth. His erection remained a solid, warm brand against her belly.

"Do you want me to fuck you?"

His coarseness drew another shocked gasp. She'd never been spoken to like that. An arc of excitement flashed through her and her inner muscles tightened around his fingers. "Yes."

"Say the words," he demanded.

Embarrassment flamed across her cheeks. She could count the number of her sexual partners on one hand and none of them had treated her like this. His tongue continued to flick back and forth over her nipples. His fingers continued their relentless torment between her legs. Sheridan moaned and squirmed against him. She opened her eyes and stared at him. "I want you to fuck me," she said, shocking herself.

His expression filled with triumph, but it was quickly replaced by desire. The look he gave her was so hot it scorched her. Quickly and efficiently, he reached into the bedside drawer and pulling out a condom, he sheathed himself. She watched in silent fascination. He was so comfortable with his body. There was no hesitation, no awkwardness. They would be just two consenting adults who wanted each other something fierce.

And then he was back between her thighs only this time his cock replaced his fingers. She felt him pressing against her entrance and a moment later, he plunged inside. They both groaned.

"Oh, fuck," he said on a sigh.

"Oh, my goodness!" She gasped at the feel of him inside her. He was so big. Too big. She felt herself stretching to accommodate him, filling her like no other had. And then he began moving, slowly at first, but as desire built inside her, he seemed to know and picked up his pace.

With her arms around his neck, she clung to him. As her need grew she was frantic and dug her fingernails into his back. He pounded into her, his face a picture of tension and need. She closed her eyes and gave herself over to the incredible sensations he produced.

She climbed higher and higher, her breath coming fast. And then she was there, at the peak. Reaching her climax, she cried out on a gasp of ecstasy. Moments later, he orgasmed on a shuddering sigh.

Their breathing was harsh in the silence. He rolled off and lay on his back beside her before taking care of the condom. Reaching for her hand, he gave it squeeze and then lay back with his hands stacked beneath his head as if what had happened between them was commonplace.

And maybe for him, it was.

Feeling suddenly shy and exposed, Sheridan reached for the bed sheet and tugged it up around them. He chuckled softly, but didn't say anything, only turned on his side and drew her close. Within moments, he was asleep.

Sheridan eased herself out from under his arm and climbed off the bed. Much as she'd like to spend the rest of the night in his arms, that would be foolhardy. She'd gone with him for a bit of fun, to lift her spirits and restore her self-esteem. There was nothing like being desired by an attractive man to soothe her battered ego. But that's all this was. A one night stand to help her get over her ex.

She'd used a fake name, and given they lived in a city of nearly five million people, it was unlikely they'd run into each other again. She'd had her fun. They'd had a great night, but this was where it ended. It was time to take stock of her life and get on with making the best of it.

As she eased out of Joel's bedroom, she sent one last wistful glance toward the bed. He slept with one arm thrown wide, his face relaxed. The sheet had slipped. Even asleep, he was gorgeous. She swallowed a sigh and left.

Joel woke with the sun pouring through the window. It beamed right onto his bed. He squinted against the brightness. Preoccupied as he was with the gorgeous Sharon the evening before, he hadn't bothered with the curtains. Now as the sun burned a hole in his pupils, he covered his head with the pillow and groaned.

Of course, the empty bed beside him did nothing to improve his mood. He hadn't really expected to find her there in the morning. Neither of them had shared their phone number. They'd both been on the same page: This was a one night stand. Still, the sex had been amazing and he was willing to admit he'd ask her out if they ever ran into each other again.

Padding across the bedroom naked, he went into the bathroom. He caught a glimpse of himself in the mirror. The rumpled hair, the self-satisfied grin, the fingernail marks down his back…

He'd had a great time partying his way through Europe. With a ten-million-dollar inheritance courtesy of his father— the late Henry Craigdon, he'd managed to enjoy himself everywhere he went. There had been plenty of places to discover and to let his hair down—and just as many beautiful and willing women to help him celebrate. Even the memory of his difficult breakup with Mary-Jane Packham hadn't dampened his mood.

Padding down the hallway, he smiled ruefully at the clothing that lay scattered across the floor of his living room.

Of course, Sharon's clothes were no longer there. The little black dress that had fit her like a glove and the lacy black underwear… He grew hard at the thought of how he'd helped her out of her dress, sliding down the zipper, cupping her firm ass…

What came after still blew his mind.

Maybe it was best they hadn't exchanged numbers. In his experience, women lost some of their appeal over time. What had once been sexy soon became commonplace. In those early days of a new relationship, they were tearing each other's clothes off every second they could get, but a year or two down the track and it was a different story altogether. He and MJ were the perfect example.

He glanced at the pale mint-green sofa that took pride of place before the huge wall of glass that overlooked the harbor. That spot had been MJ's favorite place to curl up in front of the TV. In the early days, they'd snuggled together and often ended up making love on the plush white rug. But looking back, it didn't seem all that long before the shine began to wear off.

From the beginning, MJ was angling for a ring and Joel had been just as adamant he wasn't interested in that kind of commitment. She persisted, somehow convincing herself that he'd change his mind. Five years on and right after the death of his father, they'd had an almighty row that had ended things for good. That was one of the reasons he'd hightailed it to Europe. Joel could still hear the argument echoing off the walls of his living room.

"But we've been together for years! I've given you the best years of my life! We were going to get married!" MJ cried when he told her it was over.

He'd sighed wearily and shook his head. "No, MJ. We were never going to get married."

And then she'd got nasty. "Now you've inherited millions,

you don't have time for me. What? You think you're too good for me now?"

He'd fought off a wave of irritation that she thought he could be so shallow. He'd done his best to reassure her. "No, MJ. Nothing like that."

She'd then unleashed a tirade. "Bullshit. I don't believe you. I was good enough for you when you were a cop with a generous trust fund, but now that you're a multi-millionaire, I've been given the flick. You asshole! You promised me marriage!"

He'd bitten his lip against a surge of impatience. "Now who's talking bullshit? We were never going to get married. Not now. Not ever. It has nothing to do with the money. You can't deny we fought more than we loved. I can't live my life like that. I told you. We're done. I want you to move your stuff out and don't call me again."

He recalled how MJ's face had filled with anger. In that moment there had been a brittleness about her that had shocked him. He couldn't believe he'd once found her beautiful.

On the way out the door, she'd glared at him and had delivered a barely veiled threat. "You're going to regret this, Joel Craigdon. You mark my words."

He'd been relieved she'd left without damaging his apartment. He wouldn't have put it past her to throw some of his stuff around the room and Joel had some nice stuff to destroy. He'd been fortunate to have the trust fund set up for him by his mother, and given to him when he'd turned eighteen. He'd spent the bulk of it buying the ritzy harbor side apartment and in particular, indulging his passion for fine art.

He was proud of the collection of original paintings and sculptures he'd picked up along the way. One of his favorite pastimes was to attend exhibitions of emerging artists. His mother had often complimented him on his fine eye when it came to art.

"You must have inherited that creative side from me," she'd laugh and then add a bit more to his trust fund. That, along with his detective pay, was plenty to allow him to live a comfortable life.

And now there was the extra ten million dollars to add to his bank balance...

Though he'd mourned the loss of his father, Joel hadn't been as close to Henry as some of his other children. Joel and Henry had locked horns early about Joel's career choice. Joel couldn't understand his father's opposition to him becoming a police officer. After all, Joel's oldest brother, Jett had gone into policing.

But for some reason, Henry had other plans for his third son. Just like Henry had planned that his second son would enter the priesthood, so Joel was meant to become a lawyer. In an effort to pacify his father, Joel had applied for and been accepted into law school at Sydney University, but after a year of learning about contracts and torts and negligence, he knew it wasn't for him. He'd braved his father's anger and had told him he was quitting. He'd already been accepted into the police force.

The row that erupted was savage in its intensity, and though his father threatened to cut him off, Joel wouldn't be deterred. He'd graduated from the police academy with honors. He never once regretted his career choice. In fact, one of the reasons he'd decided to return to Australia after spending months gallivanting around Europe was because he missed his job. He also missed his family and friends, but it was his work as a detective in the fraud squad that kept his adrenaline pumping.

He never knew what kind of investigation he'd be hit with next. Over the years, he'd been instrumental in the convictions of several high-profile criminals arrested for money laundering. Drug money that ran into the millions. It seemed like there was an endless supply and with the police on top of it, criminals were forced to come up with more and more creative ways to hide it.

Fortunately for the police, there were still plenty of people willing to tip them off. Some of them were anonymous sources. Others came from registered police informants. Of course, the informants always wanted something in return, be it a lighter sentence, an early release or preferential treatment. Occasionally an informant came from a competing drug ring, the motivation being something as simple as revenge.

Regardless of how it happened, Joel didn't care. What mattered was making good on the information and locking up felons who carried on the illegal behavior. And those convicted weren't always the stereotypical criminal. Occasionally Joel was tipped off to some white-collar crime that involved large sums of money. Like the case he was working on right now.

McClintock Properties wasn't the usual kind of company to land on his radar, but right now it looked like someone inside the company was siphoning off large amounts of cash into an offshore account and no specifics had been reported to the proper authorities. According to the anonymous tip they'd received, nearly thirty million dollars had been transferred between February and May. What made it even more complicated was the connection to his half-brother, Christopher Barrington. As head of contracts for McClintock Properties, Christopher held a position of trust there. And he'd obviously earned that. But Christopher was also disgruntled about being left out of their father's will. While some of the Craigdon siblings had inherited millions, Christopher had inherited nothing. He hadn't been happy about that. In fact, upon Joel's return to Sydney, his older brother Callum told him Christopher had filed a lawsuit against the estate. He was suing for more than a hundred million dollars.

Though Joel had some sympathy for the treatment his half-brother had suffered at the hands of their late father, he wished Christopher had approached the family in an effort to settle the matter amicably before rushing off to the courts.

Could Christopher be behind the large offshore transactions? Perhaps he was stockpiling his own inheritance…

Right now, all Joel had was a tip-off that the money was leaving the country. With the identity of the tipster unknown, he had no idea if the information was reliable or even true, but come Monday, he'd serve the CEO of McClintock Properties with a search warrant for access to the company's bank accounts and then the fun would begin…

Chapter Three

Joel pulled the unmarked police car to the curb outside McClintock Properties and switched off the ignition. He glanced at his partner. "You ready?"

Detective Ralph Tilocca patted the pocket of his jacket. "Yep. The search warrant's in here."

Joel nodded and a familiar surge of anticipation filled his veins. It was always this way at the start of a new investigation and though it wouldn't take long for him to get bogged down in the minutiae of details that usually left him pulling his hair out, this moment in time was the best feeling ever and was one to be savored.

Joel and Ralph strode through the marble foyer and went straight to where a well-dressed man in his thirties sat behind a desk.

"Can I help you?" the man asked, adjusting his glasses.

"Yes. I'm Detective Craigdon. This is Detective Tilocca. We'd like to see Zane Forrest."

The man's tone and expression remained pleasant. "Do you have an appointment?"

"No," Joel replied bluntly.

"Oh, I'm sorry. I'm not allowed to let people in to see Mr Forrest without an appointment. He's a very busy man."

Joel tried to stem his impatience. "I think you missed the

part when I introduced us as detectives. Get your boss on the phone."

The man flushed with embarrassment and hurriedly did as Joel asked. He spoke into the mouthpiece in a voice too low for Joel to hear. A few moments later, the man ended the call and looked back at them.

"I've spoken to Mr Forrest's executive assistant. She'll be down in a few minutes."

Joel nodded in satisfaction. "Thank you." He turned away and he and Ralph wandered over to the opposite wall where a Tim Storrier painting hung. The vibrant blue of the night sky and the orange and red and yellow of the fire burning below it were eye catching. Joel had once spent a week of the school holidays on a road trip through the outback. The vivid colors of Storrier's painting reminded him of that time, particularly the nights they'd spent camping outside Alice Springs.

"Do you think it's an original?" Ralph asked, squinting at it.

"Yep. It's real all right. Look at the quality. Look at the signature."

Ralph looked at the painting again. "Is that how you tell?"

"There are a lot of things that tell you whether it's an original piece of artwork, but look around you," Joel replied. "Does this look like the kind of place to hang a replica?"

Before Ralph could offer a response, they heard the unmistakable sound of high heels clicking on the marble. Joel turned just as the woman reached them.

"Detectives, I'm Giselle Warner. I'm Zane's EA. I understand you'd like to see him?"

Joel nodded. Giselle looked to be mid-twenties and though she was quite striking with her tidy figure and glossy dark brown hair and blue eyes, it struck him she didn't hold a candle to Sharon.

Dammit, I have to stop thinking about her. It was a one night stand. That's all both of us wanted…

"If you come with me, I'll take you to his office. Mr Forrest has someone with him at the moment, so you might have to wait a little while…?"

"That's fine," Joel replied.

Using a security pass, Giselle whisked them up in the lift to the top floor. The décor up there was every bit as plush and expensive as in the foyer. Giselle's stilettos were silenced by the thick carpet that ran the length of the corridor that opened out into a spacious reception area.

"Please, take a seat." She indicated four chairs placed in a half-circle against the wall behind them. Another brightly colored Storrier painting hung above them.

"Can I get you some coffee?" Giselle asked.

Both men declined and sat down to wait. Joel reached for a glossy magazine that boasted a beautiful woman on the cover. The model wore a bikini and was tanned and toned and smiled with perfect white teeth. She was apparently married to some Hollywood star and had just created her own line of perfume. Joel couldn't even be bothered to open the magazine. And for all her airbrushed gorgeousness, the model still didn't turn him on like Sharon had.

Dammit, there I go again, thinking about her when I should have gotten her well and truly off my mind. There are plenty of other beautiful women out there. Take Giselle…and the woman on the cover…

His thoughts were interrupted when the door opposite the reception area opened and Giselle reappeared with a gray-haired, older gentleman dressed in an expensive-looking suit and carrying a leather briefcase. Joel frowned. He'd never met the CEO of McClintock Properties, but from what he knew about Zane Forrest, the man was closer to his age than his father's. And then he heard Giselle speak.

"Thank you for coming in, Mr Jackson. I'll get that paperwork to you right away."

The man nodded his thanks and headed toward the lifts. Giselle turned to them. "Mr Forrest will see you now."

They followed her into the biggest office Joel had ever seen. Even his father's office at Craigdon Enterprises hadn't come close to this one. It was tastefully decorated with dark furniture and walls of rich green and gold. A floor-to-ceiling bookshelf lined one wall. It was filled with books and interesting ornaments that looked both exotic and expensive. It reminded Joel of the décor in an exclusive gentleman's club…and seated behind an impressive desk, Zane Forrest looked every bit the wealthy gentleman.

He stood as they entered. He was dressed in an immaculate navy-blue suit and a shirt that was so white it was blinding. His thinly striped blue-and-white tie was Italian silk and cost more than Joel made in a week. And then as Joel raised his gaze to the CEO's face, he stilled.

It was the man from the nightclub… It was…Sharon's brother. Now that he knew they were related, the similarities in their physical appearance were obvious. Both had blond hair and blue eyes. Both were tall, athletic, fit-looking.

Of all the people to run into…

Joel was still trying to process the shock of his discovery when the man held out his hand toward them.

"Zane Forrest. It's nice to meet you."

Joel recovered his composure and shook the proffered hand. "Detective Joel Craigdon. This is Detective Tilocca."

Zane's handsome face reflected his surprise, but he said nothing until they'd taken a seat. "Craigdon. Are you one of Henry Craigdon's sons?"

"Yes. Is that a problem?"

"No, of course not," he said in a tone that indicated otherwise. Zane sat back in his chair. "So, Detectives. What can I do for you?"

"We're investigating the possibility of large-scale

transactions being made from within McClintock Properties to an offshore account," Joel said.

Zane leaned back against his chair, his eyes wide with surprise. "Are you for real?"

Joel eyed him steadily. "Yes."

Ralph cleared his throat and reached into the pocket of his jacket. "We have a search warrant giving us access to all of your company's bank accounts. We'll conduct a thorough search and ascertain for ourselves whether the information we've been given has any merit."

Zane continued to regard them with surprise. "You have to be kidding! This is a law-abiding company. We deal in large sums of money, but all of it stays right here."

"What about international investors? Surely you deal with them from time to time?" Joel asked.

Zane nodded. "Of course. But the money doesn't come through McClintock accounts. Those buyers deal directly with their lawyers. We're paid on completion of the sale through the same channels." He eyed Joel. "Your information is wrong."

Joel shrugged. "Then you have nothing to worry about."

"What happens now?" Zane asked.

Ralph responded. "We do a forensic investigation of the company's bank accounts. If we find nothing suspicious, then you're good to go."

"And what if you do find something suspicious?" Zane asked.

Joel regarded him steadily. "I thought you just said McClintock doesn't conduct overseas transactions?"

Zane nodded once, but his expression was grim. "That's correct, Detective, and I stand by that remark. If you do find transactions of that nature, they weren't authorized by me."

"You mean, someone in your company could be stealing from you?"

"No. I refuse to believe any of my employees would do that."

Joel eyed him steadily. "How many people work for you, Mr Forrest?"

"Seven hundred, give or take."

Joel grinned. "And you're prepared to personally vouch for all of them?"

A flush of embarrassment crept across the CEO's face. "All right, Detective. I get your point. Of course I can't vouch for each and every one of them, but this is a family company. We're tight. Each and every one of our employees are issued private shares in the company. It's how my father started this business and a tradition I've been proud to continue. It's in the best interests of all McClintock employees to ensure the business succeeds. When the company does well, so do the shareholders."

Joel nodded. "I'm impressed."

"You should be," Zane replied. "I know of no other company in this country that offers its employees a slice of the business. As far as the bank accounts go, only my sister and I have security clearance to access them. There's no way she'd steal from McClintock. She loves the company as much as I do."

Joel held Zane's gaze another long moment. The man appeared genuine, without guile. Either that, or he was an excellent liar. Right now, Joel would keep an open mind. The CEO of McClintock Properties might be the brother of the hottest woman Joel had been up close and personal with, but that didn't mean Zane Forrest was above the law.

Sheridan thought about the past few hours she'd spent on what she hoped would be McClintock Properties' next large-scale development. If the purchase went through, the land would house a new hotel-like apartment complex that would be built on route to the new Western Sydney International Airport. While it was still nothing more than a large tract of scrubby ground, initial conversations Sheridan had conducted with the seller had been productive and after meeting Simon Blackhall and his business partners, she was confident she could negotiate a deal that benefited both parties. It was envisaged the project would be completed around the same time as the new airport opened in 2026.

Parking her Mercedes coupé in the underground staff car park, she climbed the internal steps that led to the foyer. She'd been out of the office longer than she planned. She was caught up in a traffic accident on her way to Badgery's Creek. The delay had impacted Simon Blackhall's schedule and she'd been forced to wait outside his office for more than half an hour while he dealt with another appointment.

Still, the trip west had been worthwhile. There was nothing like meeting a prospective vendor in the flesh to ascertain their true intentions. After several years of negotiating deals on behalf of McClintock Properties, she'd learned a few tricks. It was easier to bluff someone over the phone. In person, it took considerably more skill. Not everyone had the ability to lie to your face. She'd discovered she had a knack for reading people and it came in very handy when she was knee-deep in negotiations that ran into the billions.

So she made it a point to meet her potential sellers early in the negotiations. Both parties got to size up the opposition and more often than not, a mutual respect was generated. Sheridan found the outcome for both parties was generally better as a result and it saved wasting time in pointless one-upmanship. Sheridan much preferred to cut through the nonsense and get right to the point.

Like her decision to sleep with a complete stranger the previous Friday night…

It had been dangerous on so many levels, and yet she'd done it. Nobody had even known where she was. She'd sent a text to her brother on the way to Joel's place that she had a headache and had decided to go home. The police wouldn't have known where to start looking if she'd turned up missing.

Thankfully, her instincts that she could trust Joel had proved reliable and she'd come out of the adventure with only the memories of fantastic sex with the most exciting man she'd slept with. It was a shame there was little to no chance she might run into him again. Not that she wanted to repeat the experience. That was the thing with one-offs. They weren't meant to be repeated. She was sure if she went down that path, she'd inevitably be disappointed when the second time around didn't live up to the memory.

No, her night with Joel had served its purpose. She now looked back on her lukewarm relationship with Dwight and couldn't believe she'd settled for that. Their sex life had been pleasant, but it had never set her on fire or left her yearning for more. Now that she'd been given a taste of how good sex could be with the right person, she'd never settle for mere pleasant again. Joel had done her a favor and saved her from mediocre sex for the rest of her life. If she ever saw him again, she just might thank him.

The thought made her smile. Putting her shoulder to the door that led out into the main foyer, she pushed the panel open and stepped onto the shiny marble that matched the steel and glass of the impressive entry to McClintock Properties. Though the business had been started by their father, she'd always been proud of how Zane had carried on, keeping her father's legacy alive—and not only maintaining it, but making it grow beyond anyone's expectations.

With briefcase in hand, she strode toward the bank of lifts. She pressed the button and waited. A few minutes later, the doors slid open and two men dressed in dark suits alighted. Her gaze zeroed in on the taller one and her heart skipped a beat. She gasped in surprise.

His head immediately swiveled toward her.

She knew the instant he recognized her. His eyes went wide and his mouth opened. Just as quickly, he recovered himself. He glanced at the man beside him and then back at her. With the barest of nods, he acknowledged her presence and then walked on by. She watched in stunned surprise as Joel from the nightclub headed across the wide foyer then out onto the street.

He didn't look back.

Chapter Four

The two-story concrete monolith that housed the City of Sydney police station sat smack in the middle of George Street. Across from the station was the iconic Town Hall. Constructed of Sydney sandstone and completed in 1889, it remained the largest and most ornate late-nineteenth-century civic building in Australia. Renowned for its high Victorian interiors and rich decoration, the sheer grandeur of it had always filled Joel with a sense of pride.

Of course, he only caught a glimpse of it from his workstation and right now he was knee-deep sifting through McClintock Properties' bank accounts for suspicious activity. After more than four hours at the job, Joel knew exactly why and how Zane Forrest enjoyed such an impressive office.

The company regularly turned over millions of dollars a month. Some months, it was as high as a billion, particularly when it coincided with the sale of a large-scale property development. Joel had no way of knowing what the net profit was, but from all indications, the business was doing well. And that made it so much easier for someone to siphon off large sums to an overseas account. But so far, in that regard, he'd come up with zilch. He looked across at Ralph.

"Any luck?"

"No, mate. You?"

"Nope." He grinned. "But I tell you what, I wouldn't mind owning one of these accounts."

Ralph chuckled and they continued to scroll through hundreds of entries, looking for something untoward. Joel's mind wandered. He couldn't believe the girl he'd met last Friday night and taken home to his apartment was the sister of Zane Forrest. It seemed like an incredible coincidence. He had figured by her designer dress and high heels she had money, but there'd been nothing about her to suggest she came from *that* kind of money.

Not that it made any difference. He'd also grown up in a wealthy family. Money held little appeal. Inheriting ten million dollars had been nice, but it wouldn't change him. He'd enjoyed being able to afford the high life in Europe while on vacation and it was nice to have that kind of money there, but thanks to his trust fund and his police salary, he'd never had to worry about paying his bills anyway. That was a freedom he appreciated and never took for granted. He knew most people didn't have the choices he did.

"I think I've found something."

Ralph's quiet words penetrated Joel's thoughts. A burst of adrenaline surged through him. Pushing away from his desk, he moved to Ralph's desk, leaned over his partner's shoulder and looked at the screen.

"Right here." Ralph pointed to an entry.

Joel squinted. There was a transaction for close to half a million dollars with the reference "O.S.A." A little further down, they found another one.

"Let's do a search on O.S.A," Joel said, stirring with excitement. "It's a strange reference. All the other transactions are referenced with names."

Ralph tapped the keys on his keyboard and they both waited while the search results loaded. A moment later, the screen filled with entries.

"Well, well, well." Joel folded his arms and grinned. He scanned the dozen or so entries. Every one of them referenced at least six figures. Joel did a quick calculation in his head and guessed the total approximated close to thirty million dollars.

Ralph ran a hand over his buzz cut and whistled. "What I wouldn't give to have that kind of money sitting in *my* bank account."

"It seems like our information was good, after all. The person behind these transfers hasn't even tried too hard to conceal it. I mean, "O.S.A.? What are the odds it stands for off shore account?"

"Yeah. Even "overseas account" would cover it."

Joel was filled with a surge of anticipation as a plan of attack formed in his head. "I'll put in a request to AUSTRAC and see if they can tell us where the money's gone. If my guess is right, we'll be granted a search warrant for McClintock Properties' computers. We need to locate which one of them was involved in the transfers. That won't necessarily tell us who did it, but it'll help narrow it down. Zane Forrest said only he and his sister had access to the bank accounts, so let's start with them."

He thought of Sharon and wondered what role she played in her brother's company. The last time he'd seen her she'd been dressed in a designer suit, killer heels and carried an expensive briefcase. She walked with the confidence of someone who was used to giving orders...

The truth was, he really wanted to see her again.

Now there was a possibility she was involved in criminal activity. He sure could do without that complication.

Sheridan logged in on her computer. There were a handful of emails from Simon Blackhall, but the negotiations for land out near the new airport was the last thing on her mind.

It had been two days since she'd run into Joel outside the lifts. Now thoughts of him filled her every waking moment and plenty of her dreams. Upon returning to her office, she'd immediately made casual enquires of her brother and discovered Joel and the man he'd been in the company of were detectives from the fraud squad.

So, he was a detective… That explained the air of authority, but not exactly the plush harbor side pad. Detectives made good money, but she wouldn't have thought they could afford a multimillion-dollar apartment like that. Maybe he was just renting? Still, the monthly rent on a place like that wouldn't be cheap…

She didn't know why thoughts of him consumed so much of her time. They'd had a one-night stand. So what? Just because it was a first for her didn't mean it wasn't commonplace for some. It had been his suggestion. No doubt she was one in a long line of women who'd enjoyed fleeting moments in his bed.

A flash of jealousy went through her and she frowned with annoyance. She had no right to feel jealous of the other women in his life. She'd known from the outset this was no-strings-attached sex. A crazy moment when she'd acted reckless and free, just that once. The experience had also served to restore her faith that she was a desirable woman—something that had taken a blow after discovering her boyfriend of six months was cheating.

It was only much later she thought to question Zane about why two detectives from the fraud squad had visited him. She'd been shocked by what he told her. *How could someone in our company be stealing from us? And why would someone go to the trouble of sending the money to an overseas account?* It would be harder to access the money and more questions would be asked. If the motivation was simple theft, surely it would be easier to transfer it to a domestic account. Still, what did she know?

She'd never moved money overseas. She was head of McClintock's finance and negotiation department. She made sure the company had enough money to cover their monthly costs, as well as future projects and she also negotiated the price on land and building contracts. Most of her staff had high-level access to confidential information, but she and Zane were the only ones with access to the bank accounts.

There was no way her brother would steal from his own company. It didn't make sense.

Zane had told her he'd said as much to the police. He was sure the investigation would come to nothing. The police didn't even know for certain if a theft had really occurred.

"How did it come to their attention, then?" she'd asked.

"They said they received a tip-off."

"A tip-off? From whom?"

"They didn't say. They turned up with a warrant to search our bank accounts. I'm guessing they'll find nothing. I mean, you and I are the only ones with that kind of high-level access. I know I haven't been sending large amounts of money offshore. How about you?" he joked.

"Of course not. The very idea that either of us would do that is ludicrous." She paused. "It seems odd someone contacted the police and gave them information like that. It can't possibly be true. Why would someone do that?"

"I don't know." Zane's expression was grim. "But if there's any truth to the allegations, we need to do a full security overhaul. We both know we aren't behind any offshore transactions. If something shows up, it's possible our systems have been breached."

"Let's wait until we know the outcome of the police investigation. No sense spending money on upgrading our cyber security if there's no need."

"True, but it's been a few years since we upgraded. It wouldn't hurt to get someone in to do a thorough assessment and make sure we're still secure. No sense waiting for a hacker before we react. That's plain stupid."

"All right," Sheridan agreed. "Let's see what the police come up with. If they find nothing, we do an in-house overview of our cyber security protocols to see if there's anything we need to tighten. I agree. It's better to play it safe."

Zane regarded her somberly. "And if they do find something?"

She held his gaze. "I trust you with my life. There's no way I'll believe it's you. Just like you trust me. So, if the police do find something… I guess we'll deal with that if and when it becomes necessary."

Zane nodded briefly. "Fair enough." Zane paused. "How did you do with Simon Blackhall? Is he still on board?"

Sheridan filled Zane in on her meeting and confirmed her gut feel that Blackhall was in their corner.

"Good," Zane replied, nodding his head in approval. "You've done well."

Sheridan smiled. "You're looking at your gold star negotiator. Did you expect anything less?"

Zane laughed. "Careful, that ego of yours is in danger of growing too big to control." He paused again and then changed the subject. "How did you do last Friday night? I got your text. You said you weren't feeling well."

Sheridan scrambled to remember the excuse she'd sent to her brother to explain her early exit from the night club.

"Yes. I had a headache. It must have been the music. Or maybe the vodka?" She grinned as if the night had been of no consequence, while all the time she was inundated with images of Joel, gorgeous and naked, rolling around with her on his bed. *Joel.* The detective. There was no way she could let that spill to her brother.

Zane had always been protective. Most of the time, Sheridan thought it was cute. They'd lost their mother to a stroke when they were teenagers. Maxine McClintock had only been in her late thirties. It was a shock to all of them.

As her older brother by two years, Zane always looked out for her. If he knew about her and Joel, he'd make things uncomfortable for the officer and they didn't need the detective wondering why the CEO of a company under investigation for fraudulent activity might have suddenly become prickly.

Her office phone rang, distracting her from her thoughts. She picked up the receiver.

"Yes, Jane?"

"I have Dwight Britton on the line," her secretary replied. "I can tell him you're busy."

Sheridan swallowed a sigh. There probably wasn't an employee in the office who didn't know about her messy breakup.

"Thanks, Jane. I appreciate your show of support, but it's fine. I'll take the call." With that, she depressed the flashing button and answered. "Dwight. What can I do for you?"

"Sheridan! It's so good to hear your voice!"

She gritted her teeth. "Don't do that, Dwight. Whatever you think, whatever you say, it's not going to make a difference. We're not getting back together."

"But, Sheridan! I love you!" he whined.

"Yeah, right. You call that love? Cheating on me? I don't think so. I can do without your kind of love."

"I already told you how sorry I am!" Dwight protested. "She was all over me! I was drunk! What was I supposed to do?"

"You were supposed to tell her you were involved with someone and that she should turn her attentions elsewhere."

"I tried! Believe me! She was so persistent…"

Sheridan made a sound of disgust. "Oh, please. I don't want to hear it. We're over, Dwight. Get it through your head.

Stop calling me. Stop texting me. Stop hanging around outside my building."

"I never—"

"I've *seen* you. More than once. It isn't cool. We called it quits six months ago. You need to move on."

"But you don't understand…"

"Oh, but I do," she replied, her voice hard.

"You… You said you loved me!"

"You're right. And I believed I did. But that wasn't the you I know today. Although now I've had time to look back on our relationship, I'm not sure what I ever saw in you."

"Ouch! That hurts! When did you get so mean?"

Sheridan sighed. "You know what, Dwight? I'm done. This conversation's over. *We're* over. Get it through your head before I'm forced to go to the police and get a restraining order."

At the thought of the police, images of Joel—naked, muscular, fierce—washed over her. Her nipples tightened. Dwight had never made her react like that. It made her realize with even more certainty that she'd settled for far less than she deserved by being with him.

"The police?" he screeched in her ear, bringing her thoughts back to the present with a rush. "You have to be kidding! All I'm trying to do is talk to you, to make you see how sorry I am. I made a mistake. I admit it. But let's not throw away everything we had over a simple slip up. I promise it won't happen again. You're the only woman for me."

She sighed again and wearily ran a hand through her hair. "I'm sorry you feel that way, Dwight, because it's definitely *not* reciprocated. I might have thought I loved you once, but I don't now and I won't ever love you again. You need to accept we're over and find someone else."

"Is that what *you've* done?" he asked, suddenly suspicious. "Is that why you're being so cold, so cruel? You've *replaced* me already?"

Sheridan clenched her jaw against a surge of impatience. "No, Dwight. There's no one else. The time we've spent apart has helped me realize you weren't the man I thought you were. That's just the way it is. Your infidelity has little to do with it. That might have been the catalyst for our breakup, but I know now I never felt as strongly about you as I should have. I want more from the man I intend to make a life commitment to and you can't give me what I need. It's as simple as that."

"Please, Sheridan! Give me a chance!" he begged.

Sheridan could tell he was close to tears. She bit her lip and counted to five and when she spoke again, she deliberately softened her tone.

"You're better than this, Dwight. Someday you'll find the girl you're meant to be with and you'll thank me. It probably doesn't feel like that right now, but trust me. We would never have made each other happy in the long term. Let's just accept that and move on."

And then his mood turned nasty. "This is all your fault! If you weren't so frigid, I wouldn't have looked for attention elsewhere. You only have yourself to blame."

Fury ignited along her veins. "How dare you! Your inability to keep your dick in your pants had nothing to do with me. Let's make that very clear."

"I'm sorry, Sheridan. I didn't mean that. It's just that I'm so upset. You—"

"I'm sorry, Dwight," she interrupted coldly. "I have another call waiting," she lied. "I have to go. Good-bye." With that, she hung up the phone.

Trembling with anger, she buried her face in her hands, grateful she was alone in her office.

What did I ever see in him?

She could barely remember what attracted her to him in the beginning. He was pleasant enough to look at. Tall and athletic, but a little on the thin side. He didn't hold a candle to Joel, but was attractive enough. And he'd pursued her relentlessly. For more than a year, he'd flattered her with compliments, cards, comments.

He had a background in IT and worked beside her in finance. He genuinely seemed to have her best interests at heart. If she had a headache, he'd express concern she was working too hard. When she had to deal with a difficult client, he offered to sit in on the meeting. He was always doing little things to make her life easier. Finally, she'd agreed to go on a date with him and the rest, as they say, was history. Still, she'd made him work for her affection. They'd dated for three months before she slept with him.

That seemed strange now, knowing she'd had sex with a stranger the week before. Her actions with Joel were definitely out of character. She was embarrassed even to think about that night. It was hard to believe fate had seen fit to throw them together once again, this time on a professional footing.

Not that anything would come of the investigation. Wherever the police had gotten their information, it was wrong. She was certain of that. And as soon as the police came to that conclusion, Detective Joel would have no reason to stop by. It irritated her that the knowledge left her with a sinking feeling of disappointment...

Chapter Five

With one hand, Joel pulled his fine cashmere coat tighter around him to ward off the winter chill. With the other, he angled his umbrella to keep from getting soaked. It was the kind of cold rainy night most people would choose to spend indoors and normally that's where Joel would be. But tonight just happened to be the opening of the exhibition of an up-and-coming artist who was touted as the next Pro Hart. Joel had received a personal invitation from the gallery owner.

Hannah Burke had a knack of sniffing out the "next big thing." Joel had bought several original pieces from her over the years and they now filled his apartment. This time she'd followed up her invitation with a phone call and had urged him to come along.

"This guy has it all, Joel," she'd gushed. "The way he uses color! You need to see it to believe it! And his technique! Broad brushstrokes that shouldn't work, but somehow do. It's magic! Riley Hammond's going to be the name on everyone's lips."

Hannah's excitement was contagious and had been enough to pique Joel's interest. Picking up original pieces from an artist on the brink of being discovered always filled him with satisfaction. Apart from the thrill of getting in on the action early, he'd managed to accrue a number of assets that were now worth significantly more than he'd paid for them.

Pushing open the double glass doors, he gave his umbrella to the doorman and shook the rain from his coat. Folding it up over his arm, he made his way inside the gallery. Hannah spotted him almost immediately.

"Joel, I'm so glad you made it." She pecked him on both cheeks, European style.

"Thanks for the invitation." He gave her a friendly wink. "It's always good to catch up with you," he added truthfully.

She blushed under his regard. Hannah Burke was nearing fifty, but she looked much younger. Good genes and a healthy lifestyle had helped her maintain a trim figure and a face that was almost wrinkle-free.

She patted a non-existent stray piece of hair and gave him a sideways look. "You're a charming devil, Joel Craigdon, and way too handsome for your own good. I love the beard. It looks good on you. I'm sure you know that."

He shot her a look of innocence and she laughed. Taking his arm, she steered him toward the back of the room where a well-stocked temporary bar had been set up.

"What are you drinking?" she asked.

"I'll have a beer, thanks."

Hannah turned to the good-looking barman and put in a request for a beer and a glass of champagne. When their drinks arrived, she touched her glass to his.

"Cheers, Joel. Here's to you finding the perfect Riley Hammond piece. May your night be very successful."

He grinned cheekily. "And yours, too."

She tilted her glass in his direction. "Touché." She took an elegant sip of her champagne and he drank from his beer. Looking over his shoulder, she spied someone behind him and quickly offered her apologies.

"Excuse me, Joel. I must continue to mingle. Please, take a

look around at the paintings and see what you think. I'm sure you won't be disappointed."

With that, Hannah moved gracefully past him and disappeared into the crowd. Joel turned and surveyed the people who'd made the effort to gather on such a dismal night. He recognized a few familiar faces—fellow art enthusiasts and a few serious collectors. And then his gaze snagged on someone he knew on an altogether different level.

Sharon Forrest. Or was it Sharon McClintock? He hadn't thought to ask Zane why he went by the name of Forrest.

She wore a crimson halter dress with a dangerously low neckline. Her generous breasts filled the opening with smooth golden flesh. A long gold necklace nestled in her cleavage, its pendant sparkling under the light. In an instant, his body was hard as a rock and oxygen was in short supply. She laughed at something someone said and shook her head. Her long curly hair floated about her.

He didn't remember the curls, more like soft waves the first time. She must have straightened her hair… No matter, she was still the most beautiful woman he'd seen. Knowing how she felt, naked beneath him, as he kissed her, with her long legs wrapped around his hips…

The images flooded his mind and it was all he could do not to groan. His cock throbbed. His breath came fast. His fingers yearned to touch her.

Get a grip, Craigdon. You're at an exhibition, for God's sake. If you don't get yourself under control, *you'll* be the exhibition!

The stern talking to seemed to work, along with several more gulps of beer. When he finished, he turned back to the barman and asked for another. Feeling more in control, he circumvented the crowd and went to study the paintings. Hannah was right. The use of color was both clever and imaginative.

Joel had always preferred bold, bright colors over pale and these paintings had it all. Anyone would make a valuable addition to his collection. No doubt Hannah would be pleased. From the price marked on each piece of artwork, she stood to make a sizable commission. And so she should. Not every gallery owner would take a chance on an unknown artist. Hannah was one among a handful of curators who were willing to take risks. Some paid off better than others. She deserved every success.

And then, as if he'd lost control over his actions, Joel turned and sought out Sharon in the crowd. She was easy to spot. Her above-average height and bright red dress were like a beacon. He'd taken three steps toward her before he came to his senses and pulled up short.

"Joel! It's good to see you!"

Joel took a moment to recognize the woman who greeted him. Monique Hanley was another art collector and a regular at this sort of thing. Before he'd hooked up with MJ, Monique and Joel had once engaged in a hot and heavy affair. She'd been an interesting bedmate, preferring a certain kind of dominance. It had been fun for a while, but gradually the novelty had faded. Their sexual adventures became increasingly exhausting and Joel hadn't been all that into bondage in the first place. Sometimes sex the regular way was just plain fine. Eventually they'd parted ways.

Now she looked him up and down like he was a succulent dish she couldn't wait to taste. He forced a smile.

"Monique. You're looking ravishing, as always."

She appeared pleased by his compliment and kissed him on the mouth. "You're such a tease."

"What brings you here tonight?"

"Same thing as you. Where have you been? I haven't seen you around for months."

"I spent some time in Europe, after my father's death. I've only been back a couple of weeks."

"That explains your absence. I was sorry to hear about your father."

Joel shrugged. Monique had never met Henry Craigdon. She hadn't been in Joel's life long enough to meet any of his family. He knew when he'd started the affair that it wasn't a long-term thing.

"I heard you and your girlfriend parted ways. What was her name again? Melissa? Molly-Anne?"

"Mary-Jane," he supplied dryly. He wasn't surprised the news had gotten out. He and MJ had been together for five years. They'd attended many exhibitions together and were quite well known among the artsy types who always seemed to show up at these events.

Monique's deep-throated laughter filled the room. "Ah, Mary-Jane. That's right." She shot him a look beneath her long false eyelashes. One long red fingernail scraped slowly, seductively along his arm. "So, does this mean you're footloose and fancy free?"

Sheridan usually enjoyed the rare opportunities she got when Zane escorted her to an art exhibition. More often than not he invited the latest woman in his life, but for some reason he was between women right now and he'd ducked his head into her office earlier that afternoon and asked if she had plans.

"Hannah Burke has a new exhibition. Riley Hammond. An up-and-coming artist. Tonight's opening night. Would you like to come?"

She smiled with genuine pleasure. Dwight had been totally uninterested in art and Sheridan hadn't wanted to attend the upmarket cocktail parties that accompanied the opening nights on her own. With Zane only occasionally extending her an invitation, she hadn't enjoyed as many of them as she'd wanted.

"I'd love to. What time?"

"Seven. I'll pick you up just before. And bring a coat and an umbrella. It's meant to rain tonight."

Zane had always been punctual and as usual, picked her up on time. She'd walked into the packed gallery feeling excited and full of anticipation. She was the one who'd chosen many of the artworks around the office, including the Tim Storrier painting that decorated the front lobby. Zane had been so impressed with her selection, he'd purchased another for his reception area.

The night was going well. She'd already accepted two glasses of champagne and was currently on her third. She wasn't normally a big drinker and she could feel the alcohol going to her head. It was probably because she'd skipped lunch, being too busy on the phone with Simon Blackhall to bother running out for a sandwich. She could have asked Jane to get one for her, but she didn't like to take advantage of her EA like that.

And then the sound of a woman's throaty laughter caught her attention. She looked through the crowd and spotted Joel. Her heart skipped a beat.

He's here. Joel. The man she'd spent the night with and who'd filled her dreams ever since…

"Oh, God."

She didn't realize she'd spoken aloud until she registered Zane's frown of concern.

"Are you all right?" he asked.

She blushed. "Yes, I'm fine. I just… I just saw someone I know."

"Oh?"

"Yes. That detective. The one at McClintock last Monday."

Zane glanced in the direction she indicated. "You're right. It's Detective Craigdon. He must be an art collector in his spare time." Zane turned back to her. "Don't worry about him. He admitted there might not be anything to his information. It's only a matter of time before he realizes that's true. Don't let him bother you."

Sheridan grimaced. *If only it were that simple… Joel Craigdon bothers me on so many levels, none of which are linked to any investigation, real or imagined.*

And then her mind snagged on something else. "Craigdon? Did you say his name was Craigdon?"

"Yes."

"As in, *those* Craigdons?" she asked, referring to McClintock's toughest business rivals.

"Yes. He's one of Henry's sons."

Sheridan absorbed the information in silence.

A week earlier she'd thought she'd done something wild and spontaneous by spending the night with a stranger. They'd had great sex and never planned to see each other again. She'd just discovered that not only was the man she'd gone home with a detective investigating her family's company, he was also the son of her father's fiercest competitor.

Moreover, Joel had also been born with the proverbial spoon in his mouth and she'd always gone out of her way to avoid that kind of man. Without exception, every single one she'd chanced to meet had proven they were no more than spoiled brats living off a trust fund. She'd come across her fair share of them at university. They all had an air of expectation, of entitlement, that they didn't have to work for what they wanted. She'd been raised in a wealthy household too, but she'd been taught to be grateful for what she had and to never look down on those who didn't have as much. A spoiled, rich boyfriend was the last thing she wanted.

Can things get any more complicated?

The woman with Joel laughed again and Sheridan's gaze was drawn back across the room. To her consternation, the woman was now pressed up against him and had a hand around his neck, ostensibly whispering in his ear. A hot shaft of jealousy burned through her at the sight of the other woman's hands on him.

How dare she touch him like that! Who does she think she is, with her nails like claws, botoxed lips and fake eyelashes?

An angry flush heated Sheridan's cheeks. She cursed under her breath. *What am I doing? I'm acting like a jealous lover!* She had no hold on the man.

So, they'd spent a night together, a night she'd never forget. But that didn't mean she had any right to demand his fidelity. They were never meant to see each other again. He was free to see or date who he pleased…as was she.

Too bad he'd ruined her for any other man. She couldn't imagine anyone else measuring up to the perfection that was Joel Craigdon. The thought sent another rush of irritation surging through her. She made a noise of disgust in her throat. Once again, Zane leaned toward her, concern in his gaze.

"Are you *sure* you're all right?" he asked.

Sheridan gritted her teeth. "I'm fine. But it's a little stuffy in here. I think I'll go out on the balcony and get some fresh air."

Zane nodded and stood back so she could pass. Sheridan swiped another glass of champagne from the bar and weaving her way through the groups of art lovers, eventually found herself on the small balcony that overlooked the street below. The rain had stopped, leaving the night air cool and fresh. Breathing in deeply, her shoulders slumped on a sigh.

"Surely it isn't as bad as that. In fact, I've already seen at least one piece I'd like to call my own."

Sheridan gasped at the sound of Joel's lazy drawl. The

husky tones reminded her too vividly of scenes she was trying hard to forget.

"I'm sorry. I didn't realize you were here. I-I'll go." She took a step toward the door.

His arm shot out from the darkness and grabbed her elbow, staying her movement. "No. Don't go. I promise I don't bite."

His teeth gleamed in the dimness. Light that spilled out onto the balcony from inside shrouded his face in shadows. Even so, she caught the glint of amusement in his eyes…and something else. The desire in his eyes rekindled an answering need deep inside. Heat washed over her and centered in her core. His gaze drifted over her, pausing noticeably at her cleavage. Her pulse quickened and her nipples tightened. Fire followed in the wake of his gaze.

"What are you doing here?" she asked, inwardly cursing the breathlessness in her voice.

"I'm seeking to add to my art collection. How about you?"

"You're a collector?"

"Yes. I have been for quite some time. In fact, I bought my first Pro Hart when I turned eighteen."

There was no hint of arrogance in his announcement, but still she was miffed. He lived a life of wealth and privilege and didn't care who knew it.

"Lucky you," she said dryly.

Taking note of her expression, he hurried to explain. "Don't get me wrong. I know full well how lucky I've been. Not many people have the opportunity to collect art the way I do, and especially not from such a young age. I appreciate and am grateful for the wealth I've grown up with that's allowed me to lead this kind of life." His gaze was full of challenge. "Some people would say it's unfair, that I've been given too much. That might be so, but it's the way it is. I won't apologize for it."

She stared at him, weighing his sincerity. She'd pegged him as just another spoiled, rich, trust fund brat, but he'd surprised her. On another level, she was impressed with his sophistication. Not everyone appreciated art. She was also a fan of Pro Hart and had one of his paintings in her living room. Discovering Joel's passion for art rivaled hers only made him more desirable.

As if I need anything else to get my heart pumping with need…

Just being this close to him had the memories of their night together flooding the forefront of her mind, overwhelming her. A light breeze lifted his black hair and sent a whiff of expensive cologne in her direction. All at once she was back there, in his apartment, in his bed, experiencing pleasure the likes of which she hadn't ever known.

As if reading her thoughts, he stepped closer. So close, she could see the dark flecks in his beautiful blue eyes. Unable to help herself, her eyes drifted closed and she leaned in toward him.

His lips were every bit as soft and sensual as they had been the night they'd met. He pulled her in tight against him and her arms came up around his neck. Clinging to him, she kissed him back, matching his passion with fire of her own. His hand stole lower and cupped her ass. He pulled her even closer against him.

The kiss was like a brand on her soul, driving her wild with desire. Her breasts were full and taut with need. Fire burned low in her belly. She opened her mouth and their tongues entwined. He tasted like beer. Once again, the malty taste took her back to that night.

"What the hell's going on?"

Chapter Six

Zane's voice finally penetrated the fog of desire in her head. Sheridan jumped away guiltily, her breath coming fast.

"N-nothing," she stammered, flushing.

Joel recovered more swiftly. Calmly, he held his hand out toward her brother. "Zane. It's nice to see you again."

"What the hell are you doing with my sister? You barely know each other!"

Joel glanced at Sheridan, obviously prepared to allow her to set the tone. She opened her mouth to blurt out the truth and then closed it again. She was fully aware of the risks she'd taken by going home with a stranger and she didn't need a lecture from her brother, no matter how well-intended.

"Zane, back off. This is none of your business."

Zane's frown deepened. "Of course it's my business! You're my sister!"

"Who's plenty old enough to make her own decisions," Sheridan replied.

When Zane opened his mouth to protest again, she stepped toward him and placed a restraining hand on his arm. "Please, Zane. It's fine. I don't need you getting involved in this. Joel and I know each other…from before."

Zane's frown was replaced with confusion. "From before?

When? What the hell are you talking about?"

"It doesn't matter," Sheridan said.

"But—"

"Please, Zane. Go back inside. There's nothing to worry about."

Zane looked like he wanted to protest further, but instead turned a hard gaze on Joel.

"I'm not sure how the two of you came about, but I'm telling you now, forget it. My sister is out of bounds to the likes of you."

Joel regarded him with a lazy expression, but steel glinted in his eyes. "Why? Because I'm a Craigdon? Or because I'm a cop? Who do you have a beef with, Forrest?"

The two men sized each other up, neither of them giving ground. Sheridan made a sound of annoyance in the back of her throat.

"For goodness sakes! Stop it, both of you! Neither of you have a say on what I do or who I spend my time with." She turned to her brother.

"Zane, I'm no longer a teenager who has to ask for permission. Not from my father. Not from you."

Zane's hard gaze remained fixed on Joel. "You don't understand! He's a Craigdon! Don't you know what that means?"

"No, Zane. I don't judge people by their family."

"Have you forgotten his father was a notorious womanizer, among other things! Don't you care about that?"

His words gave her pause. All of a sudden, she remembered another time when Henry Craigdon had approached her at a charity fundraiser. It had happened a couple of years earlier. Joel must have seen something in her expression, because he frowned. Hastily, she pushed the unpleasant memory aside.

Sheridan lifted her chin in a show of defiance and stared at her brother. "As a matter of fact, I don't. I don't hold anyone responsible for the sins of their family. I take people how I find them and make up my own mind whether they're worth my time. I suggest you do the same."

With a grunt of disapproval and a final hard look in Joel's direction, Zane stormed back inside. Sheridan moved closer to the rail of the balcony and stared into the night. The clean crisp air filled her lungs. There was nothing like a good downpour to lift her spirits. Or another kiss with the most exciting man she'd known.

"I'm sorry about that," she said.

"No, I'm the one who's sorry."

She frowned. "What for?"

"I shouldn't have kissed you."

"I think you're forgetting it was a mutual thing."

"Whatever. I should have known better."

"Why? Because you're a Craigdon and I'm a McClintock and our families are sworn enemies?"

"No. Because… It feels way too good when I kiss you and right now I don't know how you fit into my investigation. If at all. I need to keep my distance until this case is finalized."

She stared at him in disbelief. "You actually think I could have stolen money from my own brother?"

He held her gaze, his expression somber. "I don't know what to think. It's early days. Like I said, I need to keep my distance until this is over."

Anger ignited inside her. "Well, you don't have to worry about that! I wouldn't spend a second of my time with a man who thinks I'm capable of something like that! You can take your kisses and shove them!"

With that, she turned on her heel and stormed away, berating herself all the while for being so stupid.

As soon as the Australian Transactions Reports and Analysis Centre, otherwise known as AUSTRAC, confirmed the transactions leaving the McClintock accounts were headed offshore, it took a judge less than twenty-four hours to issue a search warrant for the McClintock Properties' computers. Promptly at ten o'clock, a week after their last visit, Joel and Ralph returned to the McClintock offices and asked to see Zane Forrest.

Though it was the same fellow manning the front desk as the last time they'd been there, he put them through the identical routine, asking if they had an appointment, to which they showed their badges. This time, instead of further questions, he promptly picked up the phone. After speaking quietly into the receiver, he ended the call and looked up at Joel.

"Giselle will be down in a minute."

The same attractive brunette who'd accompanied them on their previous visit arrived a short time later. This time, her demeanor was far less friendly. It was obvious she was aware their return to her building didn't bode well for her boss. She gave them the barest of courtesies as she walked with them to the bank of lifts that whisked them to the top floor.

As the doors to the lift slid open, they stepped off and walked into the vast reception area where Giselle told them to take a seat. This time, there was no offer of coffee. Joel had a few moments to consider this upcoming meeting with Sharon's brother. No doubt the man was still seething over his discovery that his sister and a Craigdon were somewhat friendly with each other.

Well, that was too bad for Forrest. Joel hadn't gone out of his way to spend the night with the daughter of his father's sworn enemy and it seemed Sharon hadn't been any the wiser about his true identity, either. It was just one of those things they had to deal with and Forrest better start dealing with it now because Joel was there on official police business and his investigation had just ratcheted up a notch.

After more than fifteen minutes spent waiting on the couch flicking mindlessly through the glossy magazines, Zane appeared in front of them.

"Sorry to keep you waiting, Detectives," he said in a tone that indicated he wasn't sorry at all.

They followed him into his office. Though Zane suggested they take a seat, all of them remained standing. Zane looked from one to the other, and though outwardly he appeared calm, Joel sensed a nervous tension in the air.

"So, you're back. I take it you have news?" Forrest stated.

Joel nodded. "Yes. We've done a forensic examination of the company's bank accounts. It looks like the information we were given is good."

Zane's eyes widened in surprise. "You mean you've found something?" he exclaimed.

"Yes," Joel continued. "There are several transactions— fifteen in total—of large sums of money that have been transferred to an overseas account. None of them were reported to AUSTRAC and that's where the problem begins. We're still waiting on more specific details, but given the fact you told me McClintock Properties has no international dealings of that nature, we can only suspect something untoward is going on. With that in mind, we have a search warrant for your computers, laptops and iPads."

Ralph pulled the warrant out of the pocket of his jacket and handed it to Zane, who glanced at it. A moment later, Zane's jaw dropped.

"You want to take *all* of them? There are more than seven hundred employees. They each have a computer. What are they supposed to use in the meantime?"

"We'll start with those belonging to members of the executive, and any other staff members with high-level security clearance."

"Of course," Zane replied giving Joel a hard look. "But I've told you already. It's only me and my sister who have access to the bank accounts."

Joel tried not to react to the mention of Sharon. Instead, he offered a nonchalant shrug.

"Those devices will be the first ones analyzed, but just because someone doesn't have official company clearance doesn't mean they can't get into the system's files by other means. If we don't find what we're looking for in the first instance, we'll be back. In the meantime, I suggest you put in a bulk order at Harvey Norman for computers."

Zane shook his head, looking a little disorientated. "This is outrageous! You can't do this! We're trying to run a business!"

"You can get upset all you like, Mr Forrest," Joel replied, "but I'm afraid we're acting within the powers of a warrant. Now either you hand over the hardware voluntarily, or I'll have you arrested for obstruction. What will it be?"

Sharon's brother glared at Joel. "You might have a veneer of polish, but you're a Craigdon through and through. Make no mistake."

Joel shrugged, as if the man's opinion of him was of no consequence. Inwardly he wondered what had gone on between their respective fathers to cause such animosity.

"I still can't believe what you're saying! That someone is *stealing* from us!" Zane added, looking distressed. "If I had to come up with the name of someone I thought capable of doing this, I wouldn't be able to do it and yet you tell me you've found *fifteen* illegal transactions! Incredible!"

Joel felt a twinge of sympathy. "I'm sorry, Mr Forrest. But this is serious. The amount of money transferred from McClintock accounts totals just under thirty million dollars. We're talking about a significant amount of money."

Zane continued to look dazed. Joel felt another stab of sympathy, but forced himself to remain ambivalent. *Who knew?*

Forrest's confusion might just be an act. Someone had transferred that money and it wasn't some ordinary employee who had a stroke of luck. No, whoever had pulled it off had either been given access or had acquired access over time—by legitimate means or otherwise. The access to funds and these illegal transactions were evidence of a relatively sophisticated operation carried out by a pilfering team or someone who knew what they were doing.

Ralph stepped forward. "Is that your computer?" he asked, indicating an HP all-in-one desktop. Its wide screen took up a sizable portion of the CEO's desk.

"Yes," Zane replied.

"What about a laptop?" Joel asked.

"It's in my briefcase, along with my iPad." Zane scrubbed a hand over his face. "God, this is a nightmare. How am I supposed to get any work done? I have all my files on those devices."

"Surely you have a backup?" Joel asked.

"Yes, of course," Zane replied impatiently. "But first I'll have to go out and replace everything you take."

"Like I said," Joel replied. "I suggest you put in an order with Harvey Norman."

"You'll get them back once we finish with them," Ralph offered.

"Unless of course, they're needed for evidence," Joel added.

"How long will that take?" Zane asked.

Joel shrugged and then deliberately exaggerated. "Once our forensics people have gone through them, provided they add nothing further to the case, maybe a month or two."

"A month or two? This is a billion dollar company! A month or two is a lifetime! We might as well shut the doors if we have to wait that long."

Joel regarded him steadily. "Could be even longer."

Zane muttered an oath. "Look. Just take what you need and leave. This is difficult enough."

Joel nodded. "We'll need your sister's devices, too. Along with those of any other executive staff members."

At the mention of Sharon, Zane frowned. He gave Joel a narrow-eyed look that said he hadn't forgotten what had happened on the balcony of Hannah Burke's art gallery. He finally offered a reply.

"Of course. I'll get Giselle to give you a list. You'll find Sheridan on the floor below this."

Joel cocked an eyebrow in question. "Sheridan?"

"My sister. You know, the one who you had your tongue down her throat the other night. She's head of finance and contract negotiations."

Joel frowned. *Perhaps he had more than one sister…* "Don't you mean Sharon?"

Zane looked at him like he'd sprouted two horns from his head. "Sharon? Who the hell is Sharon?"

Joel flushed. "Your…sister?"

Zane gave a bark of laughter. "My sister? What the hell is this? What, you don't think I know her name?" He shot Joel a strange look. "Where the hell did you come up with Sharon?"

Joel fought to keep his embarrassment in check. "How many sisters do you have, Mr Forrest?"

"Just the one. Her name is *Sheridan.* I don't know what the hell you're talking about…this Sharon girl. Somebody gave you the wrong information." He shook his head and turned away.

Embarrassment crept up Joel's neck and inched its way across his cheeks as realization set in.

She gave me a fake name…

Why was he surprised? Had he expected her to be honest with him about who she was before she agreed to come home with him and spend the night with him, a complete stranger? The truth was, he didn't know what he'd expected.

So, it was Sheridan… He liked the name. It suited her much more than Sharon. At the thought of seeing her again, his pulse surged in anticipation. It was supposed to be a one night stand. That's how it had started out. But he couldn't stop thinking about her. It had gotten even worse since the night at the gallery. He'd woken every night since with a hard-on so painful he'd been desperate for release. The more he thought about her, the more he wanted to spend time with her again. Both in and outside the bedroom.

Joel swallowed a sigh. His problems with Sharo…*Sheridan* would have to wait. Right now they had other things to tend to. Together with Ralph, Joel loaded up Zane's computer and other devices, labeled them with evidence tags and logged them manually on an evidence register as they proceeded. After thanking Zane for his co-operation, they headed toward the lifts.

"What the hell was Forrest talking about, you with your tongue down his sister's throat? She's part of our investigation."

Joel flushed. "Forget about it. It was nothing. We barely know each other. If she's responsible for these thefts, she'll be held to account."

Ralph gave Joel a searching look and then nodded. "Fair enough. We're going to need more manpower," he said as they dumped Zane's hardware on the backseat of the unmarked police vehicle.

"Yeah." Joel pulled out his phone. He made the call to the station and was told they'd send a few more officers over right away.

Joel ended the call and looked at Ralph. "You wait here for the others. I'm going to pay a visit to the finance department. Let's hope our CEO's sister is as forthcoming as her brother."

Chapter Seven

Sheridan gnawed on the end of her pen while she answered another bunch of emails. Most of them had to do with her latest airport project. Negotiations between McClintock and the Blackhall consortium were going well. They'd almost agreed on terms. She was hopeful contracts for the purchase of the land could be finalized within the next week or so.

Zane would be pleased. Sheridan had bargained hard. A raft of other developers were sniffing around the much-coveted property, but not everyone had the ability to charm and persuade like she did. Besides, she'd offered Blackhall a good deal.

Sheridan believed in playing fair. The secret to her success in business negotiations was making sure both parties walked away with something. She'd done the figures. Apartments in the newly created suburb were expected to sell in the millions. Even with the generous terms she'd offered the seller, there was plenty of money to go round.

The phone at her elbow buzzed. Taking the pen out of her mouth, she picked up the receiver.

"Yes, Jane?"

"Sheridan. I have a Detective Joel Craigdon out here. He wants to see you."

Her heart immediately went into overdrive. Joel was outside her office. Her thoughts went straight to their last meeting. Or rather, the way they'd parted. She'd been furious with him for thinking she might be capable of stealing from her family's company.

Now that she'd had time to calm down and think about it, she understood he'd only been doing his job. After all, apart from physically loving her in the most intimate of ways, he barely knew her. He certainly didn't know what kind of person she was.

She drew in a deep breath. Refusing to see him was childish. Besides, she had nothing to hide. Squaring her shoulders, she offered a reply.

"Okay. Send him in. Thanks, Jane."

She hung up the phone, pushed away from her desk and headed straight for the small bathroom off one side of her office. She looked in the mirror and fluffed her hair and then quickly reapplied her lipstick. Nerves danced around in her stomach. It was ridiculous to feel so edgy and excited at the thought of seeing him again. So, they'd slept together. Big deal. And they'd shared another hot and heavy moment out on a balcony. Again, no big deal.

The pep talk didn't make any difference. By the time the sharp knock came on her office door, she was trembling with nerves and anticipation. With a final look in the mirror, she spun around, strode over to the door and opened it.

He stood on the other side staring at her. He looked tense and angry as he gave her a mocking once-over. He wore another dark-colored suit, white shirt and expensive tie, looking every bit as gorgeous as he had all the other times she'd seen him. She drew in another breath and eased it out in an effort to slow her racing heart.

"H-hi," she stammered. Heat exploded across her face. *God, I feel like a gawky teenager…*

He glared at her. "Can I come in, *Sheridan?*"

She closed her eyes in embarrassment. *Of course he knows my real name now...*

Avoiding his gaze, she stepped back and allowed him room to enter. A waft of expensive, familiar cologne reached her nose. With it, a barrage of erotic memories bombarded her. She pushed them back. Feeling the need to explain, she barricaded herself behind her desk and forced herself to look directly at him.

"I'm sorry. I'm not sure why I used an alias. At the time, things were all happening rather quickly and—"

"At the time you didn't seem to mind."

A blush heated her cheeks. "You're right. And I should have given you my real name. The thing is, that was my first time."

"Bullsh—"

"I don't mean that was my *first time*," she hurried to explain in an effort to ease the annoyance that now flooded his handsome face. "What I meant was, it's the first time I'd had a one night stand. I... I didn't know the rules."

"There aren't any rules," he said dryly.

She shrugged, even more embarrassed at her lack of sophistication. "So you're an expert?" She couldn't keep the tartness from her tone.

He merely shrugged.

She gritted her teeth. "Okay, so there aren't any rules. I didn't know the protocol, whatever. I hadn't even given any thought to sharing names. When you asked me, it just came out. It wasn't a conscious decision to lie to you. At least, not until that moment."

He made an impatient movement of his hand, as if whatever else she had to say was of little importance. Piqued, she clenched her teeth, determined not to say another word. What was done was done. They'd both been consenting adults. It wasn't like either of them had done anything illegal.

The thought made her frown. She recalled her conversation with Zane about the reasons Joel and his partner had last paid a visit. A flutter of nerves filled her stomach. "What are you doing here?"

"Someone is moving large sums of money from McClintock to an overseas account and they haven't done it via the legal channels. I have a search warrant for all of the computers and other such devices in this office. We've already collected your brother's. Shortly a team of officers will be here to claim the rest. Your brother has given me a list of people who are on the executive staff. Your name is on top of the list."

Sheridan gasped and her heart thumped. "This is outrageous! McClintock Properties is a blue chip company. We do not go about breaking the law. To imply someone from this company is illegally transferring money…" She shook her head. "No, absolutely not."

"You aren't listening to me, *Sheridan*. Our forensic technicians found evidence to the contrary. They've already found fifteen transactions, in fact. All of them headed offshore and none of them went through the proper channels." His gaze hardened. "In case you didn't know, every time you make an international transfer it must be reported to AUSTRAC. In McClintock's case, we're talking large transactions and not a single one of them was reported."

As she stared at him, she was filled with a sense of foreboding. Fear trickled through her veins. If what he said was true, someone in their company had been stealing… The thought was preposterous. And yet, he claimed to have the evidence…

"H-how much? How much are you talking?"

"Altogether, just under thirty million."

She gasped. "Thirty million dollars?"

"Yes."

She shook her head, dazed. "That's... No, that can't be right. There must be some mistake. Accounting should have caught it."

He leaned across her desk, so close she could see the darker flecks of blue in the cobalt of his eyes.

"No, *Sheridan*. There's no mistake. And we're determined to get to the bottom of it. If you're innocent, as you claim, you ought to be as interested as I am to identify the culprit. After all, it's *your* family's money they've stolen."

She continued to stare at him, her mind awhirl. "Yes, of course. You're right. If what you say is true, of course we must get to the bottom of it." Distracted, she ran a hand through her hair. The movement pulled her blouse taut across her breasts. His gaze immediately zeroed in.

Her belly somersaulted in need. When he lifted his gaze to hers, she saw the same desire reflected in his eyes. She closed her eyes briefly against the intensity in his gaze.

Oh, good heavens! How did it come to this? My first one night stand and the guy ends up being the chief investigator looking into my family's company. We were never meant to see each other again...

Still, she couldn't ignore her reaction to him. It didn't matter why he was there, she was glad to see him again and she couldn't ignore the little *zing* of pleasure and anticipation, knowing that until his investigation was over, he might be a frequent visitor to her office. She had nothing to hide except how he affected her. She fought hard to contain her grin.

Joel noticed the smile that tugged at the corners of Sheridan's full mouth. It was coated in a glistening red lipstick and the moment he saw her, he was taken straight back to the night they'd met. Instead of the tight-fitting black dress, she wore an equally expensive, pale gray suit. The jacket was tailored to hug her curves and flared gently over her hips. The skirt was straight and narrow and emphasized the length of her stockinged legs. The light-pink blouse that had snagged his attention when it pulled tight across her breasts seemed to mock him. Even now, he fought his body's instinctive reaction. His cock was hard, straining against his pants. It was all he could do to keep his mind on the job.

He silently cursed the luck that saw him investigating the woman who'd filled his dreams every night since he'd met her. It was early days in the investigation and there was no telling what evidence they'd dig up, but if he knew what was good for him, he needed to stay the hell away from Sheridan McClintock.

Joel scrubbed at his beard and then with a sigh, leaned back in his government-issued chair. The clock on the wall in front of him told him it was seven. Night came earlier in winter and evening had long since arrived. Lights from an adjoining office block illuminated the fact that almost everyone had gone home. Just like he should have. His shift had ended an hour ago. Holidaying in Europe and those days of doing nothing more taxing than ordering a drink seemed like a distant memory.

A roomful of McClintock computers, laptops and iPads had been delivered to the station two weeks earlier. The tech guys had been combing through them ever since. So far, they'd come up with nothing. It was frustrating as hell, but there was nothing Joel could do until they did. At least AUSTRAC had been able to provide more information on the overseas account.

The investigators had reported back that all fifteen transactions had been deposited into an account in the Caymans. A notorious tax haven, it was a handy place to park thirty million dollars. Someone was planning for the future. The question was, who?

The account had been opened in the name of a shelf company. No surprises there. They were still trying to trace it back to an individual. The problem with this sort of account was they were set up with stealth in mind. That was the sole reason the account had come into existence. To give someone a place to hide money, usually from the tax office, but that wasn't always the only motivation.

Both Zane Forrest and his sister insisted they were the only two with access to McClintock's bank accounts. If that were true, Joel wondered which was stealing from the other.

Unfortunately, the tech guys had already been over their computers. Their desktop devices, iPads and laptops had come up clean. And so had every other device they'd analyzed so far. It was beyond annoying and was the reason Joel was still at his desk long after he should have clocked off.

Scrubbing his hands through his hair, he sighed again. It was Friday night. He should be out having a good time, not driving himself crazy with this. Three weeks earlier—the same night he'd met Sheridan McClintock—he'd been at the Ivy Bar with his colleagues.

With a muttered curse, he sat forward impatiently and with a few keystrokes, logged off. He needed to go home, crack a beer and lose himself in some mindless TV before he got caught up in memories of Sheridan again. He refused to let his mind drift down that path again. It was difficult enough to keep her out of his thoughts when he was investigating her brother's company. It would be impossible if he allowed himself to remember what had happened between them that Friday night. And then again at the gallery…

He'd left without buying a painting. Hannah had called him the next day, wondering if he was all right. He could hear her unspoken question: Why didn't she make a sale? He'd apologized for leaving the party early and promised to drop by and choose a painting for his living room. There was no way he was owning up to what had happened on the balcony.

"Hey, Craigdon. What are you still doing here?"

Joel blinked away his thoughts and looked up. Brent Power was a junior detective in the fraud squad. Newly promoted, he still had an eagerness about him that Joel liked. They needed people like Brent. Cops who hadn't been worn down by time and the system.

"Just leaving now," he said and pushed away from his desk.

"Me, too. I'm meeting a few of the guys down at the Ivy Bar. Wanna come?"

Joel hesitated. He'd just finished telling himself all the reasons why he needed to stop thinking about Sheridan McClintock. Did he really want to put himself through dealing with the memories that would beset him the moment he set foot in the Ivy Bar?

"Come on, Craigdon. It's Friday night. You got any better place to be?"

Joel continued to hesitate, torn. If he were sensible, he'd thank Brent for his offer and politely decline. He'd go home to his empty apartment and even emptier bed. A bed that unfortunately no longer held the faint scent of the delectable Sheridan McClintock on his sheets…

With a muffled groan he found himself nodding. "Yeah. Okay. Just for a drink or two."

Brent grinned and patted him on the back. "Good on you! Let's go, mate!"

Sheridan looked around the group of attractive young professionals that filled every square foot of the Ivy Bar. She didn't know why she'd allowed herself to be talked into returning, but there she was with a couple of girlfriends who were on the prowl for someone to take home. She'd been friends with Bianca and Nicole since high school, but lately it seemed she had less and less in common with them.

Both women worked in the advertising industry and constantly pored over the latest fashion magazines. While Sheridan had always had a flair for style and took pride in her appearance, that interest didn't consume her every waking moment. Bianca and Nicole had also recently gotten into picking up men for one night stands. Sheridan was adamant that kind of behavior was too risky. She knew from experience that appearances could be deceiving and she wanted to know who she invited into her home. But her warnings fell flat when she recalled how she'd gone against her own advice and spent the night with Joel.

"Hey, what about that one? Over my shoulder and to the left. Dark hair, jacket, T-shirt, jeans. Looks like an executive letting his hair down. What do you think?" Nicole grinned, directing the question to Sheridan.

Blinking away thoughts of Joel, Sheridan took a quick look over Nicole's shoulder. The man sat at the bar, a drink in his hand. His dark hair was styled and swept back off his high forehead. Tinged with gray at the temples, he looked both mature and sophisticated. Though he sat alone, there was no hint of desperation in his demeanor. He appeared to be a man comfortable in his own skin.

"Good-looking, confident. I'd say he's just your type," Sheridan teased.

Nicole grinned. "That's exactly what I thought." She winked at both of them. "Wish me luck!"

Sheridan opened her mouth to caution her friend about taking strange men home, but then closed it again. If there was one thing she wasn't, it was a hypocrite. Not all strangers were serial killers. In fact, her friends seemed to have a knack for choosing men who were both courteous and respectful. Both women endlessly regaled her about the nights of excitement and passion they'd experienced at the hands of men they'd only just met. She wondered if their stories had played a part in her decision to throw caution to the wind and go home with Joel. That had been so out of character for her and yet she couldn't say she regretted it… Or that she wouldn't do it again.

And then she saw him…

Her heart leaped into her throat and her pulse took off at a gallop. She barely noticed the jaunty wave of farewell Nicole gave her and Bianca as she headed toward the mystery man at the bar. Sheridan's attention was caught on someone altogether different.

Joel stood in the entryway with another broad-shouldered, good-looking male. They both had that air of authority and confidence she now associated with men who knew how to take charge. She guessed the man who accompanied him was another cop.

From her vantage point seated at a table that faced the doorway, she watched Joel and his friend make their way to the bar. They found empty stools and immediately engaged the barman. Not far away, her friend Nicole was already in animated conversation with her mystery man.

Bianca whistled low under her breath. "Who is *that?*"

Sheridan looked at Bianca who now stared in Joel's direction. A surge of jealousy arced through her. "He-he's nobody. A cop," Sheridan replied dismissively.

Bianca's eyes widened. "You *know* him?"

Heat crept up Sheridan's neck. She kept her gaze focused on the table. "I don't *know* him. Not really. I've met him a couple of times. He came to the office the other day and spoke with Zane. That's all."

A slow smile curved Bianca's lips. "I wouldn't mind him dropping by *my* office. Whew! That man is pure sex on legs."

Once again, Sheridan forced down a surge of jealousy. She had no hold on Joel or any say about the women he chose to spend time with. Just because she didn't want to share him with one of her friends…

As if sensing their scrutiny, he looked up. Both she and Bianca were caught staring at him. Embarrassment burned across Sheridan's cheeks. She hastily looked away, but not before she saw his eyes widen in surprise and then a smile of acknowledgement slowly lit up his face.

"Oh, God! He's even more gorgeous when he smiles! Look at that beard! I bet it feels just as soft as it looks. Imagine what it would feel like when he goes down on you! Oh, Sheridan! I have to talk to that man. Please, introduce us!"

Sheridan barely heard the excited chatter of her friend. She was trying hard to avoid looking at Joel again. All she could see was the perfection of his nakedness and the way he'd felt pressed against her. The heat of his body, the thrust of his hips, his sensual kisses that went on forever…

Almost frantically, she tightened her hold on her glass and emptied the contents of her drink in a few desperate gulps and then set it down a little too hard on the table.

Bianca threw her a strange look. "Are you all right?"

"Yes. No. Actually, I have a headache. I think I might leave."

Bianca pulled a face. "But we need to go and talk to your sexy cop. At least stay long enough to introduce me."

"First of all, he's not *my* sexy cop. And secondly, I'm really not feeling well. I need to go." On the verge of panic, Sheridan felt under the table for her handbag.

"Oh my God! He's headed this way!" Bianca squealed.

Sheridan's pulse rate hit overdrive. Her fingers brushed against her handbag and she clutched it like a lifeline. With her heart thumping, she kept her face averted and pushed back her chair. There was no way she could stay and risk a repeat of the last time she was there. As much as she hadn't been able to get the detective off her mind, she wasn't going to succumb to his charms again. Especially now that he was caught up in an investigation involving her brother's company.

"I really need to leave."

She darted a glance in Joel's direction and discovered he was already halfway to their table. With a hasty farewell to Bianca, Sheridan pushed her way through the crowd in the other direction, headed straight for the exit.

Chapter Eight

Joel watched as Sheridan shouldered her way through the press of bodies and disappeared into the crowd. He was filled with disappointment and was then irritated with himself. It was probably best they stay clear of each other. After all, he was investigating criminal activity that had taken place in her brother's company. The same company where she worked. Not only worked, but held a position of responsibility and trust—and even though they'd found no evidence of wrongdoing on her devices, that didn't mean she was in the clear.

From the moment he spied her he'd tried hard to ignore her. He told himself all the reasons why he should stay the hell away from her, but it was like she was a magnet and there was nothing he could do to resist. He'd once again been overwhelmed with images of them together, naked in his bed. He was off his stool and halfway across the room moving toward her when she got up abruptly and left.

Her hasty departure was like a bucket of iced water thrown over his face. He blinked, feeling slightly disorientated and then gradually became aware of the attractive brunette who'd been seated next to Sheridan. The woman's smile was openly flirty. She waved him over, clearly interested in getting to know him better.

"Hi, I'm Bianca," she gushed, extending a slim arm.

He shook her hand. "Joel."

"Joel. A strong name. It suits you." She shot him another flirty smile.

"It looks like your friend's abandoned you," he said, glancing after Sheridan.

Bianca waved away his concern. "Oh, don't worry about her. She's not feeling well." Bianca leaned forward and ran the tip of her finger down his arm. "I, on the other hand, am feeling great."

He forced a smile. He had zero interest in the woman in front of him, despite her not-so-subtle signs of encouragement. All he could think about was Sheridan.

Why had she bolted the minute she saw him? Had she been overwhelmed by memories of their time together in his apartment and the gallery and wasn't ready to face him, or was it a guilty conscience that had her scurrying for the door? They'd found nothing to link her to the transactions, but perhaps she was involved on some other level? Or maybe she'd been smart enough to use someone else's device?

The truth was, he had no idea if or how complicit she was in the illegal transactions and he knew he'd best stay the hell away from her until she was in the clear. He didn't need his boss asking questions about his ability to remain impartial if it were discovered a girl he was keen on was up to her neck in a fraud.

Now that Sheridan had departed the club, he swiftly lost interest in being there. Cutting off Bianca mid-sentence, he politely excused himself and ignoring her sulky pout, he headed back to the bar.

"I'm going to call it a night," he told Brent as he sat his empty glass on the bar.

"But you only just got here!" Brent protested.

"Yeah. I'm not feeling so hot. I think I'll go home and get an early night."

"Hey, this place is buzzing, Joel! Take a look around! Surely you can find something that takes your fancy." Brent gave him a wink, followed by a knowing grin.

Swallowing a sigh of irritation, Joel forced a smile. "It's all good, mate. I'm beat. But you make sure you have a good time, okay? I want to hear all about it next week."

With that, Joel lifted his hand in a brief motion of farewell and left.

It was late, well past midnight, but Christopher Barrington didn't care. These hours when he could escape the minutiae of his boring life and pretend to be someone else were some of the happiest moments of his existence. Ever since his prick-of-a-father had seen fit to leave Christopher out of his will and pass his millions on to his other children, Christopher's life had been headed down the toilet.

For all of his forty years he'd been overlooked by his biological father. Henry Craigdon had still been single when he'd had an affair with Christopher's mother, but he hadn't been inclined to do the right thing by Evelyn Baker when she discovered she was pregnant. Instead Henry had first denied the baby was his. *What a prick.* Evelyn had been working as Henry's executive assistant at the time of the affair. She'd been forced to give up her job in disgrace.

Eventually, DNA proved beyond a shadow of a doubt that Henry was Christopher's father, but his mother had still been forced to resort to the courts to force Henry to make a financial contribution toward Christopher's upbringing and education. And what a joke that had been.

Henry had somehow managed to find a judge he could influence and the order for child support had been a joke. It had started at twenty-five dollars a week and over the ensuing years, it barely increased by ten percent. Then Evelyn met and married Frank Barrington and Frank was more than happy to support his new wife and her young son. When Christopher turned twelve, Frank asked his permission to legally adopt him.

Christopher ought to have felt grateful for Frank's generosity, but all it did was highlight the deficiencies of Christopher's biological dad. Anger and resentment festered over the years and consolidated into a ball of rage. Christopher had counted down the years to Henry's death and had quietly celebrated when it had happened unexpectedly—and well before his time.

Then the prick had dealt him the cruelest blow of all— Henry had not only left him out of the will, he hadn't made mention of Christopher, his first born, at all. Just like he'd treated him in life, Henry had treated Christopher in death the same. As if he didn't exist. Even thinking of it now, some four months after they'd buried the prick, it still had the power to hurt and to send Christopher's temper spiraling.

With a muttered curse, he forced the hurtful memories aside. It was Friday night and Christopher was determined to enjoy himself. This wasn't the first time he'd helped himself to Zane Forrest's office. The CEO of McClintock Properties had the flashiest office Christopher had ever seen. Not even the law offices he'd recently attended in the city were as posh as this. With the rest of the staff long gone, Christopher had the building to himself and he intended to have a good time.

Taking a seat behind Zane's desk, he drew himself close to the keyboard. Tapping in his boss' login details, he waited for the computer to load. He chuckled at the memory of how easy it had been to discover Zane's password. A little hunting around and he'd found a small address book in the top drawer of Zane's desk. On a hunch, he'd opened the book to "P" for passwords. Sure enough, there were several written there, along with the login details for his PC.

People were so predictable. It disappointed Christopher to discover Zane was just like so many others. He liked Zane. He was a good boss. He demanded excellence, but he was fair. Christopher had worked in the contracts department for more than five years now. It wasn't a job he particularly enjoyed.

McClintock Properties was Henry Craigdon's biggest competitor and it was no secret Michael McClintock had despised Henry. The feeling was mutual. Christopher had only taken the position at McClintock to annoy his father. The sad thing was he wasn't even sure Henry had noticed.

But despite his reasons for taking the job, slowly the work had begun to grow on him and to his annoyance he found he was good at it. Lately he'd discovered he was even better at impersonating Zane online to impress women. After all, who didn't want to date the CEO of a Fortune 500 company? Besides, it was a good distraction from the disappointment of being disinherited by Henry.

With a surge of anticipation, Christopher opened Zane's Skype account and clicked on the picture of a woman he'd been flirting with for the better part of a week. She was blond and busty and beautiful and just smart enough to hold his interest, but not smart enough to work out the subterfuge. He'd given her the virtual tour of Zane's office. It was no surprise she'd been impressed. He was sure by tonight they'd set a time and day to meet face to face and then they could really have fun.

There was no need for him to come clean with his true identity. After all, where was the harm? He didn't intend for this to turn into anything serious. The women he duped need never know they hadn't dated the real Zane Forrest. If things went well with the face to face, sometimes he invited them back to Zane's office.

Inevitably Christopher would make good use of the wide leather couch that stood against one wall. The women thought they'd received attention from the great man himself and Christopher had a good time. Where was the harm? It wasn't his fault they weren't smart enough to do their research and work out he looked nothing like his boss.

Joel arrived back at work on Monday morning feeling out of sorts. He'd spent the weekend catching up with various members of his family over lunch at his mother's house. He'd regaled them all with tales of Europe and some of the adventures he'd had, but one look at his brother, Callum and his new fiancé, Grace, and Joel was filled with a surge of longing.

Grace was halfway through her time in rehab. She'd been receiving treatment for an addiction to alcohol and had been given day release. Though Joel didn't know her well, he knew Callum had given long and careful consideration before leaving the seminary and choosing a life with her. That told Joel a lot about the kind of woman Grace must be.

He also admired her for her willingness to seek help for her addiction. It wasn't something everyone had the courage to do. Grace was now a month into her treatment. She looked healthy and relaxed. She'd chosen to spend her day out with her children and Callum's family.

Grace's children, Seth and Alyssa, were noisy and cute. It was obvious they already felt comfortable around Joel's family. And why wouldn't they? During Grace's rehab, Callum had moved back home. Grace had been allowed to have her weekly contact visits with her children at Craigdon Manor. It was a plan that looked like it was working out for everyone. His mother, Elizabeth treated them like they were her grandchildren, showering them with food and gifts, expressing interest in their schooling, their hobbies, their new pet.

Both of the kids had been ecstatic over the arrival of the puppy. Callum had gifted the dog to Grace after her family dog died. Given that Callum was allergic, it was a loving and thoughtful gesture and Joel was sure Grace saw it as such. Callum had also been instrumental in getting Grace unsupervised visits with her children and though they were still living with their grandparents, Grace and Callum were hopeful she'd be successful in having them return to live with her full time once the matter came back before the court a few months down the track.

The way Callum and Grace looked at each other, it was clear the pair were in love. Joel was sure they only let go of each other's hands to eat. The loving looks, the tender kisses, even the casual caresses—none of them had gone unnoticed by Joel and it left him wanting the same thing for himself. Which totally surprised him.

Before he'd left for Europe, making a deeper commitment to his long-time girlfriend was the last thing on his mind. MJ had been angling for a proposal for months, but Joel had shied away. Now, after spending a single night and a few stolen kisses with Sheridan McClintock, he found himself wanting more. Not just more of her delectable body in his bed, but more of *her*. She intrigued him, challenged him, excited him— and they barely knew each other. He wanted to spend more time with her, get to know her. Let her get to know him.

The thought of her with another man filled him with jealousy. He wanted her for himself. If that meant marriage, then maybe he'd have to give that kind of commitment some serious consideration. He was surprised the thought didn't fill him with panic like it usually did. His mom had always told them when they found the right person, they'd know. Right now, he couldn't imagine life without Sheridan in it and he barely knew her. Perhaps his mom was right…?

With a sigh, he pulled off his jacket and hung it in his

locker. Of course, getting to know Sheridan McClintock was a little difficult at the moment. Until they'd wrapped up the current investigation, he needed to keep his distance. It would be easier to remain distant from her if he were confident she'd been involved in illegal activity. He was a pretty good judge of character. She hadn't tweaked his radar in any way other than having opportunity.

He detoured to the tearoom on his way to the squad room and poured himself a coffee. He carried it to his desk and set it down.

"How was your weekend?" Brent asked, already seated in front of his computer.

"Fine," Joel mumbled. "And yours?"

Brent's grin widened. "Oh, yeah, baby. I had the best time! Don't forget I told you to stay!"

Joel managed a smile. "So you met someone at the Ivy Bar?"

"You bet I did! Right after you left, this chick came up to me and asked if I wanted to dance. We hit it off right away. Boy, she has some moves, and believe me when I tell you they're not limited to the dance floor." He winked at Joel.

Joel chuckled. "Well, I'm glad you had a good weekend. Let's hope we make as much progress on the McClintock matter."

"Oh, yeah. Speaking of the McClintock case, I had a call from one of the techies just before you arrived."

"Yeah? What did he have to say?"

Brent idly scratched his head. "They spent all weekend going over every device we took from the McClintock offices. Seems like they missed something the first time. Second time round, they found what we were looking for."

Joel's heart started in excitement. "They located the transactions?"

"Yeah. All fifteen of them. They were hidden in coding,

but once they knew what to look for, it was fairly simple to track them all down."

"Whose device did they come from?" Joel held his breath while he waited for the answer.

"The head of finance. The chick. Sheridan. They were found on her computer. What the hell kind of name is that, anyway?"

Joel's ears buzzed and he barely heard the rest of what Brent had to say. The technicians had found evidence the illegal transactions had been made from Sheridan's computer! He shook his head once in instinctive denial, but then his resolve firmed. Thank God he hadn't pursued her any further. In the blink of an eye she'd gone from having a chance involvement to being his number one suspect.

Tamping down his disappointment, he compressed his lips into a thin line. "Have they sent through a report yet?"

"Probably. Check your inbox. They said they'd email it through right away."

Joel digested the information and as he logged into his computer and opened his emails, he braced himself for what he'd find. Sure enough, the report was sitting in his inbox. In bold black type it set out the evidence they'd found which established Sheridan McClintock's computer had been used to initiate all fifteen of the illegal transfers. Either Sheridan was the guilty party, or someone else used her login details.

Joel clung to the slight possibility that someone else had accessed Sheridan's computer and transferred money on fifteen separate occasions without her being aware of it. It was a long shot and if he hadn't been personally invested in her innocence, he probably would have dismissed the possibility as quickly as the idea formed.

Still, he prided himself on being thorough and keeping an open mind and he always looked at a case from every angle. This one was no different.

Ralph Tilocca appeared in the doorway of the squad room. Joel pushed away from his desk.

"Morning, Ralph. Don't get too comfortable," he advised his partner. "We're heading out."

Chapter Nine

Doing his best to keep a clear head, Joel swung the unmarked squad car close to the curb outside McClintock Properties. He and Ralph climbed out and headed for the glass front doors. The two of them went straight up to the man behind the front desk and flashed their credentials.

"Detectives," the man greeted them in a pleasant enough tone. "You're back again."

"Yes," Joel replied. "We're here to see Sheridan McClintock."

"Give me a moment. I'll call her office and let her know you're here."

With his hands jammed in his pockets. Joel turned away and studied the Tim Storrier original he'd spied the first time he'd been there. It reminded him of his most recent purchase. The Riley Hammond painting he'd bought from Hannah had arrived and he'd hung it on the wall behind the bar in his apartment. The bright colors of the contemporary piece of artwork provided a pop of color in his living room. Overall, he was pleased with the purchase and he was sure Hannah was just as pleased to make the sale.

Of course, every time he thought of that night at her gallery, his mind returned to those hot and heavy moments with Sheridan on the balcony. His blood had heated the instant he spotted her in her seductive red dress and things hadn't cooled a bit when he kissed her.

To the contrary, the mere touch of her lips ignited a fire so hot in him he thought it might consume him. His head had been filled with the feel of her in his arms, her curves pressed against him, the softness of her lips, the exotic smell of her perfume… And then her brother had discovered them and put a sudden halt to the desire that raged through Joel's veins. Joel couldn't help but wonder what might have happened if they'd been in a more secluded location.

Would she have let me fuck her like I knew she wanted me to? His body instinctively hardened at the thought. And then he cursed. She might very well be tangled up in his investigation. Even if she were innocent, the fact her computer and login credentials were involved made things complicated. If he were smart, he'd forget all about Sheridan McClintock and the way she made him feel.

He wished it were that easy…

Not only were things complicated by the ongoing investigation, after that night at the gallery, it was also clear Zane had a beef against Joel's family, or more specifically, his father. While Sheridan had seemed more inclined to judge people on their own actions, he'd noticed the shadow that had passed over her face when Zane called Henry a womanizer.

Was it the fact Joel's father had been unfaithful in his marriage that concerned her, or was there more to it? It bugged him that he didn't know.

The *ding* of the lift, indicating its arrival on the ground floor, registered. Spinning on his heel, he watched as Sheridan alighted. He tried not to notice how good she looked in her designer outfit and impossibly high heels. The bright red jacket fit her snugly around the waist and the matching short skirt emphasized the length of her shapely legs. She wore a white blouse that tied at her throat and contrasted starkly with her bright red lipstick, the exact same shade as her suit.

Sheridan's heels clicked on the marble tiles as she came toward them. She walked with confidence, although she avoided his gaze when she held out her hand toward them.

"Detective Craigdon. Detective Tilocca. You wanted to see me?"

Joel briefly shook her proffered hand and kept his expression neutral. "There have been some new developments. Is there somewhere we can go and talk in private?"

She nodded briskly. "Of course. We can go to my office." With that she turned on her heel and strode back the way she'd come.

Joel and Ralph followed. In the close confines of the lift, Joel tried not to breathe in too deeply. As he stood beside Sheridan, he found if he turned his head just slightly her exotic perfume wafted to him. That immediately brought back memories of their time together and right now it was the last thing he needed to be reminded of. Clearing his throat, he eased himself away from her.

Thankfully they reached their destination in short order and Joel gratefully stepped out into the corridor. He knew the way to her office from the last time he'd been there, but politely stood back and let her take the lead.

"So, what are these new developments?" she asked without preamble as they filed into her office. She turned to face them with her arms crossed over her chest.

Joel took a moment to appreciate the two Brett Whiteley prints that hung on the wall behind her. He also recognized a Fiona Hall sculpture on the coffee table that stood parallel to a two-seater leather couch. He'd been too angry the last time he'd been there to notice them. He liked her even more, knowing she was an art connoisseur with similar tastes to his own.

Forcing his mind back to the job, he eyed her steadily. "We've had our tech guys do a forensic examination of several McClintock devices. They've found evidence that fifteen illegal transactions were made from your desktop computer, using your credentials."

She gasped in shock. "No, it can't be."

"I'm afraid so," Joel continued. "We're talking a total of just under thirty million dollars and every single dollar of that was deposited into an offshore account."

The color had left her cheeks. She shook her head in denial. "No, you have it wrong. It wasn't me. There's been some mistake. There's no way those transactions were made by me."

"I didn't say they were made by you," Joel replied.

She frowned in confusion. Ralph stepped in. "The evidence doesn't lie, Ms McClintock. We know the transactions were made from your computer, with your login details. What we don't yet know is who was operating the device when the transactions occurred."

"Who else has access to your computer?" Joel asked.

She looked bewildered. "No one."

Joel shot her a dubious look. "No one? So no one comes into your office? Ever? You keep it locked at all times?"

"No, of course not. But no one knows my login details."

His gaze bored into hers. "Are you sure?"

She made an impatient sound in the back of her throat. "Of course."

"Does anyone have a reason to set you up? Any disgruntled employees?" Ralph asked.

Sheridan remained silent for a moment. She looked genuinely puzzled. "The only person I can think of is my ex-boyfriend, but he doesn't work here any longer, or know my login details."

"What's his name?" Joel asked.

"Dwight Britton."

"How long since he worked here?" Ralph asked.

"He was asked to leave nearly seven months ago."

Joel lifted a single dark eyebrow. "He was asked to leave?"

She flushed. "Yes. We broke up right before Christmas. We used to work together. I'm sure you can imagine it was…uncomfortable after the relationship went south. Zane suggested he find another place of employment. He gave Dwight a letter of recommendation to sweeten the deal."

"How long did he work here?" Joel asked.

"Four or five years. He started out in our IT department as a junior technician and worked his way up. He eventually was given a job in my department."

"What did he do there?" Joel asked.

"He was responsible for our computer systems."

"How closely did he work with you?" Joel demanded.

She flushed again. Her chin lifted in defiance. "We were work colleagues for more than a year before we started dating. Even then, we were always professional around each other in the office. It's one of the reasons I resisted his advances for so long. Office romances are tricky and often lead to difficulties, especially when the relationship turns sour…"

Her voice drifted off. Joel ignored the stab of jealousy and gave her a hard look. "It sounds like you've had plenty of experience. Is it your common practice to date your co-workers?"

She looked away, embarrassed. "No. Dwight was the first."

"Do you have your login details written down anywhere?" Ralph asked, breaking the tension.

Sheridan nodded. "Yes, in my phone, but I keep it in my contacts under Apple Blossom."

Joel threw her a droll look. "Apple Blossom?"

She shot him a rebellious look. "Well, I was going to go with Apple Macintosh, but I thought that was a bit obvious."

Joel gave a bark of laughter and shook his head in disbelief. "For a woman who comes across as smart as you do, you sure have some dumbass moments. Does Dwight have access to your phone?"

She eyed him steadily. "No. It's password protected."

"Let me guess; it's your birthday?"

Her guilty blush told Joel all he needed to know. He sighed. "How long did you and this Dwight guy date?"

"About six months."

"Who broke it off?" Joel asked.

"I did."

"Why?"

She frowned. "Does it matter?"

Joel moved into her personal space, purposefully making her feel uncomfortable. "Someone used your computer to carry out illegal offshore transactions. Your brother's company is short a little under thirty million dollars. Right now, you're our prime suspect. Unless you can convince us there might be someone else with means, motive and opportunity who could have carried out the fraud, you're in big trouble. So yes," he added, "the reasons behind the breakup and who instigated it is important if you want us to look in someone else's direction. Understand?"

By now he was close enough to see the dark flecks in her blue eyes. A tiny pulse beat a frantic rhythm in the side of her neck. Her perfume enveloped him, taking him back to the night they'd met and all the intimacy that had followed. Now, the combination of her scent, his memories and her closeness irritated him.

With a muttered curse, he moved away from her, giving them both some breathing room. Ralph shot him a quizzical look. Joel clenched his jaw and silently counted to ten in an effort to get himself back under control.

She's just another potential suspect being interviewed. Stop getting all worked up over her. I need to quit the reminiscing and focus on the job…

She seemed unaware of Joel's internal battle as she took a seat, propped her elbows on her desk and rested her chin in her hands. A faint flush of embarrassment stained her cheeks. With her gaze focused on the leather blotter in front of her, she spoke again.

"Dwight Britton was cheating on me. When I found out about it, I broke things off. He apologized, said it would never happen again, pleaded for me to take him back… All the usual things. Recently he called and did the same." She cut a glance toward them. "But I was having none of it. And I won't. There are some things no one can forgive…or forget."

She made an impatient motion with her hand. "Of course, there were other things in our relationship that weren't quite right, even before the infidelity. Things I wasn't happy about. I guess Dwight wasn't happy, either. No one cheats on their partner without good reason, right?" She offered a slight smile, but neither Joel nor Ralph reacted.

"Anyway," she continued, "I ended our relationship and we went our separate ways. Zane was upset about Dwight's cheating and to make things easier for me, he asked him to leave McClintock Properties."

"And Britton went quietly?" Joel asked.

Sheridan grimaced. "I wouldn't say quietly. But like I said, Zane gave him a glowing reference and I'm almost certain Dwight was rewarded with a very generous severance package." She shrugged. "I was happy to leave it to Zane to work out the details. I was just grateful I wouldn't have to face Dwight in the office every day. Like I said, office romances. They never work out well for anyone."

"Were you in love with him?" Joel demanded. He could feel Ralph's questioning gaze upon him. After all, the question wasn't strictly necessary to their investigation. He didn't want to admit, even to himself, how important her response was to him.

Her expression turned introspective and perhaps a little sad. He held his breath.

"Yes. At least I thought I was," she finally said. "I'm not someone who jumps into relationships without careful consideration, no matter what you might think. Dwight courted me for a year before I agreed to go out with him."

Joel tried to reconcile her statement with the woman who'd gone home with him. "Did you live together?" he asked.

She shook her head. "No. We'd only been dating for six months before we broke up."

"That's a long time for some people. Certainly long enough to have committed to living together."

She eyed Joel steadily. "Like I said, I'm not someone who rushes into this sort of thing. Even though I was careful, he managed to break my heart. Makes me question…"

For a moment, she looked so sad and resigned it was all Joel could do not to leap over the desk and pull her into his arms. He wanted to reassure her that Dwight was a fool for cheating on her and Joel couldn't believe any man who'd managed to steal this woman's heart would be stupid enough to trample all over her emotions.

With a muffled curse he shook his head in an effort to rid himself of his inappropriate thoughts. He barely knew the woman and right now, she was his prime suspect and positioned in the crosshairs. It was possible her disgruntled ex-boyfriend had motive to steal from her brother's company after being laid off for a personal transgression that had nothing to do with his employment—and as her boyfriend, it was also possible he had gained access to her computer and login details…

But Dwight Britton had left the company before Christmas. The earliest of the fraudulent transactions had occurred in February, well after Sheridan's ex had been shown the door.

Had the man sat back, biding his time, waiting for the perfect moment to strike? And if he *had* waited, how did he get access to Sheridan's computer when he no longer had access to the building? Was Britton a viable suspect, or were they clutching at straws?

Joel swallowed a sigh. They'd track down this Dwight Britton and find out what he knew, but Joel didn't hold much hope he was their perpetrator. He glanced at Ralph. His partner nodded. They had all they needed for now. Needing to re-establish the professional nature of their relationship, Joel moved closer and held out his hand to Sheridan.

"Thank you for speaking with us, Ms McClintock. We appreciate your cooperation."

She shook Joel's proffered hand. He ignored the warm tingles that ran up his arm at her touch.

She averted her gaze. A flush stole across her cheeks. "Let me know if I can be of any further help," she mumbled.

He nodded. "We will."

With that, he and Ralph left.

Christopher Barrington was on his way to see Sheridan about the tender on their latest airport project when he spied his half-brother, Joel, and another man in her office. Always curious about situations that appeared out of the ordinary, he positioned himself on the far side of the wall, adjacent to her open door. He was too far way to hear anything clearly, but the body language of both Sheridan and Joel told him plenty.

It was obvious Joel was there on official business. From the look of shock, quickly followed by confusion that traveled over Sheridan's expressive face, whatever news Joel had given her had been completely unexpected. And then Christopher caught the word "fraud" and a frisson of unease crept through his veins.

Had someone discovered I pose as Zane on the Internet and elsewhere? Surely they wouldn't call the cops over something like that? It had all been a bit of fun. There was no harm in it. Still, he was concerned Zane might not think of it like that. Though Christopher didn't particularly care for his job at McClintock, the place had begun to feel like home. He needed to lie low for a while and stay the hell away from Zane's computer.

As Christopher continued to spy on his boss's sister, he saw Joel move closer to Sheridan. So close, they were almost breathing the same air. Christopher watched with interest as Sheridan's cheeks turned red. He glanced at Joel. His half-brother's body was tense and expectant. Awareness crackled in the air between them.

Well, well, well. What do we have here?

Christopher chuckled silently to himself. He could well understand Joel's reaction to the woman. She was one hot piece of ass. The thought of her getting it on with his half-brother filled him with irritation. Not only was she a beautiful woman, she was also sister to the CEO. And very wealthy. Christopher wouldn't mind a piece of her for himself...

He stored away the intriguing discovery of Joel's interest in the woman and watched as she shook hands with both cops. It hit him they were making their departure, so he quickly strode away in the opposite direction, toward the lifts. By the time Joel and his buddy were in the corridor, Christopher managed to conceal his concern over the reason for Joel's visit and reacted with just the right amount of surprise when they stood face to face.

"Joel. Fancy seeing you here! To what do we owe this pleasure?"

Surprise flared briefly in Joel's eyes, followed quickly by irritation. Christopher guessed news of his lawsuit against the Craigdon estate had already reached Joel's ears. Still, he needed to find out the purpose behind Joel's visit; to make sure he was in the clear. To that end, he kept his fake smile firmly fixed in place.

Joel eyed him coolly. "Our visit here doesn't concern you, Christopher. If you want to know anything, I suggest you speak to your boss."

Christopher tamped down a surge of annoyance and smiled once again. "Come on, Joel. We're brothers. Surely I deserve more than that?"

Joel remained tight-lipped. He stepped forward and pressed the "down" button. His hand tapped impatiently against his thigh.

Christopher tried a bit harder. "How's MJ? I haven't seen her around lately. You guys still good?"

Joel's expression hardened. "Fuck off, Christopher. MJ's none of your business."

Christopher faked concern. "Really? Because back there you seemed awfully chummy with the delectable Sheridan McClintock. I'd hate for you to be doing the dirty on your long-term girlfriend."

Joel's eyes flashed with anger. He took a step toward Christopher, his fist clenched. For a minute, Christopher thought he might hit him.

Joel glared at him, his breath coming fast. "Leave Sheridan McClintock out of this. And for your information, Christopher, MJ and I broke up months ago."

As if on cue, the lift arrived and the doors slid silently open. Without a backward glance, Joel and his partner stepped inside. The doors closed behind them.

Chapter Ten

As the lift descended, Joel worked to contain his anger. The run-in with Christopher was the last thing he'd needed. He'd forgotten his half-brother worked at McClintock and now the prick had picked up on what had passed between him and Sheridan. The thought of Christopher having something over him was infuriating. It also put him on edge.

"Is he really your brother?" Ralph asked.

"Half-brother. We share the same father."

"Who is he?"

"Christopher Barrington. He works in McClintock's contracts division."

"What's his story? There seemed to be a bit of tension between you."

Joel's short bark of laughter was devoid of humor. "Yeah. You've got that right."

As the doors slid open and the men stepped out, Joel explained about his father's will and how Christopher had been disinherited. "The old man should have treated him better, but what happened has nothing to do with me."

"So his father was worth billions and he didn't get a dollar?" Ralph mused.

"Yeah."

"When did your father die?"

"In February."

"Missing out on such an inheritance is enough to make some people really angry. The first of these fraudulent transactions occurred back in February. Do you think this half-brother of yours could be behind the missing money?"

Joel slowed to a stop. It wasn't the first time he'd considered Christopher in connection with this investigation, but when the evidence pointed to Sheridan, he'd gone down a different path.

"It's possible," he said slowly. "He's worked here for a number of years. He holds a position of trust. He also has access to Sheridan's office."

"Did we seize this guy's computer?"

"Yes. Along with those of all of the staff in his division. They came up clean."

"Yeah, but so did Sheridan McClintock's the first time. Maybe the techies missed something else?"

Joel shrugged. "Who knows? He certainly seemed eager to know the reason behind our visit. He tried hard to play it casual, but I saw the tightness around his eyes. He really wanted to know what was going on."

"The urgings of a guilty conscience?"

Once again, Joel shrugged. The two of them continued across the foyer and all the way outside. Joel squinted against the bright sunshine then reached in his pocket for his sunglasses and pulled them on. He tossed the keys to his partner.

"How about you drive? I've had about enough of dealing with cantankerous people today. That run-in with my half-brother has soured my mood."

"Where to?" Ralph asked as they climbed into the unmarked car.

"Let's go and talk to Dwight Britton."

"Do we know where he went after he left McClintock?"

"No, but I'll bet the McClintock HR department has a clue." Joel made a call to Zane who promised to call him back with the information. Moments later, Zane came through. Joel ended the call and looked at Ralph, feeling bemused.

"Seems like Ms McClintock's ex-boyfriend has found a new home at Craigdon Enterprises."

"You mean your father's company?"

"Yeah. Though it isn't my father's anymore. He left it to my cousin, Logan."

Ralph winced. "Ouch. Don't you have siblings who work there?"

"Yeah," Joel replied grimly. "And my brother, Nicholas works there fulltime. Has since he left school. He's taking the change in ownership pretty hard."

"Can't say I blame him," Ralph muttered. "What's Britton doing there, anyway?"

Joel's gaze narrowed as he stared out the window toward the towering building that housed McClintock Properties. "Who knows? McClintock and Craigdon are both in the property development business. They've always been fierce competitors. Britton left McClintock with a beef to grind. I guess it makes sense on some level for him to seek a job with the enemy."

Ralph put the car in gear. "Let's go and talk to him then."

Sheridan closed the door behind her unexpected visitors and returned to her desk. Seeing Joel up front and personal again had rattled her. He hadn't mentioned their almost-meeting at the Ivy Bar the previous Friday night, but she was sure it had been on his mind. Along with the night they'd spent together in each other's arms and their lip-locking episode at the gallery...

She needed to put all that aside and focus on the reason for his visit. Someone had transferred huge sums of money from McClintock accounts and they'd done it, not only from her computer, but using her login. No matter that she didn't want to think about any of her work colleagues doing such a thing, the evidence had been found. It wasn't a matter of *if* it had happened, but who had done it. The one thing she was certain of was that neither she nor Zane were the culprits.

Could it have been Dwight?

He was certainly upset enough when she ended their relationship. He'd begged her to forgive him. Told her he loved her, that he couldn't live without her. Said she was his everything. Too bad he hadn't remembered that while he was screwing the brunette he'd met in a bar a few hours before.

No, it couldn't be him. He wouldn't be that vindictive. And of course, she hated to admit it, but she didn't believe he was that clever. Yes. He was an IT expert with high security clearances… But to hack into her phone—okay, so her password was her date of birth, but so what? He didn't know that. To log into her computer without her knowing, to access classified and password protected accounts, to set up illegal offshore accounts, to transfer the money, not once but on fifteen separate occasions… Her mind boggled at what was involved.

She didn't have a clue how someone might go about such a thing. There was no way Dwight would know how to do it. He was a disgruntled ex-lover and former employee, but relationships ended all the time. People didn't go to such lengths to get back at an ex, especially when it involved illegal behavior. Dwight was so finicky about obeying the law he wouldn't even risk getting a parking ticket.

No, it couldn't be him. Problem was, she couldn't come up with another feasible suspect. She ran through her staff in her mind and considered and dismissed every one of them in turn.

At last she gave up on a sigh. She had no choice but to leave it to the police. She'd always had faith in their ability to solve crimes. Maybe that trust came from binge-watching episodes of *Law & Order*, but however she'd arrived at it, that's the way she felt.

As Ralph wove the police vehicle in and out of the traffic headed in the direction of Craigdon Enterprises Joel was filled with a surge of anticipation. He was curious about the kind of man who had once laid claim to Sheridan McClintock's heart. According to Sheridan, she and Britton had only dated for six months, but she'd also admitted she thought she'd been in love with the man prior to their breakup.

Is Britton big and buff and macho, bursting with muscle and testosterone? Or does Sheridan prefer men more elegant and refined? Designer suits, impeccable ties, thousand dollar loafers… Joel was probably a loose combination of both. He wondered if she'd found him appealing because Joel was the antithesis of the men she usually dated or if he had more in common with Britton than he knew.

"I guess we should find out if Britton's at work today," Joel commented and once again pulled out his phone. He put in a call to his brother.

"Hey, Nick. How're you doing?"

"Good, mate. What are you up to?"

"I'm in the neighborhood. In fact, I'm on my way to speak to a Craigdon employee."

"Yeah? Who?"

"Dwight Britton. Do you know him?"

There was a brief pause. "Dwight Britton. Can't say that I do," Nicholas replied.

"He came from McClintock Properties. Worked there until just before Christmas."

"Are you sure he works here?" Nick's tone was uncertain.

"I think so. That's what he told McClintock's HR department."

"It's just that Dad had a policy to never employ people from McClintock. He was convinced anyone coming from there was out to spy on him."

Joel gave a half-chuckle. "Sounds a little paranoid."

"Yeah, maybe. But that's the way it was. There was bad blood between Dad and Michael McClintock."

"Is it possible this Britton guy was employed after Dad's death?"

"You mean, by Logan?"

"Maybe."

"I don't know. I'll have to find out."

"We're only a few minutes away. If you can find out whether this Britton fellow's at work today that would be good. I don't really care how he came to be employed there."

"No worries. I'll call you back."

Ralph had circled the block two times looking for a parking space before Joel's phone rang.

"I checked with HR," Nick said. "You're right. Dwight Britton's on the Craigdon payroll. He works in our IT department. He started here a week after Dad died."

"Right. Do me a favor, don't tell him we're here."

"What's this about?" Nick asked, his voice filled with curiosity.

"We're just following up on some enquires. Some unusual activity associated with McClintock Properties. Nothing for Craigdon to worry about."

Joel heard Nick's sigh of relief. "Good to know. Things are still a little crazy over here. With Dad gone, it's taking some adjustment for everyone. The last thing we need is a police investigation."

"I'm sure you and Logan will keep things on track," Joel reassured him.

"Yeah. It's more me than Logan. Ever since he appointed me managing director, he's taken a step back. Which has been a good thing. We both know Logan's never been interested in the family company."

Joel felt a wave of sympathy for his brother. What Nicholas said was true. It was the reason their father's decision to overlook Nick in favor of their cousin had come as such a shock.

"Text me when you arrive," Nick added. "I'll meet you downstairs and take you to Britton."

"Thanks, bro. Appreciate that. We'll see you shortly."

Giving up on finding a spot to park, Ralph pulled the police vehicle into the bay reserved for emergency services. Joel sent a text to his brother and the two cops climbed out and headed for the skyscraper that housed the offices of Craigdon Enterprises. Over the years, Joel had only sporadically visited his father at the company headquarters, but he'd been there often enough that when he stepped inside the wide entryway that led to the bank of lifts, he was immediately reminded that Henry Craigdon was no longer there and would never be there again.

Never again would his father greet him brusquely and demand to know what investigation Joel was working on. Never again would they argue over the way they took their coffee: Henry with milk and two sugars; Joel liked it black.

They might have been at loggerheads in the early days over Joel's career choice, but Henry seemed to have gotten over his disappointment that Joel hadn't gone into law. They had a healthy respect for the other's achievements and though they weren't openly affectionate toward one another, Joel was sure his father had loved him.

Joel and Ralph had barely cleared security before Nick came striding toward them. "Joel. Good to see you, mate."

Joel introduced Ralph to his brother. They two men shook hands. Ralph indicated with his head the security station in the foyer.

"What's with the metal detector? I thought you were property developers."

Nick grinned. "Yeah, it's probably a bit over the top. Dad had it installed about ten years ago. Some idiot came in one day threatening to shoot him."

"Was he armed?" Ralph asked.

"No," Joel responded, taking over the story, "but Dad wasn't taking any chances. At the time, he had more than a thousand employees working here. He took his responsibilities to them seriously."

Nick scoffed. "I think he was more interested in keeping himself intact, but whatever. I'll talk to Logan about having it taken away. I always thought it was over the top. Just like the use of security access passes in the lifts. No one can go up without using their pass to activate the floor where they wish to alight. More overkill, if you ask me. It's not like we're storing gold bullion on site. But apparently Dad thought it was needed and so it was installed."

"Before or after the metal detectors?" Ralph asked with a wry grin.

"Before, actually. Long before," Nick replied. "I'm not sure why Dad felt so vulnerable, but he was the boss and that meant he made the decisions."

"McClintock's has them too," Joel said. "Not the metal detectors, but an electronic pass is required in order to access each floor."

"You know how competitive they were," Nick muttered.

Joel grinned. "I wonder who installed them first."

Ushering them toward the lifts, Nick informed them he'd

asked Dwight Britton to meet him in the conference room on Nick's floor. Joel and Ralph could speak to the employee in private. No one else in the office need know they'd been there. Joel murmured his approval.

The lift whisked them to the top floor. Nick showed them to the conference room and told them he'd see them later. Joel opened the door. A highly polished, pale Tasmanian oak conference table that seated twelve people filled a vast portion of the room. Floor-to-ceiling glass made up one wall and framed a spectacular view of Sydney Harbour.

A man of about thirty, with a head of thick brown hair, slim athletic build and glasses stood as they entered. His brown eyes shone with a keen intelligence, but other than that, he was unremarkable. Joel disliked him on sight.

"Dwight Britton?" Joel asked.

"Yes." The man regarded them suspiciously. "Who are you?"

"We're Detectives Craigdon and Tilocca. We're from the Major Fraud Squad."

Britton's eyes narrowed. He looked quickly around the room. "Where's Nick?"

"Don't worry," Joel reassured him. "Nick knows we're here. How do you think we knew where to find you?"

A flash of panic filled Britton's eyes, but just as quickly disappeared. Making a visible effort to relax, his expression turned affable. "Craigdon? You must be one of Nick's brothers. A younger brother, for sure."

Joel ignored the man's attempt at flattery. He gave Britton a hard stare. "We'd like to ask you a few questions. I suggest you take a seat. We could be here for a while."

Britton did as he was told and Joel and Ralph took a seat opposite him. Sitting shoulder to shoulder, the detectives were a formidable sight. Not that it seemed to bother Britton, at least outwardly. He folded his hands together and casually rested them on the table and then gave them a benign smile. "Ask away."

Joel filled Britton in on the reason for their visit. He watched the man closely when he told Britton that they knew about the thirty million dollars that had been transferred out of McClintock accounts. Britton's light brown eyebrows rose a few degrees as he expressed his surprise.

"Thirty million dollars? That's a sizable sum."

"Yes, it is," Joel agreed.

"And what does this have to do with me?"

Joel eyeballed him. "We spoke to Sheridan McClintock. She told us you were unhappy about your breakup. We're looking at everyone who might have a beef against McClintock Properties and in particular, for employees with motive or employees who had access to those accounts."

Britton's languid expression slipped slightly at the mention of Sheridan's name, but he quickly masked it behind another benign smile. "How long has the money been missing?"

"The first transaction occurred in February," Ralph supplied.

"February? I'm sorry, Detectives. I'm confused. I'm not sure if Sheridan told you, but I left McClintock Properties in December."

"We're aware of that," Joel said tightly.

Britton spread his arms wide. "Look, Detectives. I appreciate you have a job to do and I'm happy to do all I can to help but the thing is, even when I was employed there, I never had access to McClintock bank accounts."

"So you're saying you know nothing about the missing money?" Joel asked.

"That's exactly what I'm saying." He paused. "Do you mind if I ask where the money went?"

"To an illegal offshore account," Ralph replied. "We're working on discovering who set it up. From there it's only a matter of time before we know who made the deposits."

Britton nodded slowly. "Good." He turned to look at Joel. "Follow the money, Detective. Isn't that what they say?" He chased the comment with a sly wink.

Joel's hands clenched into fists. It took all of his self-control not to wipe the smug expression off the asshole's face.

This is the jerk Sheridan had been in love with? What the hell did she see in him?

With an effort, Joel held his temper in check. Pushing away from the table, he pulled out a business card and tossed it on the table. "Here's my number. If you remember anything you think might help, call me."

With that, he turned on his heel and without waiting for Ralph, he left.

Chapter Eleven

Twice Christopher strode across the wide expanse of carpet where his partitioned office was located in the center of the room, intent on confronting Zane about the appearance of the two detectives. Both times his steps had faltered just before he reached the lift. Seeing Joel and his partner interviewing Sheridan had been unsettling and Joel's lack of explanation for his presence there was equally disturbing.

Does Zane know I hacked into his computer and Skyped girls, all the while pretending to be the CEO? Had Zane somehow guessed Christopher had taken it a step further and been entertaining women in Zane's office, continuing the same subterfuge? Okay, so it probably wasn't his finest moment, but Christopher didn't think it warranted a call to the fraud squad. Had he misjudged his boss?

But why didn't Zane say anything to me first? Christopher had worked there for more than five years. Long enough to be considered a valued employee. He'd always thought he and Zane had a good working relationship. They weren't close, but he never expected them to be. Christopher worked in the contracts department, two floors below the senior executive team. He was hardly the man's confidante. Still, Zane had always come across as fair and decent and Christopher would have expected to be called into the man's office and interrogated before the police were called in.

Maybe he was worrying about nothing? Having two detectives meet with the CEO's sister might have nothing to do with him. In fact, the more he thought about it, the more unlikely it seemed they'd been there to talk about him. For a start, if they were here about him they'd likely have been holed up in Zane's office, not his sister's. Secondly, surely if he'd been the subject of a complaint, the police would have questioned him, not merely brushed him off. Especially when one of those officers was Joel. There was no love lost between him and his half-brother. If the police had anything on him, Joel would have been at pains to point it out.

Yes, he was concerned about nothing. He was sure of it. Best go talk to Zane and find out the truth, then he could put his mind at rest. Filled with a new determination, he pushed away from his desk for the third time and strode with confidence out of the room.

Punching at the "up" button on the lift, he waited impatiently for it to arrive. Now that he'd finally found the courage to confront Zane, he wanted to get it over with. To his relief, when he asked Zane's executive assistant if her boss had a few minutes to see him, she nodded in the affirmative.

"He's between appointments at the moment, Christopher. I'll buzz him and let him know you're here."

Christopher nodded gratefully and did his best to control his nerves. Now that the moment was upon him, he had to steel his resolve. From the corner of his eye, he saw Zane's EA pick up the phone. She spoke quietly into the receiver before hanging up.

"You can go right in, Christopher."

Taking a surreptitious inhale of breath, Christopher found his way to Zane's office. Of course it wasn't the first time he'd been there, but the sight of the over-the-top opulence once again boggled his mind.

His gaze skittered away from the couch. He knew too well how that felt. The ambience of the room was different with the light pouring in from the floor-to-ceiling windows. Once the sun had gone down and the city lights of nearby skyscrapers twinkled like thousands of Christmas lights, it became an intimate, cozy escape. As Christopher well knew, firsthand.

"Christopher, it's good to see you." Zane pushed away from his desk and shook Christopher's hand. Both men took a seat.

"What can I do for you?" Zane asked. "Is this about the deal Sheridan's putting together with Blackhall? He's playing hardball, but we sure want to get our hands on that real estate."

Christopher shook his head. "No. But I heard Blackhall had gone coy on the price. Still, no one can close a deal like your sister."

Zane grinned. "You're absolutely right about that. So, if this isn't about the airport deal, what can I do for you?"

Christopher forced a grin. "I ran into a couple of detectives on my way to see Sheridan. One of them was my half-brother. I saw them talking to her. I guess I just wanted to make sure everything was okay. You know how much McClintock Properties means to me. Is everything all right?"

Zane waved away his concern. "Everything's fine. The police are convinced someone's been stealing from us. They say they've found evidence, but I'm not so sure. I mean, surely someone would notice if thirty million dollars hasn't been accounted for in the books."

At Zane's first words, Christopher relaxed. This wasn't about him impersonating his boss at all. That was good. Then the full import of what Zane had said registered and Christopher gasped. "Thirty million dollars?"

"Yes, that's what the police say." Zane's expression turned grim. "If it turns out they're right, someone in accounting has a hell of a lot of explaining to do."

"I'll say," Christopher muttered, his mind still reeling with the knowledge that thirty million dollars was missing and no one in the company had noticed before now.

"So, which of the detectives is your brother?"

Christopher blinked. "Excuse me?"

"You said one of the detectives you saw with Sheridan was your brother. I was just wondering which one."

"Half-brother," Christopher corrected. "And it's Joel Craigdon."

Zane's mouth tightened. "So you're related through your mothers?"

"No. We shared the same father. I was born quite a few years before Henry married Joel's mother."

"Henry Craigdon died earlier this year."

"Yes. In February. A heart attack."

Zane's lips twisted in distaste. "He and my father were fierce rivals up until my father's death."

Christopher smiled. "I believe you gave Henry a run for his money, too. Your father taught you well." It always gave Christopher immense pleasure to discover someone who'd gotten the upper hand against his late father in business. The prick was so proud of all he'd achieved in the business world. It was good to hear he'd been given his comeuppance every now and then.

Unaware of Christopher's dark thoughts, Zane regarded him curiously and there was an edge of something different in his voice. "If Henry was your father, why don't you work for Craigdon Enterprises?"

A flash of resentment, hot and urgent, burned through Christopher's veins. With one innocent question, every grievance he had against Henry and his family came bursting to the fore. His lip curled up in disgust.

"Henry didn't want me. I used to beg him to let me work in the business. I didn't care if he put me in the mailroom, in a basement office, or on a building site. I just wanted to be part of it. But he didn't offer me as much as a job doing the staff coffee run." Resentment roughened his voice. His chest was tight with anger. For a moment, he forgot he was in Zane's office until the man cleared his throat.

"So working for McClintock is your second choice?"

Christopher shook his head, eager to set the record straight. "No. I mean, yes. I had my heart set on working in my family business, but when that didn't work out, I looked elsewhere. I like it here. I worked here long before the old man died. I'm grateful for the opportunity to work for you."

He glanced at Zane, hoping the man bought his smooth lies. Zane's expression remained dubious. Christopher thought fast. Working at McClintock was far from his dream job, but it wasn't terrible. Besides, it would give him the opportunity at some point to wreak havoc on his late father's company. Cutting Christopher from his will was Henry's final insult. He might not be around to feel the pain personally, but Christopher had resolved to make someone pay. Right now, he had Craigdon Enterprises firmly in his sights. Anything he could do to disrupt their profits, he'd consider a win. And of course, there was the lawsuit he'd filed against the estate. If the family thought he'd take this lying down, they were in for one helluva surprise.

He forced a smile to conceal the extent of his anger and offered a casual shrug. "I like this kind of work," he lied again. "And I'm good at my job."

Zane nodded. "Yes, you are and we at McClintock are grateful for your input but make no mistake, I won't tolerate any divided loyalties. Your allegiance is to McClintock Properties. Anything else won't be tolerated." Zane gave him a hard look. "Do you understand?"

Christopher hurried to reassure him. "Yes, of course."

Zane's gaze remained fixed on his. "Just you make sure you keep your nose clean. If I get even a hint you're selling us out to Craigdon…"

Christopher was genuinely appalled at the thought. "No, never! You don't know how much I despise that family. My father treated me worse than a stray dog while he was alive. Even when he died, he still kicked me in the guts."

"What do you mean?"

"He's worth millions. Billions, even. And yet that lousy prick left me nothing in his will. Zero. Not a single dollar. He didn't even make mention of me."

Sympathy showed in Zane's eyes. "Wow. That's tough," he said quietly.

A fresh wave of anger washed over Christopher. "You bet it is." Christopher leaned forward in his seat. "You questioned my loyalty to McClintock. Let me tell you this. As well as being an exemplary employee here I intend to do whatever it takes to see Craigdon Enterprises go down."

Zane stared at him. Gradually, the hardness in his expression softened. He shrugged his acceptance. "I guess you have to do what you have to do. I won't pretend to know what it feels like to be treated like that. I was fortunate to have a good relationship with my dad. I will tell you one thing, though. Life's too short to hold on to grudges. Hatred and resentment can eat you up inside. Destroy your life. Still, it's none of my business as long as it doesn't interfere with McClintock pursuits and interests. Understood?"

"Understood."

The two men shook hands. On the way back to the lifts, Christopher ran into Sheridan. Her form-fitting designer suit emphasized her shapely figure. She was pure sex on legs. He wondered if he stood a chance with her. To tell the truth, he hadn't really given it any thought over the past five years he'd worked there. But now that he knew she and Dwight were no longer an item, and that Joel was keen on her, she'd suddenly become even more attractive.

He smiled his most charming smile. "Sheridan. I was just talking to Zane. Do you need any help with that airport project?"

She blinked in surprise. "No, thanks. I think I have it under control, but thanks for your offer."

She attempted to step past him, but he stood in her path. "Anytime you want me to look over the terms of the contract, just give me a call. I'm happy to help."

"Thank you, Christopher. I appreciate that."

Once again, she tried to step around him, but he held his ground. "I was wondering if you'd like to go out for a drink?"

She arched a single eyebrow and he blushed. "That is, I didn't mean right now. But sometime. Maybe this Friday? What do you say?"

"I'm sorry, Christopher. I'm flattered. I really am. But I'm going to have to decline." This time, when she stepped away from him, he let her go. Tamping down his irritation, his gaze followed her along the corridor until she disappeared from view. She'd certainly seemed receptive to Joel's attention. Christopher would be damned before Joel got one up on him, especially when it came to women.

Determination surged through him. He vowed to make it his business to win Sheridan over. Not because he wanted her necessarily, although he couldn't deny she was a tasty bit of skirt, but it would be so much fun to screw Joel over and run away with his girl.

Joel made his way to Nick's office, his head still full of steam. There was something about the sly smugness of Dwight Britton that set his teeth on edge. The man had exhibited far too much confidence for someone being interviewed by the police over the possible theft of thirty million dollars. Then again, perhaps Britton's confidence stemmed from his knowledge he wasn't the thief.

It was true he'd left the employ of McClintock Properties a couple of months before the first of the transactions occurred. That didn't mean he couldn't have done it, but it definitely would have made it more difficult. Joel had checked with the HR people, that upon the cessation of Britton's employment, it was standard procedure for his staff ID to be handed in, along with his security access pass to the lifts. If he'd accessed the building after that time, he'd done it using someone else's pass and that wouldn't have gone unnoticed. It seemed more and more unlikely Britton was their man. Still, Joel wasn't prepared to let the jerk off the hook just yet.

With a sigh of frustration, Joel strode into Nick's office and threw himself down in the seat opposite his brother. Joel had already farewelled Ralph, telling him he'd catch him later at the station. He wanted to spend some time with his brother, trying to get to the bottom of how an ex-McClintock employee had ended up at Craigdon Enterprises. He also wanted to hear Nick's take on Sheridan's former boyfriend.

"So, how did it go?" Nick asked.

"What an asshole," Joel growled. "How could you employ someone like that?"

Nick grimaced. "I didn't. Like I said, he came on board right after Dad died. The place was still in an uproar. I spoke to Logan. At the time, he hadn't been aware of Dad's policy not to employ McClintock staff."

Just then, Logan filled the open doorway of Nick's office. With a discernible limp—the consequence of a bad sailing accident a few years earlier—he strode inside and perched on the corner of Nick's desk.

"Hey, Joel. Nick told me you were here. It's good to see you."

The two men shook hands. Joel murmured a greeting.

"Look, I'm sorry about the stuff-up with this Britton guy," Logan said.

Joel waved away his apology. "Don't sweat it. I understand. You didn't know."

Logan grimaced. "You're right. So much was going on right after Uncle Henry's death… I didn't take time to look at the guy's CV. We were short staffed and he seemed to know his stuff. He talked the talk and convinced me I should give him a go."

"It doesn't matter. It's a long shot he's even involved in my investigation. Just out of interest, could you pull his HR record and confirm when he started here?"

Logan nodded. "Of course, but I can tell you now it wasn't long after the funeral." Logan paused and then added, "Nick told me about Uncle Henry's policy of not hiring anyone out of McClintock Properties and I understand the reasoning behind it. After all, they're our biggest competitor. I'm happy to let Britton go if that will make both of you feel better."

"Unfortunately, you can't do that. We'll be sued for unfair dismissal," Nick said.

"You won't have to fire him if I put him away for stealing," Joel offered.

Logan frowned. "I thought you just said he was an unlikely suspect?"

"Yeah, maybe, but I haven't dismissed him entirely. He definitely had motive. He also has a background in IT. As to means and opportunity, I can't dismiss those, either. He could have used someone else's pass to access the building. It's also possible he hacked into McClintock systems from afar. It's been done before. We'll have to wait and see."

"How much money are you talking?" Logan asked.

"Almost thirty million," Joel replied.

Nick whistled. "Thirty million? That has to hurt them." And then he looked at Logan. A tiny smile played around his mouth. "This might be our opportunity to outbid them on some very lucrative contracts, Logan. Maybe even that one out at the new airport. It's about time we had some luck come our way. We were hemorrhaging money in the months before Dad's death."

Joel started in surprise. "Really? Why?"

Nick shrugged. "I wish I knew. You forget I wasn't privy to his decisions. I've looked over the accounts since Logan appointed me MD. A shitload of money disappeared on a regular basis, but I haven't been able to track it down yet."

"How much are you talking?" Joel asked.

"Maybe millions. More than half a million in one day alone."

"That's a lot of money to go unaccounted for. Are there any clues about where it went?" Joel asked, his radar engaged.

"No. Plus there are other things that don't make sense," Nick continued.

"Like what?" Joel asked.

"The number of employees Dad had on each building site."

"What about it?" Logan asked.

Nick sighed. "At any given time, there appeared to be several hundred more in attendance than were needed. And they were all paid well."

"Why would he employ more laborers than he needed? That seems a waste of money," Logan replied.

Nick nodded. "Exactly. I haven't figured it out yet, but I find it strange."

"Do you think he was losing his marbles?" Joel asked dubiously.

"No," Nick replied. "I might not be happy about the terms of his will, but I can't claim senility for him. Dad was as sharp as he'd always been, right until the very end."

"Where's the McClintock money trail lead to?" Logan asked.

Joel compressed his lips and gave his cousin a grim look. "That's what I'm trying to find out."

Chapter Twelve

oel tossed his wallet and keys down on the hall table in the front foyer and made his way across the wide expanse of his marble-tiled living room. Toeing off his boots, he kicked them aside and then worked on loosening his tie. He shrugged out of his jacket and draped it over the back of the couch. It had been another tough day at the office and he was no closer to finding the person who'd robbed McClintock Properties of nearly thirty million dollars.

Night had already fallen and with it, a drop in the temperature. Though the harbor side suburbs of Sydney never experienced anywhere near freezing, it was cool enough in the winter to require a jacket.

Walking over to the bar, he opened the fridge and reached inside for a beer. He twisted off the lid and chugged down at least a third of the bottle. Wiping his mouth with the back of his hand, he took his beer and threw himself down on the couch with a sigh.

It was so quiet. Elevated above street level on the fifth floor, he rarely heard the noise of the traffic. At best the occasional sound of a horn from a passing ferry was all that disturbed his thoughts. He normally embraced the peace and quiet and the solitude which came from living on his own, but tonight he was restless and he didn't know why.

Liar…

Of course he knew why. The lack of progress with his investigation was annoying, but that wasn't the reason for his present discontent. No, that had everything to do with Sheridan McClintock. The gorgeous, exciting woman who had him tied up in knots… The very same woman who filled his dreams and too many of his waking moments. The woman he couldn't get off his mind. That admission sent another surge of irritation and unease flooding through him.

What is it about her that has me so enthralled? There was no question she was beautiful, but he'd dated beautiful women before. Hell, during his sabbatical in Europe he'd slept with a fair number of them, too. And yet, none of them had the hold over him like she did. Not even MJ, and he'd given her five years of his life.

He wished he knew what it was about Sheridan that attracted him so strongly because then he could go about overcoming it. The simple fact was, as much as he wished things were different, she was involved in a police investigation—an investigation he was in charge of. Everything came back to that.

Biting off a frustrated curse, he stood and headed out to the balcony. The ocean breeze held a winter chill, but he ignored it. Leaning over the railing, he took another swig from his beer and tried not to think about Sheridan.

What he needed was a distraction. Perhaps he should go out and pick up a woman? Someone warm and willing, for the night. For no-strings-attached sex. That had always cheered him in the past.

Even as he finished the thought, his mind rebelled hard and fast. After being with Sheridan, he couldn't imagine sleeping with anyone else. Though she'd been a beautiful stranger he'd picked up for the night, right from their very first meeting, it felt like something special. The chemistry had been electric.

Maybe he should get a dog? It had worked for Callum and Grace. In fact, the puppy had spent the first week of his adoptive life in Joel's apartment. At the time, Joel had been horrified that a noisy, messy puppy had taken up residence in his laundry room, but now he wondered if getting a canine friend might be just what he needed.

It would certainly be nice to come home to someone who looked forward to his arrival. They could go for walks, play fetch in the park, maybe even engage in conversation. Okay, so it would be completely one-sided and the dog wouldn't be able to give him any advice, but so what? It would be someone to listen to him and sometimes that's all he needed.

The idea grew on him, felt comfortable. Yes, he would get a puppy. Something small and manageable. Tomorrow was the first day of the weekend and he had the next two days off. He'd go first thing in the morning to the animal shelter and pick out his new best friend.

Feeling better than he had in weeks, Joel finished his beer. And then he went and spoiled his reprieve by wondering if Sheridan liked dogs.

"Ugh!" he groaned. He was hopeless! A completely hopeless case! Even the decision to get a dog brought her to mind.

He should get royally drunk, so drunk he wouldn't have to think about anything. It was Friday night and he was alone. Right now getting drunk held a vast appeal.

As if in agreement with his decision, another gust of cold wind blew across the water and found its way up the side of his building. With a shiver, he collected his empty bottle and headed back inside.

Christopher took a sip from his whiskey and then set the highball glass back on the bar. After being reassured that Joel's official visit to McClintock Properties had nothing to do with him he thought he owed it to himself to celebrate and there was nothing like single malt to do the trick.

Harry's Bar was one of his favorite hangouts in the city. Almost hidden down a narrow lane, it was a modest-sized bar with tables tucked discreetly away in the shadows. It wasn't trendy or fashionable like some of the other bars in the city and that was part of the appeal. The hordes of beautiful people didn't flock there. There were no photographers from the social pages, no celebrities, no Instagrammers or bloggers. No one but ordinary people enjoying a private drink or a slice of conversation.

The subdued lighting throughout was conducive to secret assignations and the 90's country rock music coming from the speakers was loud enough to provide cover for most conversations. It was a meeting place for those who preferred to fly under the radar and it suited Christopher's needs perfectly.

Taking another sip from his whiskey, he savored the rich warm taste of the alcohol in his mouth and then relished the feeling as it slid down his throat. Some of his tension eased. Glancing around him, his gaze landed on a woman who looked vaguely familiar. Attractive, slim hips, big boobs, blond hair… He wondered how he knew her. And then it came to him.

Mary-Jane. MJ to those close to her. Joel's ex-girlfriend. Christopher had never cared to learn her surname. The truth was, he'd never paid her much attention at all, but given his recent run-in with Joel, he wasn't feeling kindly toward his half-brother and all of a sudden, he found he was very interested indeed in snagging Mary-Jane's attention.

Collecting his drink, he moved further down the bar and took the empty seat beside her. He offered her his best smile.

She blinked at him and seemed to have difficulty focusing.

He glanced at her half-empty wine glass and suspected it wasn't her first, or even her second. And then she burped and he was overcome with alcoholic fumes and his suspicions were confirmed.

"Sh-shorry," she slurred.

"Hey, nothing to be sorry for," he quipped and gave her another smile.

She frowned. "Do I know you?"

"Of course you do, MJ. It's Christopher. I'm Joel's brother."

She squinted at him. "Are you sure? I don't remember a brother called Christopher."

Christopher's smile slipped a little. Irritation coursed through him. "All right, I'm not strictly a brother. I'm his half-brother."

Once again, her eyes narrowed on him. "Oh, Christopher! Now I remember. You're Henry's bastard." She followed that with a laugh.

Christopher gritted his teeth. "Charming. So glad you remember me."

His sarcasm was lost on her. Instead, she leaned forward and touched him on the arm. "Did you hear what Joel did? He dumped me! The asshole! All the crap I put up with—the nights when he came home late from work, the weekends when he just couldn't get away. He spent more time at the station with his cop buddies than he did with me. And did I complain? Of course not."

Christopher privately found that hard to believe. Women like MJ were born to complain. Still, he made the appropriate sounds of sympathy and was rewarded with a smile.

"You understand, don't you, Christopher? You're one of the good ones. Not all men are pricks. Only those with the name Joel Craigdon. We'd been together five years! Five years! I gave him the best years of my life! And how does he reward me? The moment he comes into some money, I'm given the flick! Now that he's inherited ten million dollars, I'm not good enough," she wailed.

Once again, Christopher murmured words of sympathy. "I agree. He's treated you appallingly, MJ. He should be made to pay."

She blinked at him. "Pay? How am I going to do that? I don't have any money."

Christopher tamped down his irritation. *What the hell had Joel seen in this twit?* No matter. She'd serve Christopher's purpose for bringing a little chaos into his half-brother's life.

"I'm not talking about money, MJ."

Her eyes clouded with confusion. "Then what are you talking about?"

He looked at her and smiled. "I'm talking about a baby."

She frowned. "A baby? What baby?"

"Joel's baby."

Her frown deepened. "Joel has a baby? He *cheated* on me? That asshole!"

"No, no, MJ. You misunderstand. Joel doesn't have a baby. *You* do."

She looked at him blankly. "I do?"

He hurried to explain. "Well, not a real one, of course. You're going to pretend you're pregnant."

"Why would I do that?"

"Don't you want Joel back?"

"Of course I do!"

"Then this is the way to get him."

"What way?"

With an effort, Christopher held on to his patience. This is what he got for trying to help out someone when they'd had a few too many drinks.

"You're going to trap him into marriage with the oldest trick in the book, MJ. You're going to tell Joel you're pregnant. There's no way he's going to walk away from the mother of his child."

"But I'm not pregnant."

"Joel doesn't know that."

Another wave of confusion washed over her face. "But how can I be pregnant? We haven't been together since before Henry's funeral."

"So? Tell him you haven't said anything because you were waiting for him to return from Europe."

She looked down at her flat stomach. "But I don't look pregnant."

"You can buy a prosthesis."

She gave him a blank look. "A what?"

"A prosthesis. You can buy them off the Internet. A different one for every month of your pregnancy."

"How do you know this stuff?"

Christopher smiled. "What does it matter? You want to get Joel back, don't you?"

"Of course I do! But what if he demands proof? A scan?"

He shrugged. "So, get one."

She looked at him in disbelief and then laughed uproariously. "I don't know anyone who could get me a baby scan picture."

Christopher smiled. "Then I guess it's lucky I do."

She looked at him suspiciously. "What's your price? I don't have any money." She paused and then laid a hand on his thigh and slid it up toward his groin. "Perhaps I can cut it out some other way?"

He looked down at her hand in distaste. This was about screwing with Joel, not literally screwing his ex. Besides, the brassy blond with the overinflated chest just wasn't his type.

He moved out of hand's reach. "Don't worry about payment for now. I'll let you know what I want, all in good time. Don't say anything to Joel until I have the scan for you, okay?"

"Okay."

"Give me a minute to make a call. I'll be right back."

With that, Christopher left the bar and stopped a few yards outside the door. He scrolled through his contacts and found the number of a girl he'd dated on and off who worked in an ultrasound clinic.

He'd loaned Amy some money to pay off her brother's dealer. She still hadn't paid it back. It suited him to have her in his debt. He never knew when he might need to call in the favor. Like, right now.

Amy answered the call. In short order, he explained what he wanted. After only the slightest hesitation, she agreed to provide him with an anonymous copy of an ultrasound.

"How soon can you get it?" he asked.

"I'll do my best to get it to you later in the week."

Christopher ended the call with a satisfied smile. His plan to disrupt Joel's perfect life was headed in the right direction. Now all he needed was for MJ to play her part.

Sheridan pushed the wheelbarrow of dog food down the row of kennels. A cacophony of gleeful barking escalated with her every step. There were more than fifty dogs of all breeds, shapes and sizes waiting for adoption at the animal shelter where she volunteered once a week and every one of them knew what it meant when the wheelbarrow appeared.

"Oh, Rusty! You're still here, boy! Cleo, how are you, sweetie! Toby, you gorgeous thing! Yes, it's dinnertime! Okay, okay! No need to get so excited. There's enough for everyone."

Reaching the end of the row, she set the wheelbarrow down and then started dishing out measured scoops of dog biscuits into each of the food bowls. With so many dogs to feed, it was a time-consuming process, but one she enjoyed.

What gave her even more pleasure was discovering that some dogs who'd been there the week before were there no longer because they'd gone to a loving home. That was the goal for all of them.

She'd have adopted them all if she could, but her modest Eastern Suburbs apartment didn't lend itself to more than one pet. A mixed breed, long-haired, little silky terrier named Gypsy was the love of Sheridan's life. It pained her that the dog was forced to spend so many hours alone, but Sheridan made up for it during the hours she spent at home.

Gypsy was spoiled rotten, with her own princess bed, complete with a fluffy mattress, lace-edged pillow, soft pink baby blanket and more doggie toys than she could ever possibly need. The fact that she spent more time in Sheridan's bed than she did in her own was testament to Sheridan's weakness when it came to her pet.

Making her way slowly down the row of kennels, she took note of some newcomers. An older blue cattle dog looked at her with sad, baleful eyes. A red kelpie, missing one ear, was also new this week. A Jack Russell, a fox terrier and a dog whose breed she couldn't identify were in the next kennel and eagerly awaited their food. She bent down and scratched the foxy between the ears.

"How are you, boy? Where did you come from? Are you liking it here?"

"Of course he is! A roof over his head, two square meals a day, plenty of friends. What's not to like?"

Sheridan smiled at the vet who walked up beside her. Matilda Lockheed was another single, twenty-something woman who volunteered her time at the shelter on the weekends.

"How are you, Matilda? Did you have a good week?"

"Not too bad. A couple of tricky surgeries on dogs hit by cars. Fortunately we managed to save them both. Then there was a horse out at Richmond who got caught up in a fence. Some nasty gashes. Plenty of stitches later, and she was good to go."

Sheridan grinned. "Sounds like you've been busy."

"Sure thing," Matilda replied. "How about you?"

Sheridan pushed the almost-empty wheelbarrow back toward the storage shed. Matilda kept pace beside her.

"Not too bad. I'm working on a project that's a little challenging, but nothing I can't handle."

"What about your love life? Did you ever look up that guy you met in the nightclub?"

Sheridan blushed. She'd forgotten she'd confided in Matilda about the night she'd met Joel. Of course, she hadn't told the woman she'd gone home with the handsome stranger, just that she'd met someone who rocked her world.

Feeling unusually brave, Sheridan looked at Matilda and grinned. "Um, yes. As a matter of fact I did."

Matilda's face lit up with surprise and delight. "You *did!* Ooh, tell me everything! What's his name? What does he do? How did you find him? Did you end up swapping numbers?"

Sheridan held up her hands and laughed. "Whoa! Too many questions!"

Matilda screwed up her face in mock desperation. "Please, Sheridan! I'm begging you! We both know my love life is completely dead. I haven't had a date in *months!* It's not my fault I have to live romance vicariously through you! Now stop being a tease and tell me everything!"

Sheridan laughed again. "I can't believe a woman who looks like a supermodel and is smart to boot hasn't had a date in months." She waggled her finger. "Uh, uh Matilda. I'm not buying it."

Matilda's laughter spilled over. "It's true! Now, stop deflecting and start talking!"

Sheridan stood the wheelbarrow up on its end and closed

the storage shed. Taking pity on her friend, she draped her arm casually over Matilda's shoulder as they both walked back to the waiting room.

"Okay, here goes. His name is Joel. He's a cop. Believe it or not, he walked into my place of work. Our eyes met across the lobby…and that was it."

Matilda squealed. "Oh, my God! Are you for real? So are you, like…dating?"

Sheridan blushed. "No. Nothing like that."

"So what? You meet the man of your dreams and… nothing? How does that work?"

They reached the back door of the building that housed the main office and waiting area where members of the public came to apply to adopt an animal. Sheridan pulled the door open and the women walked inside. After the brightness of the sun, it took a few moments for Sheridan's eyes to adjust to the dimness. She followed Matilda into the waiting area and suddenly pulled up short. Her heart skipped a beat.

Joel Craigdon sat in one of the hard plastic chairs that lined the wall of the waiting room. He appeared to be engrossed in a magazine on pet care. As if becoming aware of her presence, he looked up and saw her.

Heat exploded across her face, but for what seemed like an eternity she couldn't look away. Then she became aware she was staring and hastily dropped her gaze. In a sudden rush of panic, she turned on her heel and started heading back the way she'd come.

"Sheridan! Wait!"

Joel's shout could be heard clear across the waiting room. Two other people, including a young boy, lifted their heads and looked at her curiously. She gritted her teeth, knowing she had no choice but to face him.

She plastered a smile on her face. "Joel! What are you doing here?"

He stood and came toward her. With each step, her heart beat faster until she could barely breathe.

"I could ask you the same thing," he murmured. The sexiest smile she'd ever seen played around his lips.

Closing her eyes briefly, she tried hard to catch her breath. "Um, I… I work here."

His face flooded with surprise. "You *work* here?"

"Yes, well, I mean, I volunteer. It's not a paid position. I come in once a week." Her words all ran together in a garbled rush. A fresh wave of embarrassment spread across her cheeks.

He stepped back slightly, his eyes wide. "Wow. I mean, that's really… Wow. Good on you."

The admiration in his eyes unsettled her. She wasn't used to having him look at her like that. In fact, the last time she'd seen him, he'd been in her office interrogating her over allegations of theft. Well, maybe not interrogating. That was a bit harsh. But he'd been a long way from the emotion she saw on his face right now.

"Sheridan? Is everything all right?"

Chapter Thirteen

oel stared at the tall leggy redhead who came toward him. Though she was dressed casually in jeans and a sweatshirt, she could have walked off a fashion shoot. Her pale flawless skin glowed with health and vitality. Her blue eyes shone with intelligence. A tiny line marred the smooth skin of her forehead and her full lips were pursed in consternation. She was a stunning woman with a figure to match and yet as she came to a halt beside him and Sheridan, he felt nothing but curiosity.

Feeling the need to introduce himself, he stuck out his hand. "Joel Craigdon. I'm a friend of Sheridan's."

The woman's eyes widened. Her mouth dropped open in surprise. "*Joel?* I'm Matilda Lockheed. I'm also a friend of Sheridan's." The woman flicked a quick questioning glance in Sheridan's direction before returning her gaze to his.

"So, *Joel.* What can we do for you?"

"Actually, I'm in the market for a dog."

"You… You want to adopt a shelter dog?" Sheridan asked, her eyes wide with amazement.

Joel frowned, annoyed at her reaction. "Yes. Why not?"

She shrugged and looked at him helplessly. "It's just that… I hadn't seen you as the animal shelter type."

He frowned at her in mock irritation, his earlier annoyance gone. He was enjoying her discomfort.

"There's a *type?*" he asked, widening his eyes innocently.

Embarrassment turned Sheridan's cheeks crimson. She ducked her head. Joel refused to feel sorry for her. He was having too much fun.

"No, of course not. Anyone's entitled to adopt a shelter animal, provided you meet the conditions."

"Conditions?"

"Yes, you know. We… We require you to fill in an application and we need to make sure you're aware of your responsibilities as a pet owner and ensure that you have the right equipment and food and…other stuff."

Her voice drifted off. She stared at the floor and Joel could tell she was desperately wishing the floor would open up and swallow her.

The woman who'd introduced herself as Matilda appeared to take pity on her friend. She took over the conversation.

"What Sheridan is trying to say is we need to make certain you're the right person to have one of our animals. They've all been rescued from various situations and all of them, at some stage, have known what it's like to feel unloved. We take our responsibilities toward our animals very seriously and we do our very best to match them with people who will love and appreciate them and treat them well."

Joel nodded. "Of course. I'm pleased to know the well-being of your animals is something close to your heart. It's the main reason I chose to come to this shelter."

Sheridan looked at him in surprise. "Oh?"

"Yes. I did some research on the Internet. You center has outstanding reviews. I read through a good deal of them. They all described the staff and your facilities in glowing terms."

Sheridan flushed with pride. "That's very nice of them. We love working here and we do our best to treat our animals with kindness and love. Some of them have never known love from a human. You wouldn't believe how cruel some people can be. It simply breaks your heart. Why they ever take on a pet is beyond me. Those poor animals are the ones we have the most trouble re-homing. The cute and cuddly ones go quickly. The older, more reserved pets who haven't been treated well, not so much."

Joel had come there with the intention of adopting a small dog like a poodle or a Maltese or even a pug, but now he wondered if he should set his sights on something else.

"Can you show me what dogs are available?" he asked, directing his question to Sheridan.

Matilda looked at Sheridan and grinned. "Of course she can! Go on, Sheridan. Take *Joel* out to the kennels and show him what we have."

The woman practically pushed them both out the door. Joel wondered briefly why Matilda kept emphasizing his name in a slightly odd way, but no matter. When he'd set out that morning, determined to come home with a four-legged friend, he'd had no idea he would run into Sheridan. It seemed ironic that the reason he'd gone down this path in the first place was in an effort to distract himself from her and the way she dominated his thoughts and yet, here she was, volunteering at the shelter.

It was true he'd done his research and the Love & Kindness Animal Shelter certainly came across as the best, but there were others he could have gone to. A couple of them much closer to home than this one. If he didn't know better he'd think some higher power had a hand in his decision; that this meeting was meant to be.

That idea didn't frighten him like it might have before he'd met Sheridan. In fact, though he should be staying the hell away from her until his investigation had been concluded, he'd be lying if he said he didn't welcome the idea of spending a Saturday morning with Sheridan. She was easy on the eye and just as easy to be around. He enjoyed her company as much as he enjoyed looking at her.

And of course, every moment he was around her reminded him of the night they'd spent together. If he thought that memory had been exaggerated with time, he had only to remember the fire that had ignited between them at the gallery when he'd taken her in his arms and kissed her like his life depended upon it—and at the time, it had felt like his did.

This morning he'd been given an unexpected gift and he was determined to make the most of it. He firmly ignored the faint stirring of guilt. There was nothing wrong spending time with a witness. At this stage, there was no evidence she was involved on any level other than that it was her computer and credentials that had been used.

Joel liked to think he was a good judge of character. Over the years, he'd honed his bullshit radar to an accurate degree. Right from the start, Sheridan had protested her innocence. His gut told him he could believe her. Right here, right now that was good enough for him.

Hurrying to catch up with her, he offered her his best smile. "So, how long have you volunteered here?"

She flicked him a glance and kept walking. "I started coming here while I was at university. My dad died during my second year. We were close. It was a very difficult time in my life. I saw a flyer asking for people to volunteer at an animal shelter. I thought being around animals might help."

"And did it?"

"Help? Yes. That's why I'm still here. There's nothing like the unconditional love from an animal. They give and give and give and ask so little in return. A friendly greeting, a quick cuddle, food and a warm dry bed. Not much, all things considered."

"Such as what?" he asked, intrigued.

"Considering what they've been through. Like I said, all of these dogs have been rescued from owners who should never have been allowed a pet in the first place. Many have been abused, beaten, starved. They've never known an ounce of love." She paused and her voice softened. "That's my favorite part. Letting them know they're loved."

He stared at her, his heart spilling over with emotion. "They really mean a lot to you, don't they?"

She looked at him and nodded. "They're like my babies. I wish I could take them all home."

"That's why you're so particular about their new owners. You want to make sure they're going to be treated well."

"Yes. But not just treated well. We don't let an animal go with anyone if we're not absolutely certain the dogs will be loved."

"How do you bear to let them go? Over the years, you must have re-homed hundreds of animals. It must be hard."

Her slow smile lit up her face and set his heart racing. Even in a pair of casual jeans and a long-sleeved T-shirt, with her hair bouncing in a ponytail, she was beautiful.

"But that's the best part! Knowing they've found their forever family who'll love them and care for them for the rest of their life."

He smiled softly. "You really do love it here."

She looked at him, her eyes luminous. "You're right. I do. Getting to be part of the decision-making process when a new family comes in looking for a pet and then introducing them to some of our animals… Working with them to help them decide what kind of pet will suit them best. There's a lot of thought that goes into an adoption. We need to be confident the animal will not only suit its owner's needs, but that its needs will be seen to as well. It's a two-way street."

She sighed and then looked away. She gave an embarrassed shrug. "I sound a little bit loopy. Like that crazy old woman who lives down the road and owns ten or twenty cats. But I swear, it's not like that at all. I love animals and I want everyone else to love them, too."

"It's a little bit different than your day job," he mused.

She laughed and the sound of it filled him with warmth.

"Yes, that's for sure. This place couldn't be any further removed from the demands of a busy corporate office. But that's why I keep coming back. It gives my life balance. And that's important for all of us, don't you think?"

Joel stared at her. She was so different from the immaculately groomed, confident, corporate negotiator. She was also unlike the blond bombshell sex kitten he'd taken home. There were so many facets to her. He was fascinated and yearned to get to know her even more.

He'd never thought much about his work/life balance. He loved his work as a detective and if he were honest, he was probably happiest on the job. When he was in the middle of an investigation, the hours, days, weeks slipped by and he hardly even noticed. Then it hadn't bothered him when he missed out on family gatherings, barbeques, or a party at a friend's house. Though MJ had complained incessantly that he always put his work before her, it hadn't been a problem for Joel.

Now he wondered if he'd been cheating himself out of something far more important. His life was passing at a clip. Already he was twenty-eight. Not old by anyone's reckoning, but not so young, either. Plenty of people had put down roots and started a family by then. It was something Joel had resisted. Perhaps because he'd never before found a woman he wanted to spend his life with. Since meeting Sheridan, everything had turned on its head.

She was staring at him with an expectant look on her face and he realized he hadn't responded to her question.

"Um, yes. I guess so. I haven't given it much thought."

She smiled and his heart tripped over again. "Well, you

should. It's not good for any of us to hurtle through life only intent on the final destination. We never allow ourselves time to appreciate what we have, if we do that. I'm always telling Zane to slow down and smell the flowers. He works too hard."

Joel nodded slowly, absorbing her words of wisdom. "I think you might be right. Maybe my decision to get a dog was my subconscious telling me I need to slow down, diversify, have something more than work in my life."

She smiled again. "Maybe."

They rounded a corner and were beset by noisy and frenzied barking. Sheridan laughed and shouted over the din.

"Don't mind them! They're excited to see you!"

She kept walking down a concrete path that ran down the middle with large enclosures either side that served to contain the mix of dogs. There were so many different breeds, shapes and sizes.

"Jaxon! Sit down! There's a good boy!" Through the bars of the enclosure, Sheridan patted a greyhound on his head. He licked her hand excitedly and she chuckled.

She turned to Joel. "What kind of dog are you looking for?"

"I'm not too sure," he answered honestly. "I live in a city apartment with a balcony, but no outdoor green space…" His voice faded as he noted her change in expression.

Of course she knew where he lived. She'd been there. He watched as her eyes darkened and her chest rose and fell with quickened breath. His pulse had also picked up its pace. Through his mind tumbled images of them removing their clothes in the living room, coming together skin-to-skin, and then him carrying her to his bed.

His body reacted predictably to those images. He half-turned away from Sheridan in the hope she might not notice. He stole a look at her and saw her color was high. He was probably kidding himself that she wasn't aware that he was rock hard with need.

In an effort to steer the conversation to a safer topic, he cleared his throat. "I think a dog on the small side would be more practical. I had in mind a Maltese or a poodle, or even a pug, but after listening to what you said about those dogs that are hardest to re-home..." He looked up at her and grinned. "I think I'd like to adopt one of those."

The smile that lit up her face was as bright as her unshed tears. She swiped at her eyes, embarrassed at her show of emotion, but kept smiling just the same.

"Oh, Joel! That would be amazing! We have so many beautiful dogs. I'm sure you could fall in love with one of them. Come on; come with me. I'll show you."

Her excitement was contagious and he couldn't help but grin. If he'd known getting a dog would make him feel this good he would have done it a long time ago. And then he took a moment to consider that thought and realized it wasn't the act of getting a dog that had him in such a buoyant mood. It was Sheridan. She made all the difference.

Hell. What am I doing? Things are moving way too fast. This woman's becoming far too important. She's involved in my case!

The rush of thoughts flooded his mind and filled his gut with unease, but he didn't care. There would be time enough later to reflect on what was happening. Right now, he wanted to savor every moment he had with her. With his mind made up, he followed her further down the path until she came to a stop outside one of the enclosures.

Three small dogs ran toward her, barking excitedly and dancing around, making it difficult for Sheridan to unlock the gate. Laughing and cajoling the dogs, she eventually pulled it open.

"Hurry!" she urged, waving Joel inside.

The dogs continued to bark and jump. Sheridan burst into laughter and bent low, giving all of them her attention. A scratch behind the ears for one. A cuddle for another. And then she picked up an odd-looking dog with floppy ears and soulful brown eyes that looked like a cross between a spaniel and a terrier.

The dog squirmed in delight in Sheridan's arms and licked her wildly on the face. She laughed again and held the dog close, not at all put off by the dog's enthusiasm.

Joel smiled. "Who's that little fellow?"

She looked up at him and grinned. "This is Roxy."

"Roxy," Joel repeated. "Is Roxy a boy or a girl?"

Sheridan rolled her eyes. "A girl, of course."

"Okay."

"All of our dogs have been de-sexed, microchipped and vaccinated, so you don't have to worry about puppies."

He must have looked a little horrified, because Sheridan laughed again. He had to admit, the thought of having to deal with a litter of pups in his apartment was enough to have him breaking out in hives.

"Good."

She shot him a dubious look. "Have you ever had a dog?"

"No. Is that a problem?"

"No, not necessarily, but dogs aren't like motorbikes. They can't be taken out when it's convenient and then parked back in the shed. A dog needs regular exercise, even a little one. Will you have time to take a dog for a walk every day?"

"I guess I'll have to make time." He gave the small dog in Sheridan's arms a pat. "What's Roxy's story?"

"She was brought in by a motorist about four weeks ago. He found her wandering along the road. She was half-starved, sick and bleeding. Something had bitten her on the leg. Probably another dog. The wound was infected and quite nasty. It was lucky Matilda was here. She's our resident volunteer vet."

At the mention of her friend's name, Sheridan gave him a quick searching glance that he couldn't quite work out.

He reached out and patted the dog again and this time she pressed her head into his hand. When she looked up at him with her big dark eyes, he couldn't help but smile. He gave her a scratch between the ears and she made a sound that was remarkably human.

Sheridan laughed. "She likes you. And why wouldn't she? There's definitely a lot to like."

Just like that, the air around them turned dangerous. She stood close, close enough that if he leaned in a little and bent his head he could kiss her. Her gaze had locked on his; her eyes were shadowed with desire. The smell of her perfume lingered on the air and it was all he could do not to take her in his arms. Which was ridiculous, of course. They were in the middle of fifty-or-so barking dogs and one was being held between them.

Don't do it! Kissing her again will only complicate things. And yet they both wanted it. That's what made this situation so dangerous…

He deliberately stepped away, putting some distance between them. "What kind of dog is she?"

His question effectively broke the spell that had fallen between them and he quietly sighed with relief. He had no sense if he allowed himself to get involved with this woman. At least, now.

Sheridan busied herself patting Roxy. When she responded, her tone was cool and efficient.

"It's a little hard to tell. Matilda thinks she has a lot of terrier in her and perhaps even a bit of spaniel. And you might recognize some poodle in her if you look at her coat. She's multicultural; that's what we like to say."

"I think she's the one. I'd like to adopt her."

"Are you sure? There are plenty of others you can meet."

Joel shook his head. "No, Roxy's the one. I don't need to look at anything else. Sometimes you just know, right?"

He gave her a meaningful look, but her gaze remained fixed on the dog.

"You seem very decisive," she said. "I like that. And I agree. I think you know right away when you've met the right one. The right dog, I mean."

She turned away from him, but not before he caught the color spreading across her face. It pleased him to know she was jittery around him. He was jittery around her, too. It was a strange feeling to be nervous around a woman. He'd grown up confident in his own skin and had always accepted the appeal he held for women.

Over the years, he'd dated more than his fair share. And then MJ had come along and for a good while, he thought they might make it. But somewhere along the way she'd changed from easygoing and fun to clingy and contemptuous. She began to find fault with everything he did. She resented the time he spent away from her at work. She resented lots of things. Even before the death of his father, their relationship had deteriorated.

MJ had accused him of dumping her because he'd just inherited ten million dollars. It was clear she thought he no longer had use for her, that now that he was loaded he could do better.

She couldn't have been further from the truth. Joel had never been motivated by money. He would have gone into law like his father wanted if money drove him. While he appreciated and acknowledged he'd grown up in a wealthy family and enjoyed all the privileges that kind of lifestyle provided, the thought of not being surrounded by millions of dollars didn't upset him.

He didn't dispute he liked nice things—art, a comfortable apartment, beautiful women. But he truly believed he'd be just as happy without them. Well, maybe not the art. Or the beautiful women. One woman in particular. The same woman who stood only a few feet away, holding the first addition to his family.

"What are you doing after? Would you like to get a coffee?"

As soon as the questions fell out of his mouth, he kicked himself. *What the hell am I doing?* He should keep his distance, not use any excuse to remain in her company. Of course, he could always tell her he needed to ask her a few more questions about the case.

Bullshit. He was a detective. He could see her on official business any time he liked and she was smart enough to know that. Best fill in the application, collect his dog and get out of there.

And then she surprised him. "Sure," she said. "I get a break in ten minutes. If you're certain about adopting Roxy, then let's go and complete the paperwork and then you'll be good to go."

She gave him a smile that touched his heart and once again he was lost. *I'm an idiot! Why am I doing this? I'm hopeless! Totally hopeless!* But he couldn't keep the grin off his face.

Chapter Fourteen

They agreed it would be best to leave Roxy at the shelter and come and collect her later. Sheridan gave Joel directions to a nearby café where the coffee was good and the pastries were even better. On their way there, she had time to reconsider her decision, but she was tired of pretending she didn't like this guy. There was something very special about him.

He was sexy, charming and handsome. He was fun to be around. He liked dogs. He also hadn't seemed to notice how gorgeous Matilda was. Sheridan had watched him closely. He'd reacted with nothing more than polite curiosity when Matilda introduced herself. For Sheridan, his desirability went up another notch.

Okay, so he was investigating her family's company and that certainly complicated things, but she knew he wouldn't find any evidence that she'd done anything wrong, so it was only a matter of time before he dismissed his concerns about her. It still niggled a little that he thought she could be capable of stealing, but she'd decided to let that go. Far better to look to the future and concentrate on what they might have between them when all the obstacles to their relationship could be removed. She hoped it would be a seamless transition.

"Just here," she said and pointed toward a quaint café tucked between a hairdressers' and a butcher shop. The brightly decorated sign outside the building read: Janice's Café.

Joel found a parking spot not far away and together they walked to the café. It was a beautiful winter's morning with bright sunshine and a cloudless blue sky. The air was sufficiently chilly to be aware of it, but it didn't detract from her enjoyment of the day.

After spending on average fifty hours a week at the office, the weekends were the times Sheridan looked forward to the most. It was the time when she got to spend quality time with Gypsy, along with the other animals at the shelter.

Joel held open the door for her and she murmured her thanks and walked inside. The staff welcomed her in a familiar way. She was a regular there, usually arriving after her shift.

"Sheridan! It's good to see you!" Janice called from behind the counter.

Sheridan smiled at the middle-aged owner with the purple hair and numerous piercings.

"Hi Janice. How've you been?"

"I couldn't be better!" Janice replied, following it with a wink.

Her gaze slid to Joel and then back to Sheridan. Curiosity shone in the woman's eyes, but she was too polite to ask questions. Which was just as well, because Sheridan wasn't quite up to the point where she wanted to make introductions.

"If you don't mind, we might sit out the back," Sheridan said and with a quick look in Joel's direction, pushed open the wooden door that led to a cozy courtyard.

Large terracotta pots stood in all four corners, filled to overflowing with bright flowers. Ferns and other greenery hung in baskets from the roof. The effect was like being seated in a wonderful garden. That was one of the reasons Sheridan loved the place.

Apartment living meant no ready access to outdoor space. She didn't even have a balcony. It was only when she took Gypsy to the park that she was able to kick off her shoes and dig her bare toes into the grass and revel in the feel of nature. Most afternoons she didn't have a lot of time to really indulge herself, so being able to come to Janice's Café on Saturdays was always a treat. This was the first time she hadn't come alone. No wonder Janice was full of questions.

After ordering coffee and pastries, there was a moment of awkward silence before they both began to speak at once.

"So, what made you decide—?" Sheridan asked.

"Tell me about—?" Joel said.

They both laughed, a little embarrassed. Joel indicated with his hand. "You first."

Suddenly nervous, Sheridan cleared her throat. "I was just wondering what made you decide to get a dog."

Joel shrugged. The motion emphasized the broadness of his shoulders and stretched his black T-shirt taut across his muscular chest. She tried to forget how firm he felt beneath her fingers...and her lips...

"I'm not exactly sure," he replied, dragging her attention back to him. "Ever since MJ and I broke up, I've lived on my own. I don't mind it, but it's a bit lonely at times. I came home last night and decided it was time to get a dog. Is that weird?"

Sheridan's mind had snagged on the mention of his ex-girlfriend. *MJ*. She fought off a stab of jealousy. Of course he'd had girlfriends in the past. But this one had apparently shared his apartment, so she must have been special...

The expectant look on Joel's face reminded her she hadn't answered his question. "Um, no. I don't think that's weird. A bit spontaneous, maybe. Are you really sure you want to do this?"

"If I wasn't sure before I came here, one look at Roxy's face has convinced me. I mean, how could you not want to take her home?"

He grinned and Sheridan laughed. He was so easy to talk to. She wondered if he'd be as forthcoming about his ex-girlfriend.

"So," she said, striving for casual. "Tell me about MJ."

Joel scowled, but didn't dismiss her request. "There's not much to tell. We dated for a while. She moved in. We got on for a while. Then we didn't. She moved out."

"You make it sound so simple. Are you so clinical about all of your past relationships?"

Joel shrugged. "Probably. When something's over, it's over. I'm not one to get sentimental about these things."

"How long were you together?"

"Five years."

Sheridan blinked in surprise. "Five *years?* That's a long time."

Once again, Joel shrugged. Sheridan dared another personal question. After all, it wasn't that long ago he'd interrogated her over her relationship with Dwight. Fair was fair.

"Who broke it off?"

Joel looked at her, a tiny smile tugged at his lips. "Touché," he said quietly and then drew in a deep breath. "I did."

"Were you in love with her?"

Once again, he acknowledged her almost-identical question with a smile. "No."

She sat back in shock. "No? You were together five years. How could you not have been in love with her?"

He looked away. "What's love? I cared for her. We had fun together. I never wanted to see her come to harm. Isn't that enough?"

"Of course it isn't! It's obvious you've never been in love."

His mouth twisted in an imitation of a smile. "Of course. You're an expert. You were in love with that asshole Dwight Britton. The same asshole who could very well be responsible for the theft of nearly thirty million dollars from your family accounts. Yeah, what a catch."

His sarcasm angered her, but she let it slide. He hadn't known the Dwight she had. Dwight hadn't always been a jerk. Many times he'd been sweet and kind and thoughtful. He'd leave little notes and flowers and occasionally a box of her favorite chocolates on her desk or in her car or even on her pillow. Each time, he had touched her heart.

Of course, he wasn't perfect. There were times when he was downright annoying. But that was okay with her. She didn't want perfection. She only wanted someone to love and someone to love her—and Dwight seemed to fit the ideal. In fact, if he hadn't been caught cheating, she might very well have moved their relationship to the next level. Now she shuddered at the thought.

To have settled for nice and pleasant instead of raging fire and galloping hearts… Until her night with Joel, she hadn't realized how wonderful sex could be. Her mother had died when she was thirteen. There hadn't been time for the chats. Her father was merely relieved she didn't show that much interest in boys during her teenage years. He wasn't cut out for talks of a personal nature and they'd never talked about sex.

She could have talked to Zane about it, but that wasn't as easy as it sounded. Zane was fiercely protective. He didn't even want to think about her becoming sexually active, let alone give her advice on the subject. It was a wonder she'd managed to have any boyfriends at all with her brother always looking over her shoulder, often disapproving.

Their coffees and pastries arrived, sparing her from having to answer. Joel took a bite of his Danish and made a sound of satisfaction.

"Oh, my God! This is delicious! How come I've never heard of this place?"

She merely shrugged and sipped her coffee. Joel looked at her for a moment and then set his cup down. He reached over and placed his hand over hers.

"I'm sorry, Sheridan. I shouldn't have said that about Dwight. I was out of line."

"It's fine," she said dismissively.

"No, it's not." He paused. High color swept over his cheeks. "The thing is, I was jealous. I still am. The thought of you with Dwight—with any man—drives me mad. It isn't fair and it isn't right, but that's the way I feel. Sometimes it pushes me to say stupid things and this was one of those times. I'm sorry."

He looked so sincere, she believed him. Her heart had also picked up its pace when he mentioned he was jealous. That meant he cared. She should know. The thought of him with MJ—or any woman—drove her mad, too.

She gave him a slow smile as the knowledge that they cared more for each other than they'd admitted sank in. She lifted his hand off hers and then squeezed it. His eyes went wide with surprise.

"I understand all too well," she said quietly. "The thought of you and MJ… She's your ex, but you gave her five years of your life. To me, that's a lifetime and it tells me how very much you cared about her. Are you sure you're over her?"

"Absolutely," he replied without hesitation. "We were over long before I asked her to leave. It was one of those relationships that burned itself out. I never once considered asking her to marry me."

She shook her head, confused. "Then why didn't you call it quits sooner?"

He shrugged and looked genuinely perplexed. "I can't answer that. I guess I was busy at work. For some of that time

I worked in homicide. There was always another case. The truth is, we barely spent more than a few hours together at night. I'd usually come home late, sometimes long after she'd gone to bed. And then I'd be back at work early the next morning."

"That doesn't explain why you stayed in the relationship," Sheridan said.

Joel sighed. "You're right. I guess it was easier to maintain the status quo. I didn't have the energy required to change it. In the end, we were arguing almost every time we were together and I knew something had to be done. It was toxic to both of us. Neither of us were happy. We both deserved better.

"Then my father died and I guess that was the catalyst. MJ turned up to the funeral, but she couldn't leave the place quick enough. At a time when I could have really done with her support, she wasn't there.

"That was the end of us. I'd had enough. We broke up that night. I told her to get her stuff together and leave. We had an ugly fight, but she left without me calling the police."

Sheridan gasped. "It got *that* bad?"

Joel nodded. "She wasn't happy about having to leave. I'm just glad she didn't do any damage to the place. I'm not sure if you remember, but I collect art. I have some very nice pieces. Original paintings, sculptures and other things. She could have been a lot more malicious on her way out than she was."

Sheridan slowly shook her head. "Wow. I mean, wow. Have you seen her since?"

"No, thank God. Hopefully she's moved on and found someone else."

"And that doesn't worry you?"

Joel chuckled. "Hell, no. I wish the next poor bastard better luck."

Sheridan released his hand and took another sip of coffee.

She was both relieved and pleased that Joel wasn't missing sleep over the whereabouts of his ex-girlfriend or who she might now be with. It reassured her more than anything that he was truly over his ex.

And then he leaned forward and another lazy smile played around his lips. "Do you really feel jealous at the thought of me with other women?"

She blushed and bit her lip. No point in denying it. She'd said exactly that.

"You thought I didn't pick up on it, right? That somehow that little tidbit got lost amongst everything else." His grin widened. "No such luck, babe."

Her heart tripped over in nervous excitement at his casual use of the endearment. She'd never been called that before. In fact, apart from the occasional endearment from her father, she hadn't been referred to like that by anyone. Dwight certainly hadn't been into endearments.

During their time as a couple, she hadn't given it much thought, but now she found she liked it, especially when the endearment came from Joel. With an effort, she maintained her composure and arched one perfectly groomed eyebrow. "*Babe?*"

Joel looked unrepentant. "Yeah. Do you have a problem with that?"

She laughed and her stomach quivered with butterflies. "Not at all."

"So you're not going to deny you turn green with jealousy at the thought of me with another woman?"

She blushed, but held his gaze. "No. I can't. It's true."

His eyes darkened with emotion. Desire glinted in their depths. "I never knew honesty could be such a turn on."

His voice was low and husky. It washed over her, sending shivers of desire along her nerve endings. Heat unfurled low in her belly and her nipples puckered in response. She bit into her Danish in an effort to distract herself and then washed it down with a sip of coffee. Joel's hot gaze watched her every move and she felt self-conscious. The moment she finished swallowing, he spoke again.

"God, you're so erotic. I love watching you. Talking, laughing, eating, arguing... It doesn't matter. Everything about you fascinates me."

A fresh surge of need went through her and she squirmed uncomfortably in her seat. This was getting hot and heavy and they were in no place to take advantage of it. *Perhaps that's a good thing?* Maybe, but right at that moment, she couldn't think of a single reason why.

And then, as if reading her mind, Joel's expression changed, became more somber. He sat back in his seat.

"You're right. Now is not the time or place. We're in a café... The investigation... Roxy's waiting for me to collect her and take her home. I have to stop by the store and buy her a kennel, or a bed, or something she can sleep on and then there's the dog food..."

Sheridan smiled. "It's all right, Joel. I understand. This is going a bit fast for me, too. It's good enough for me to know I like you and you like me." And then she was struck with a sudden bout of uncertainty. "Is that fair to say?"

Almost instantly the somber expression disappeared and was once again replaced with a blaze of desire.

"Oh, yes," he drawled, his voice low and sexy. "That's definitely fair to say. I like you, Sheridan McClintock. I like you a lot. And I'm glad you like me. And as soon as this investigation's over, you and I are going to get reacquainted and just so you know, it won't be in a coffee shop."

Chapter Fifteen

oel stared at his computer screen, his mind on Sheridan. He'd spent the rest of the weekend getting Roxy settled in and every time he looked at the dog he thought of Sheridan. He'd been telling her the truth when he told her he liked her and he was just as pleased to discover she liked him, too. All he had to do was tidy up the McClintock investigation and they'd be free to explore where their relationship might lead.

Now he'd met her ex-boyfriend, he couldn't understand what she'd seen in the man. He was a smug, rude, arrogant asshole. How could someone like that manage to get a woman like Sheridan McClintock to fall in love with him? It was almost beyond conceivable.

Sheridan hadn't risen to the bait when he'd ridiculed her choice of men. He admired her for her restraint. He'd been rude and churlish and he was pleased he'd found the courage to apologize. Still, giving her heart to a jerk like Britton… That was hard to accept. All he could imagine was that Britton had shown a different side to his girlfriend than the one he'd shown to Joel.

And that led him back to his investigation. No matter there was a chance Britton was his man, there was also the possibility Sheridan was more involved than he wanted to believe. The fact was, the transactions had originated from her computer and they'd begun two months *after* her ex had left the scene.

He wanted to take her at her word—his gut believed in her innocence—but right now, he just didn't know and it was killing him. He'd always been able to separate emotion from cold hard fact. It was one of the reasons he was such a good investigator. He had a knack of remaining objective, distant, apart from the action and could assess a situation from afar.

The thing he had going with Sheridan was a damn distraction and he wished to God she wasn't connected to his investigation. The truth was she hadn't given him enough reason to completely discount her. At the moment, everyone even remotely involved had to be considered a suspect.

He prided himself on his objectivity and his cool-headed assessment of the facts. Despite his affinity for Sheridan, nothing had changed in that regard and it wasn't about to change now. He sure as hell wasn't going to be taken in by a pair of beguiling eyes and memories of the best sex of his life, or the fact he might well be on the way to falling in love for the very first time.

Still, he was nothing if not thorough. Pulling up the list of police contacts on his screen, he found the number of one of the computer techs who specialized in computer hacking and put in a call.

"George. It's Joel Craigdon. Mate, just wanting to pick your brain about computer hacking."

Joel explained the situation and was interested to discover hacking into supposedly secure computer systems was easier than he'd thought.

"Does it make any difference where the hacker is situated?" he asked.

"No. A good hacker can do it from the comfort of his lounge room on the other side of the world if he has the right skills and equipment."

"The guy I'm looking at was an ex-employee of this company."

"Well, hacking's even easier if the hacker has access to usernames and passwords. It's merely a matter of dialing into the server and entering the login details."

"Is it possible to determine if a device has been hacked?"

"For someone like me, it is. You have to know what you're looking for."

Joel thought for a moment. "So a hacker leaves behind something that can be traced?"

"Yes. But it's not as easy as that. Often it looks like the entries have originated from the particular device. It's a ploy, of course and makes it that much harder for people and businesses to realize they've been hacked."

Joel thanked George for his time and ended the call, secretly relieved. Dwight Britton had just jumped higher on Joel's suspect list. The man was an IT geek who'd worked alongside Sheridan in the finance department for at least a year. He'd also dated her for six months. It was plausible he'd accessed her login details without her knowledge.

Though he hated to credit Britton with anything, the truth was Joel needed to dig deeper into the money trail. To that end, he reached for his phone again and put in a call to AUSTRAC. He was lucky enough that one of the investigators who'd provided him with the initial information was in the office.

"Max, it's Joel Craigdon. Just wondering if you have any more information on the shelf company collecting that thirty million dollars?"

"Joel. I was just about to call you. We've managed to dig up details on the director of the shelf company. It took some doing and there were several false leads, but we've come up with a name."

"Who is it?" Joel held his breath in anticipation.

"Sheridan McClintock."

Joel felt the color draining from his face. He'd almost convinced himself Britton was the culprit. Discovering it had been Sheridan all along was a terrible blow. He felt like he'd been kicked in the guts.

"Are… Are you sure?"

"Yep. She's the sole director. The Caymans bank identified her through her driver's license and passport. There were copies of both in their files. I can email them to you if you like."

"Thanks," Joel said, hardly aware he was still speaking. He ended the call and stared in shock at his screen. He'd been duped. She'd smiled and batted her eyes at him and told him straight out she was innocent. She'd found him a dog and told him she liked him and smiled at him once again. And he'd fallen for it. All along, she'd been taking him for a ride.

Anger coursed through him. He might have underestimated her, but she didn't know him very well. She didn't know how determined he was to find the perpetrator and see them put behind bars. She'd learn to rue the day she thought she could pull one over on Joel Craigdon. With steely determination, he pushed away from his desk.

Ralph looked up from the file spread before him. "Where are you off to?"

Joel glanced at him. "It's Sheridan McClintock. The thief. It's her. AUSTRAC found proof she's the one who opened the account in the Caymans."

Ralph's expression reflected his surprise. "Well, well, well. Who'd have thought? I almost bought her innocent routine. She certainly appeared genuine enough. I wonder what her motive was?" he mused.

"I couldn't give a shit about her motive," Joel growled. "She's our guy. Let's go and arrest her."

Sheridan was on the phone to her brother when Joel and his partner marched into her office, unannounced. From the grim look on their faces, they weren't there to bring her good news. A frisson of unease stole along her nerve endings.

"Actually, Zane, those two detectives are back," she told him… "Yes, the ones that were here last week. Do you mind coming to my office? It looks like they mean business." With that, she hung up the phone and folded her hands calmly in front of her on the desk in a false show of bravado.

"Detectives. No one told me you were downstairs. What can I do for you?"

Joel glared at her. "Sheridan McClintock, we're placing you under arrest."

Shock ricocheted through her. She gave up all semblance of calm. "*Arrest?* What for? Is this some kind of joke?"

Joel didn't respond. Instead, he walked around to where she remained seated at her desk and pulled her to her feet. The next thing she knew there were handcuffs securing her wrists.

"Let go of me! This is an outrage! I've done nothing wrong!"

"Save it for the judge," Joel growled. His eyes glittered with fury.

"You've made a mistake!" Sheridan protested, her alarm growing. She'd never seen Joel so angry or been in a situation like this where her word was questioned.

"We have evidence you set up an illegal offshore account and thereafter deposited in it close to thirty million dollars. You're going to be taken to the City of Sydney Police Station where you'll be given the opportunity to participate in a police interview."

Sheridan's anxiety continued to grow. She looked from Joel to Ralph and back again. Both men wore identical grim expressions. A muscle ticked in the side of Joel's clenched jaw Neither man looked her in the eye.

"What the hell's going on here?"

Sheridan almost collapsed with relief as Zane appeared in the open doorway. Joel glanced briefly at her brother.

"Your sister's under arrest for the theft of thirty million dollars. We're taking her back to the station to be interviewed."

"Like hell you are! This is outrageous!" Zane shouted.

Joel's glare turned to steel. His tone brooked no disobedience. "I'm going to have to ask you to step out of the way."

The two men stood toe to toe and eyeballed each other. For a long tense moment, neither man moved. Then, with great reluctance, Zane stepped aside and let Joel proceed. As he led Sheridan out of her office and down the corridor toward the lifts, her brother shouted out behind her.

"Don't say a word, Sheridan! I'll call our lawyer. He'll meet you at the station. Don't tell them anything until he gets there."

The ruckus had brought people out of their offices and out from behind partitions. With her head held high and her gaze directed straight ahead, Sheridan bore their curious glances and the frantic whispers that followed in her wake.

Ralph stepped forward and pressed the "down" button for the lift. The three of them stood in silence. Sheridan refused to utter a word to her captors, or even grace them with a glance. The minutes seemed to drag into hours, but finally there was a *ding* indicating the arrival of the lift. She surreptitiously eased out her breath.

The doors slid open and Christopher alighted. Engrossed in a file he held, he almost walked right into them. He came to an abrupt halt. As he looked from her to Joel and back again, a frown marred his features.

"Sheridan? Joel? What the hell's going on?"

"She's under arrest. That's all you need to know," Joel

said. He pushed his way into the lift, dragging Sheridan along with him. The other detective stepped in beside them. Christopher stood there, his face a picture of confusion. Before he could say anything further, the doors slid closed.

If Sheridan thought being dragged from her office in handcuffs was humiliating, it was nothing to being brought in through the rear of the police station and locked in one of the holding cells while the detectives did whatever it was they were doing. More than an hour passed before Joel reappeared and unlocked the door to the cell.

"Follow me," he ordered.

"Where am I going?" she demanded. "You can't hold me here! I have rights!"

"You have nothing," he snarled.

She opened her mouth to protest, outraged at his treatment, but he cut her off before she could speak.

"I don't know about you, but I heard your brother give clear instructions you weren't to be interviewed without the presence of your lawyer. We've been waiting for him to arrive. Of course, we can do it without the lawyer. You just say the word."

She glared at him and didn't deign to answer.

"I'll take that as a no," Joel growled.

Turning away from her, he strode down a long corridor with closed doors leading off on either side. Eventually he stopped outside one of them and turned the handle. He pushed the door inward and stepped back, indicating Sheridan would enter ahead of him. Refusing to look in his direction, she marched past him.

Robert Mitchell, the McClintock family lawyer was already seated at the stained Formica table. He got to his feet as she entered.

"Sheridan. How are you?" the lawyer said. He extended his hand and Sheridan shook it.

"Robert. Thanks for coming."

"Of course. I dropped everything as soon as Zane called."

"This has all been some terrible misunderstanding," she said in a rush. "I don't have a clue why the police think I'm involved. I'm innocent, Robert. You need to believe me."

Sheridan heard the trembling in her voice and hated herself for it. Being transported in the back of a police car while handcuffed and then locked in a holding cell had shaken her. She'd never been inside a police station before, let alone been locked in a cell. It wasn't a pleasant experience. The only thing she was grateful for was that the cell had been empty.

Robert held up a hand, halting her. "Don't say anything more, Sheridan. I understand you feel the need to assert your innocence, but I also need you to let me do my job. Don't answer any question unless I tell you to and whatever you do, don't forget I'm on your side. Do you understand?"

Sheridan opened her mouth. She wanted to tell him she needed to make Joel see he was wrong. She wasn't behind the theft. But one look at the steel resolve in Mitchell's eyes and she lowered her gaze and nodded. "Yes."

Through the one-way glass panel cut into the door of the interview room, Joel watched Sheridan talk to her lawyer. He'd stepped out of the room to give them the privacy she was entitled to. Of course, everything in the room was being recorded. There was nothing underhanded about it. It was standard procedure and there were plenty of signs posted around the room alerting the occupants of such.

After a few minutes, Joel opened the door and strode back into the room. In his hand he held the paperwork that provided evidence of Sheridan's involvement in the setting up of the illegal offshore account. Coupled with the forensic evidence that the fifteen transactions had originated from her computer, she had some explaining to do.

Of course, now that she'd lawyered up, he probably wouldn't get anywhere with her. Robert Mitchell was a highly respected criminal lawyer with an enviable success rate in the courtroom. But even if Sheridan chose to remain silent, Joel had enough to charge her.

"Are we ready to proceed?" he asked. He directed the question to Sheridan, but it was her lawyer who replied.

"I've instructed my client not to answer anything without my prior approval. If you're prepared to proceed on that basis, we're good to go."

Joel acknowledged the comment with a brusque nod. He'd already suspected the lawyer would run the interview along those lines. Pulling out the chair directly opposite Sheridan, Joel eyeballed her as he took a seat.

He started the interview by asking her to identify herself for the purposes of the electronic recording. He had her lawyer do the same.

"You're employed by McClintock Properties, is that right?" he asked.

Sheridan glanced at Mitchell who nodded. "Yes," she replied. "It's my family company."

"And what position do you hold in that company?"

Once again, she looked at Mitchell for guidance. Once again, he gave her permission to respond.

"I'm head of finance and contract negotiations."

"What does that entail?"

A glance at Mitchell. A nod from the lawyer.

"I'm responsible for ensuring the income generated by McClintock through the sale of property is paid to the company in a timely manner. I'm also responsible for negotiating deals on new projects the company wishes to take on."

"Is it your job to source those new projects?" Joel asked.

Another nod from Mitchell.

"No. My brother, Zane and his team are usually the ones who decide what projects McClintock will take on."

Joel kept his tone conversational. "Do you have security clearance to access any of the McClintock bank accounts?"

"Don't answer that," Mitchell said quickly.

Joel tried again. "Are there any McClintock bank accounts you *don't* have security clearance to access?"

"Don't answer that," the lawyer repeated, his tone stern.

Joel shuffled the papers in his hand. "I want to talk to you about a number of financial transactions which occurred between February and May of this year where money was dispersed from an account owned by McClintock Properties to an overseas account."

Mitchell's gaze narrowed on Joel. "She's not answering anything about any transactions that might or might not have occurred at McClintock Properties."

"Tell me about the offshore account you set up in the Caymans," Joel continued, unperturbed.

"Ms McClintock will not be answering any questions of this nature. If you have nothing further, my client and I will bring this interview to an end."

Joel nodded. He'd expected as much. Still, it didn't change anything. "As you wish," he replied.

Mitchell pushed away from the table. Sheridan started to follow suit.

"Not so fast, Ms McClintock." Joel's casual smile belied the titanium in his tone.

"What's the problem, Detective? Mitchell demanded. "My client has a right to silence. She's answered all the questions she's going to."

Joel fixed his attention on Sheridan. "You're right. You're completely within your rights to refuse to answer my questions.

Just as I'm within my rights to charge you."

She gasped. "*Charge* me? Have you gone mad? What are you talking about?"

Ignoring her outburst, Joel began to read out the charges against her. By the time he'd finished, she was ashen and her lips were pinched with fear. She looked at her lawyer, stricken.

"Robert! You have to help me."

Joel stood and walked around to where she remained seated at the table. He took her by the arm and helped her to her feet. "Oh, he can help you, all right. As soon as we're finished. Right now I'm going to take you to the charge room where you'll be photographed and fingerprinted. Then you'll be brought before the magistrate where you can apply for bail." He glanced at the lawyer. "You can reconvene with your client in the courtroom."

Not giving either of them time to argue, Joel led Sheridan out of the interview room and further down the corridor until they came to the charge room. Her eyes were as wide as saucers and the color still hadn't returned to her cheeks. When he picked up her hand to press her fingertips into the ink, he noticed she was trembling.

A surge of sympathy rushed through him. He viciously suppressed it. He couldn't afford to remember the hours of pleasure he'd spent with her, both inside and outside his bedroom, or that for a while, he'd almost been convinced of her innocence.

No, Sheridan McClintock was like any other prisoner, to be treated exactly the same way. With clinical precision, he went through the routine of fingerprinting and photographing her and entering her details into the computer.

In short order it was done. She'd remained silent throughout, though he could tell from the distress on her face that the whole procedure had been an ordeal. Once again, he fought off a wave of sympathy.

"The court is still sitting," he said. "We'll go through there now. You'll have time to confer with your lawyer before he makes an application for bail."

Joel used a private access between the police station and the courthouse which was situated next door. A few minutes later, he opened the door to the courtroom and led Sheridan inside.

Chapter Sixteen

heridan's head spun. Everything had happened so fast. One minute she'd been dealing with the usual day's events from the comfort of her office and the next she was being brought before a judge. She could barely think through her shock.

Joel had mentioned an account in the Caymans. She had no clue about that and yet he seemed convinced she was behind it. *What did he find to convince him I'm the culprit?* Whatever it was, it couldn't be true. She had nothing to do with the missing money. She wished she could have asked him, but her lawyer had advised her against answering any questions of that nature and she had to trust his advice. After all, he was the expert in these things.

She looked around the courtroom. There was a scattering of desperate-looking people seated in the public gallery and a few lawyer types in dark suits hovering around the bar table. One lawyer was on his feet engaging the judge in argument about his request for leniency for his client. It was an argument he eventually lost. Icy dread filled her stomach. Shortly, her lawyer was going to appeal to the same judge for her bail.

Oh, God. What if he refuses the application? What if I'm locked up overnight? Or even longer? Oh, God. Oh, God. Oh, God…

Her chest was tight. Her breath came fast. With an effort, she tried to get hold of her panic. Eventually it was her turn. Robert waved her over to the bar table and then pointed to the dock where the prisoners sat. It wasn't far away from the bar table, but it felt like there was a canyon between them. Two corrections officers stood guard on either side of the dock. On shaking legs, she climbed the step and sat down.

Robert addressed the bench. He outlined the flimsiness of the prosecution's evidence and emphasized Sheridan's good character, her stable employment, the fact she had no prior criminal record, was a member of one of Sydney's most respected families.

The application went on and on. Arguments resounded back and forth. A buzzing noise sounded in her ears. Panic rose within her at the possibility that bail might be refused. She only heard snatches of the legal discussion. It all turned into a blur. And then the gavel dropped with a loud bang and she nearly jumped out of her skin.

"Bail is set at ten million dollars."

With the surety paid and the paperwork completed, Sheridan stumbled out of the court registry feeling dazed and numb. Though she hadn't seen him in the courtroom earlier, Zane came forward immediately after the decision and took her into his arms. He shook with anger at the way his sister had been treated and promised her this nightmare would soon be over. He led her out of the courthouse to where he'd parked his car. Acting on autopilot, she climbed in and pulled on her seatbelt.

Seated behind the wheel, Zane shot her a look of concern. "I just don't understand how the police think you did this, Sheridan. It doesn't make an iota of sense. I don't care what evidence they say they have. There's no way I'll ever believe you're behind this."

She gave him a wan smile. "Thanks for the show of support, Zane. I really appreciate it."

"We need to find out who did this. The police obviously think you're their guy. They're not going to be looking for anyone else. If we want to find the real culprit, we're going to have to do it ourselves. I'm not going to let you go down for this, Sheridan. Not on my watch."

Once again, she was filled with gratitude for his staunch support. She wondered how Joel and his partner could have gotten things so wrong. They'd seemed like competent detectives, but she knew darn well she wasn't responsible for the theft. They'd overlooked something, or concocted evidence to suit a narrative she wasn't privy to. Zane was right. The police were done looking for the perpetrator. If she wanted to find out who was behind this, she was going to have to investigate it herself.

"Someone's setting you up. It's the only explanation," Zane continued as he swung out into the traffic. "They've left enough crumbs behind for the police to follow and draw the conclusion that you're involved. Only, the crumbs are false. Someone has deliberately tried to get you in trouble and it's worked." He looked at her, a frown marring his forehead. "Who could hate you that much?"

She shook her head, still feeling overwhelmed by the day's events. "I don't know. The only person I can think of is Dwight. We didn't exactly end things on friendly terms. And he's the only one who might have gained access to my computer and login details."

"You're right." Zane's expression turned grim. "I think it's time I had a chat with Dwight Britton. If he's the one behind this, he's going to wish he'd never even heard the name McClintock."

"Maybe it would be best if I spoke to him? He'll already be on the defensive if you call him. After all, you were the one who came down on him hard and made it clear he needed to find another place of employment."

Zane gave a grudging nod. "Okay. But keep your wits about you. If Dwight's the one behind this, he's feeling a lot more aggrieved than either of us imagined and now that the police are involved, he probably realizes the thirty million he's stockpiled is about to disappear. Make sure wherever you meet, it's in public."

Sheridan frowned. "Surely you don't think he'd hurt me?" She gave a half-chuckle. "We're talking about Dwight. He's not exactly the aggressive type."

"True from what we know of him. But you don't want to take any chances. Just make sure you're not alone with him, okay?"

"Okay," she agreed. Now that she had a plan to move forward, she was filled with a renewed sense of determination. Joel Craigdon and his cronies could go to hell. If the police weren't interested in finding the real culprit then she and her brother would. Together they were the McClintocks and they made a formidable team.

Zane dropped Sheridan at her apartment and told her to take the rest of the day off. She was grateful for his solicitude. The last thing she could concentrate on was work. She needed to formulate a plan to get Dwight talking. If he was the one behind this, he might not be all that forthcoming about it. She guessed it depended upon his motives. Was it about the thirty million dollars, or was he just trying to make her life unbearable?

If it was the latter, he'd done a good job. She'd never been more frightened or more humiliated in all of her life. She was just thankful that, so far it appeared the media hadn't gotten wind of it. That would be the last straw. To have her face plastered all over the evening news for a crime she didn't commit and then spend the rest of her life trying to convince people of her innocence… She went over how to record their conversation using her phone, checking online directions. Once confident she could do that she went to bed.

After a restless night spent drinking coffee and pacing her apartment, Sheridan was determined to force Dwight to tell her the truth. The more she thought about it, the more she was convinced this was his way of getting back at her. It was pure and simple, a petty act of revenge.

She picked up her phone and squared her shoulders and dialed Dwight's number. He answered on the third ring.

"Sheridan! How nice to hear from you! It's been so long! I've missed you!"

She gritted her teeth and forced a pleasant tone. "I've missed you too," she lied.

"You have?"

She heard the hope and anticipation in his voice and clenched her jaw. "Of course. In fact, that's the reason for my call. I was wondering if you had time to meet me somewhere. There's something I need to talk to you about."

"Um, sure," he agreed. "When?"

"Today would be good, if you can manage it."

"Sorry, I'm snowed under at work, but what about tomorrow? I should be on top of things by then. We could meet at the gun range at Condell Park. You don't know how much I've missed our weekly sessions there."

Sheridan frowned. The gun range was at least a couple of hours from the city and she was reluctant to meet in a place where they'd spent so much time as a couple. Still, she wanted him relaxed and unsuspecting. If that's where he wanted to meet, she'd go along with it.

"Sure. Is twelve okay?"

"Sounds good. I'll make sure I get the time off. See you there. I can't wait."

She almost groaned aloud at the enthusiasm in his voice, but pulled herself up just in time. "Great. See you then." With a sigh, she ended the call.

It was done.

Whistling a jaunty tune, Christopher tapped the pocket of his suit jacket, reassured by the crinkling sound of paper. Little Amy from the ultrasound clinic had come through as promised and provided him with the scan of a twelve-week baby. The date of the scan, name of the patient and medical record number had been blurred out, but he hoped Joel would be too shocked by the sight of the picture and the thought he was about to be a father, to pay too much attention to the missing details.

After witnessing the humiliating way Joel had dragged Sheridan out of her office in handcuffs, Christopher felt even more justified about bringing a little turmoil into his half-brother's life. He'd learned from the staff that Sheridan had been arrested for stealing thirty million dollars from McClintock. Though he doubted the truth of the rumors, everyone knew something was going on.

Pushing open the door to Harry's Bar with his shoulder, he took a moment to let his eyes adjust to the dimness. MJ sat at the bar alone. A half-empty glass of red wine sat in front of her. Christopher sighed inwardly. He hoped she wasn't as drunk as the last time they'd met. He needed her to focus.

Plastering a smile on his face, he greeted her with a peck on the cheek. "MJ. You're looking ravishing."

Truth be told, she looked a little overdone in her low-cut sequined top and tight leather skirt that barely covered her ass.

Still, he wasn't there to judge her on her clothing. She was a free agent. She could wear what she pleased.

Unable or unwilling to see through his insincerity, she smiled back. "Christopher. You're here. Does this mean you have it?"

He tamped down his irritation at the greedy anticipation in her eyes. "Of course. I told you I could get one. It's a matter of knowing the right people and being prepared to pay enough money."

Her eagerness faded. "I can't pay you."

"We already discussed this, MJ," he soothed.

She quickly regained her enthusiasm. "I'm sure my fortunes will change when I'm Mrs Joel Craigdon. He'll hardly deny his wife and the mother of his child the little luxuries that make life so much more comfortable, don't you think? After all, he's just inherited ten million dollars."

Christopher's mind filled with the possibilities of separating Joel from his money. Having Joel's future wife in Christopher's debt would give him a direct line of access to Joel's bank account. Life would be very sweet, indeed.

This time, Christopher's smile was genuine. "MJ, I *definitely* think. And when I'm ready to call in your debt, you'll be the first to know."

Joel poured himself another cup of coffee and made his way back to his desk. Throwing himself down into his chair, he stared blindly at his computer screen. He'd been in a funk ever since he'd discovered Sheridan's complicity in the theft. The same theft she'd emphatically denied any knowledge of. And he'd believed her. He'd never trust his gut again. It had let him down so spectacularly. *Shit! Shit! Shit!* How could he have misjudged her so completely? He'd let his cock take over and blind him to the reality.

Sheridan was their thief. She'd set up an offshore account and then over a series of fifteen separate transactions, had transferred into that account a total of just under thirty million dollars from her brother's company accounts. Those were the facts and it made him sick in the gut. Even worse, he was angry—at Sheridan for lying and at himself for falling for those lies.

His phone beeped, indicating a new text. Pulling it out of his pocket, he checked the screen.

Hi Joel, I'm in the city. Would love to have lunch if you can spare the time. Love Mom.

Joel cursed under his breath. Though he always enjoyed spending time with his mother, he wasn't exactly having a good day. He'd just found out the woman he was halfway in love with was a skilled liar and a criminal—and it had happened on his watch. He'd never been very good at keeping his feelings from his mother. She had a knack for knowing when he was troubled. He wasn't sure how she did it, but she had unerring instincts when it came to knowing her children were struggling.

Sometimes that was actually a good thing. It definitely made it easier to broach difficult discussions with her and inevitably she gave good advice. She'd lived a life full of experiences and challenges and had plenty of wisdom to offer her children as a result. Wisdom Joel often found invaluable.

He guessed it couldn't hurt to meet her for lunch. She might even be able to offer some insight into the mess with Sheridan. Besides, he hadn't eaten since the burrito at breakfast, purchased from a street vendor not far from his work. As if in agreement with his decision, his stomach growled. He sent a quick text to his mother, confirming a time and place they could meet. Pushing away from his desk, he reached for his jacket and shrugged it on.

"I'm going to lunch," he muttered in Ralph's general

direction. Not waiting for a response, he headed for the door.

He spied his mother in the crowd of lunch goers who filled the dining hall below the MLC building. She was immaculately groomed as usual and wore a tailored ice-blue suit. The skirt fell modestly to just below her knee. Her shiny leather pumps matched the color of her suit. She'd turned sixty earlier in the year but she could pass for a decade younger, even with her thick head of snowy white hair.

She smiled and came to her feet as she caught sight of Joel. "Joel! How are you?" She pecked him on the cheek and he caught a familiar whiff of her Chanel **N°5** Perfume, a scent she'd worn for as long as he could remember.

"Mom. It's good to see you." He took a seat opposite her.

"Thank you for meeting me, Joel. I had an appointment in the city and found myself with an hour or two on my hands. I thought about calling Callum, but he'll be up to his elbows in food service at Jennifer's Kitchen. With Grace still in rehab, they're a little short-handed."

"Good to know I was your second choice," he teased.

She blushed. "Actually, I called Nicholas, too. He has back-to-back meetings all afternoon."

"Okay, well, third choice, then."

"Well…"

He rolled his eyes in disbelief. "You're kidding, Mom! How many others did you call before you got me?"

She laughed and patted his hand. "Just kidding, darling. It's always good to spend time with you. I haven't seen you since we all had lunch together."

Joel sighed. That afternoon seemed a lifetime ago.

Elizabeth shot him a look of concern. "What's the matter, son?"

Joel thought about brushing off her question and forcing a casual smile, but decided against it. What the heck. This was his mother. He'd always found her easy to talk to and she'd given him good insights into his problems in the past. Right now he was topsy-turvy whenever he thought of Sheridan. How could he like someone in that way when she was nothing more than a common criminal?

Her actions went against everything he believed. He was a cop, for God's sake! He'd taken an oath to uphold the law. How could he even contemplate falling in love with someone who had such complete disregard for everything he held in high esteem?

"What's going on with you, Joel?"

The concern in his mother's voice was enough to get him talking. He blew out his breath on another weary sigh.

"There's this woman," he began. "Her name's Sheridan."

He told his mother about the night he and Sheridan had met, leaving out the hot sex that had followed. She didn't need to know *everything*. He talked about the investigation and how she seemed to be implicated and then she wasn't, but now she was again. In the meantime, he'd developed feelings for her, feelings that wouldn't go away, despite what he now knew about her.

"Before you discovered she was the thief, how did you feel about her?" his mother asked.

Joel closed his eyes briefly against the memories of him and Sheridan together. The night at his apartment... The kisses they'd shared on a secluded balcony... Spending time together at the animal shelter... Bonding over their pets...

He opened his eyes and looked at his mother. "I was more than halfway in love with her. In fact, I might have already been there. She's like no woman I've ever met. She's smart and kind and beautiful. She's fun to be around. But it's more than that. I can't describe it. Just a feeling I get when I'm around her. Nervous, excited, jittery... I've never felt like that before. Not even with MJ."

His mother regarded him steadily. "I could never see what

you saw in MJ. Oh, she was pretty enough, but I never thought she was your soulmate."

"And yet we were together five years! Five years of my life! There were plenty of times when I knew it wasn't working, but all couples go through their ups and downs, right? Even you and Dad."

Elizabeth nodded. "Absolutely. But please don't model your relationships on mine and your father's. We didn't have the best of marriages."

Joel acknowledged her comment with a brief movement of his head. "Callum emailed me about your revelations. The one about having an affair." His mother opened her mouth to speak, but Joel cut her off.

"It's all right, Mom. I'm not judging you. None of us are perfect and Dad sure as hell wasn't the easiest person to live with. Nor did he remain faithful."

"Please don't think that was the reason for my affair. It had nothing to do with pettiness or revenge."

Joel looked at her. "Then what was it about?"

Elizabeth sighed quietly. Her gaze remained fixed on the table in front of her. "I fell in love with someone who wasn't my husband."

Joel frowned. "Really? How does that happen?"

"I was a few years into my marriage when I realized I'd married the wrong man. Your father was handsome, charismatic and charming. He swept me off my feet. I should have known better. I wasn't a young girl by any means."

"How old were you when you married?"

"Twenty-seven. Your father was thirty-three. Back in those days, we were positively ancient. My parents despaired of me ever getting married."

"They must have been pleased when Dad proposed?"

She smiled grimly. "Oh, yes. They were pleased, all right. On top of that, your father was a good catch. He came from a good family and had a promising career as an accountant. They were very happy for both of us."

"So what happened?" Joel dared to ask and then wondered if he really wanted to know. Some things were better left buried, including the demise of his parents' marriage. But the question had already been asked and he could see his mother considering her answer.

"It was a gradual thing. The love didn't die overnight. But that's the thing about being with the wrong person. Little things you used to overlook start to irritate. Soon there are more and more things you dislike. It erodes any love you might have felt when you said your vows. Throw in the fact I knew by then that I was in love with someone else and it makes life very difficult."

Joel shook his head. "Wow. Did Dad know how you felt?"

"I kept it a secret for a long time, but eventually he found out."

"How?"

"It doesn't matter."

"Why did the two of you stay married?"

Elizabeth shrugged. "I had five children. By then your father was a powerful man. I wasn't going to risk losing my children in a custody battle."

"What about Dad? Why did he bother staying in the marriage?"

Elizabeth looked at him sadly. "Who knows? I think he enjoyed having me under his control, being able to remind me every day of my transgression."

"But he had affairs, too!" Joel exploded. "I'm not sure when they started, but I remember becoming aware of them when I started hanging around Craigdon Enterprises. I never talked about it with him or anyone else. I guess I was ashamed of his behavior, but I sure as hell knew what went on."

Elizabeth reached over and squeezed his hand in an act of

reassurance. "Don't feel bad about it, Joel. It wasn't up to you to take action or even to raise it with anyone. Your father and I were the only ones responsible for our relationship, and the deterioration of it. Either of us could have walked away if we'd really wanted to. We didn't."

"But what about all the other women?" Joel cried.

A waitress hovered nearby waiting to take their order. Joel glanced at her and wondered how much she'd heard. No matter. They were strangers to her. The odds were they'd never see her again. Quickly he scanned the menu and ordered a steak sandwich with a side of fries and a black coffee. His mother ordered the minestrone soup. When the girl left, Joel picked up the threads of their conversation.

"I don't understand why you were willing to stay when you knew he was being unfaithful. And not just once. I guess once might be forgivable. But it was over and over. Dad didn't care who knew. He almost seemed to flaunt it, to throw it in your face. I can't imagine staying in that kind of relationship. You deserved better, Mom. How come you didn't think like that?"

"It's hard to understand why people do what they do. Please just accept I had my reasons. It suited me just as much as it suited your father to remain in our marriage."

"It's not the kind of marriage I want," Joel muttered.

His mother looked surprised. "So you do want to get married one day?"

"Yes. I guess so. Why?"

Elizabeth shrugged. "You never showed any inclination toward the wedded state in the past."

"You're talking about with MJ?"

"Well, you were together five years. Long enough to progress to the next level."

Joel grimaced. "Yeah. Five years. And all that time, I never once thought of marrying her." He was filled with a sudden surge of uncertainty. "How do you know, Mom? How do you know if it's the real deal? How do you know if it's going to last the distance?"

She gave him a sad smile. "None of us know if our marriage is going to last the distance. We like to think it will and can hope for the best and we can try to make sure we choose the right life partner in the first place."

"But how do you do that, Mom?" Joel cried, exasperated. "You just admitted you'd married the wrong man. You gave him thirty-three years of your life! There must have been plenty of times you were miserable! How do I ensure I don't make the same mistake?"

Elizabeth sighed wearily. Her expression was filled with sadness. "I wouldn't wish on any of my children the difficulties I've endured over the years. All I can say is, I wouldn't have gotten through it without my faith in God."

Joel made an impatient sound in the back of his throat. Though he'd been raised a Catholic, over the years he'd grown away from God. He couldn't remember the last time he'd been to church.

"You need to be very sure about your decision," Elizabeth continued, oblivious to his thoughts. "When you meet the right one, you'll know. Being around her will feel different than any other woman you've been with. It will also feel easy. You shouldn't have to work at conversation, laughter, having common ground. It helps if you feel passionate about similar things. And most of all, she needs to be someone you can't imagine living without. Even then, there are no guarantees, but I can tell you, very few of those things were present in my relationship with your father, even in the beginning.

"I was swept away by the man I thought he was. I didn't take the time to look beneath his charismatic surface. I lived to regret my mistake. I hope and pray none of my children make the same mistakes."

The waitress arrived with their meals. When she moved out of earshot, Elizabeth looked at Joel with an earnest expression.

"Take a good long look at this woman, Joel. Despite what's happened, you need to listen to your heart. True love doesn't come along often. In fact, I truly believe it's a once-in-a-lifetime thing. Don't be in too big of a rush to walk away. If it's meant to be, it will work out."

Once again, she reached out and squeezed his hand. "Pray about it, Joel. Turn your troubles over to God. He's the best person to help you with this. He won't steer you wrong." Tears glinted in her pale blue eyes. "Trust me, son. I wouldn't have gotten through thirty-three years of marriage without God on my side."

Joel compressed his lips against a wave of emotion. It was difficult to see his mother upset. She was the strongest woman he knew. Perhaps it was time to give God another chance…?

Chapter Seventeen

oel returned from lunch in a thoughtful mood. He sat back down at his desk, still thinking about the things his mother had said. He wished he had the liberty of taking the rest of the day off, to really mull over their conversation, turn it over again in his mind, look at things from all angles, but unfortunately he still had the McClintock case to finalize and already there was another case on his desk.

With a sigh, he pushed the thoughts aside and opened the report he'd received on a fresh investigation that had ties to one of the big four banks. He tried to concentrate on the lines of text that filled his computer screen, but that proved difficult. He read the same paragraph three times and it still didn't make any sense. He cursed, knowing his inability to concentrate had everything to do with Sheridan McClintock.

He was so disappointed to discover she was up to her neck in criminal activity. He'd been prepared to give her the benefit of the doubt about her computer and login details being used for the transactions. After all, it was possible someone else had access to both.

But once the guys from AUSTRAC found evidence that the shelf company who owned the account in the Caymans had been set up by her, his willingness to remain open to the possibility she was innocent had disintegrated. Of course, the evidence was purely circumstantial, but sometimes that's all they had. He'd learned to accept long ago that if it looked like, smelled like, and sounded like it, it probably was.

The phone at his elbow peeled, snapping him out of his mood. With his mind still on Sheridan, he answered distractedly.

"Major Fraud Squad."

"Can I speak to Detective Craigdon?"

"Yes. I'm Joel Craigdon."

"Joel. It's Michael O'Connor. I'm one of the forensic technicians who have been examining the McClintock devices."

Joel sat up straighter in his seat, curious as to the purpose of the technician's call. As far as he knew, the forensic examination of the computers and other devices was completed. "Michael. What can I do for you?"

"Look, we've dug a little deeper. It appears the computer we thought was the origin of those transactions was hacked."

Joel stilled. He recalled his conversation with one of the other officers about how easy it was to hack into someone's system. "Are you sure?"

"Yes. It took a little time to track it all the way through, but we're certain the computer was hacked."

Joel's heart thumped. *Was it possible Sheridan was telling the truth after all?* "Can you tell the identity of the hacker?" he asked.

"No, but we've traced it back to a computer owned by a rival company. Craigdon Enterprises. I assume it's no relation?"

The breath whooshed from Joel's lungs. Caught up in a coughing fit, it was a few moments before he could respond.

"Craigdon Enterprises? Are you absolutely certain?"

"Yes. Once we knew what to look for, it was a fairly straightforward task to retrace the steps taken by the hacker. It came back to Craigdon."

"That's my late father's company. He died nearly five months ago."

"So, around the same time the first of these transactions occurred. Any disgruntled relatives? Anyone left out of the will?"

Joel's thoughts immediately centered on Christopher. But Christopher didn't work at the family company. Still, he had a security pass. He would have been able to get access. The family had never made any secret of his relationship to them. Any number of the staff knew he was Henry's son. They wouldn't have given much thought if they saw him on the premises. Then again, there was Dwight Britton.

"Can you identify the computer that was used to hack into the McClintock server?" he asked.

"Yes." The technician rattled off a serial number. "Provided someone in the company has a record of the allocation of each computer, it shouldn't be too difficult to locate. One thing we can be certain of is that the computer's still in use. The most recent transaction occurred only a few weeks ago."

Joel thanked Michael for his information and hung up the phone. His mind raced. Blood pumped through his veins. Sheridan had been set up. It wasn't her at all. Someone had hacked into her computer. How they were able to set up the Caymans account using her identification was another question, but one that he was sure he could find an answer to, given enough time. After all, many of the banks located in tax havens didn't require a face-to-face interview. Anyone could have posed as Sheridan and provided her identification documents and the bank wouldn't have been any the wiser. He should have thought of that sooner. It was just that so much other evidence pointed to it being her…

That was no excuse. He needed to call her. Apologize. Fill her in on these new developments. Apologize again.

Before Joel could do anything, the phone in his pocket rang. He pulled out his mobile and glanced at the screen and grimaced.

MJ. Great.

He hadn't seen her since he'd broken up with her, right before he'd left for Europe. She'd left countless messages on his phone that ran the whole gamut of emotions from screaming at him for being so cruel and heartless, to crying and begging him to take her back. He'd barely listened to most of them. As far as he was concerned, he'd had a lucky escape.

His finger hovered over the "decline" button on his phone. He really didn't have time to deal with her. Besides, there was nothing she could say to him that would change his mind.

They were over. Finished. Never, ever again. It might have taken him five years to realize it, but she was most definitely not the right one. Still, ignoring her wasn't going to make her go away. He needed to make sure she knew once and for all they were over. There was never going to be future for them.

With a sigh, he answered the call. "MJ. What can I do for you?"

"Joel! I'm so glad you picked up."

She sounded so relieved, he frowned in concern. "Is everything all right?"

"No! Yes! Oh, I'm sorry! I'm all over the place. Listen, I have something to tell you. It's important. When can we meet?"

"Can't you tell me over the phone?"

"No."

"Why not?"

"Please, Joel. I need to see you."

He paused, torn. His investigation had just blown up in his face. He needed to call Sheridan and update her. He needed to call Nick and find out who the hell had the use of the

Craigdon computer. There was so much work to be done. There was no way he could get away now.

"Please, Joel. It's really important." The quiet desperation in MJ's tone got to him. He found himself relenting. He'd liked this woman well enough to give her five years of his life. The least he could do was meet with her and find out what she had to tell him that was so important. He just couldn't do it right now.

"Okay, MJ. But I'm really busy at the moment. I'll have to call you back. We'll work something out."

She gushed with gratitude and then made him promise.

"I promise. I'll call you back."

As soon as he ended the call, he phoned Nick. Much to Joel's relief, his brother picked up after the second ring.

"Joel. What's up?"

"There have been some new developments in the McClintock case. We now believe Sheridan McClintock's computer was hacked."

"So she's off the hook?"

"Yes, more than likely."

"Okay. Well, I guess that's good news."

"Yes. But wait for the bad news."

Nick's tone turned wary. "Okay. Tell me the bad news."

"The forensic technicians have traced the hacker back to a computer at Craigdon Enterprises."

Joel wasn't surprised by the shocked silence that followed. "Nick? Are you still there?"

"Yeah. Shit. Are you sure?"

"Yes. In fact, I even have a serial number. Do you keep track of that sort of thing?"

"Yes, of course."

"So you'll be able to tell who's been allocated that asset in the company?"

"Yes. What's the serial number?"

Joel provided Nick with the information. "How long will it take for you to identify the employee who uses that computer?"

"I'll put a call into HR right away. I don't know off the top of my head who's in charge of recording that kind of information, but it's certainly done."

"Great. Call me as soon as you have it."

With that, Joel ended the call. He needed to tell Sheridan, but he wanted to speak to her face to face. He wanted her to know how sincere he was in his apology. But he couldn't do it now. He hadn't been lying when he'd told MJ he didn't have time to talk. Things were moving quickly. He needed to stay on top of it all.

A faint headache had made itself known. Either stress-related or perhaps a lack of caffeine. The second possibility he could do something about. He pushed his chair back and headed for the tearoom. He barely had time to fill a cup with black coffee before his phone was ringing again. He glanced at the screen.

Nick.

He answered the call without hesitation. "That was quick."

"Yes, I was lucky to get connected to the right person straight away."

"What did you find out?" Joel held his breath as he waited for the answer.

"You're not going to believe this. Then again, maybe you will."

"Who is it? Christopher?"

"Christopher?" Nick sounded bemused. "No, not Christopher. It's Dwight Britton."

Britton? Sheridan's ex. The IT geek. The memory of Britton's arrogant smugness came back to Joel in a rush. The prick. He was laughing at them. They'd been there with the asshole, him and Ralph, at Craigdon Enterprises, trying to piece together information and all the time Britton had been laughing at them.

"Where is he now?" Joel asked.

"I assume he's at work. Let me have security check if his pass was used this morning."

Nick put Joel on hold. A few minutes later he was back on the line. "According to security, he used his pass to access the lifts at half-past eight this morning. Of course we can't tell if he's left the building. This time of day I can only assume he's still at his desk."

"Good. Listen, can you get me a printout of whose pass was used on certain dates?"

"Yes, of course. An electronic record of the time and date is made each time an access pass is used."

A surge of excitement went through Joel. He scrambled through the papers on his desk until he found the report from AUSTRAC listing all fifteen of the illegal transactions. As luck would have it, each one of the transactions had occurred after hours. He punched the air.

"Yes!" He was confident that would narrow the number of potential suspects considerably. Most people didn't work late if they could help it.

"What is it?" Nick asked.

"I think we might have caught a break." He explained to Nick about the time the transactions had occurred. "I'm going to send you through a list of dates," he continued. "I need to know who accessed the lifts on each date and the time of such access." Then another thought occurred to him. "What about CCTV footage? How long do you keep the security tapes?"

"Four or five months."

Joel breathed out. "The first of our transactions occurred in February. Let's hope we still have that footage."

"I'll get on it right away and email you the files as soon as I get hold of them."

"Great. Listen, don't say anything to Britton about this. I don't want him alerted that we're onto him. We need to get our ducks in a row before we can arrest him and when that happens I'd rather catch him by surprise."

"No worries."

"And Nick?"

"Yeah?"

"Thanks. I really appreciate your help."

"Anytime."

Joel spent the time while he waited for Nick's information, bringing Ralph and their boss up to speed. He was upfront about his family company's involvement. Superintendent Kingsley eyeballed him.

"Is this going to be a problem for you, Joel?"

"No, sir."

"Are you sure?"

"Yes, sir."

"Have you had any personal dealings with this Britton fellow?"

"Nothing outside of an interview in the normal course of our investigation."

"Do you feel like your ability to remain independent will be compromised as a result of your family's involvement in this investigation?"

"No, of course not," Joel assured him. "It's a minor detail, nothing more. My family's company is involved only as the employer of this thief. I'm certain Craigdon Enterprises is an innocent party, merely caught in the firing line."

The superintendent nodded. "Very well. I appreciate you bringing this to my attention. I'm satisfied there's no conflict of interest. You may remain in charge of the investigation."

"I'm going to need some extra manpower once we get hold of all that security footage," Joel said. "We're talking almost half a year's worth of tapes. We're going to have to go through each one and match it to the time and date of each transaction and then use a process of elimination to determine who was in the building at that time. Hopefully we'll narrow it down to only a handful, maybe even less, who were there on all fifteen occasions."

"Of course. I can spare you an extra three officers. Will that suffice?"

"Thank you. I'll take whatever I can get. I'll let you know once I receive the footage. With a bit of luck it will be later today."

Joel returned to his desk and did his best to occupy his time while he waited for Nick's email. Over and over his thoughts returned to Sheridan and more than once he reached for his phone, intent on calling her.

Maybe he should just tell her, straight out, over the phone? Did it really matter whether he did it in person? The end result would be the same. He'd jumped the gun and arrested her on information that had now proved wrong and though he'd acted in good faith at the time, he was sure she wouldn't see it that way. He'd offer an apology and walk away. Probably forever.

He instinctively rebelled at the idea. The night they'd spent together had been magical. And then those other times. Even when it was as something as mundane as choosing a pet or having coffee. They were moments that stood out for him.

He didn't know what it was about her that set her apart from all the other women who'd passed through his life, but there was something about her that was indefinably special. He wanted to get to know her better. He wanted to know what she thought about the current state of politics. Whether she was into rugby union or rugby league. If she was a morning person or preferred to do her best work at night. There were so many things he wanted to know about her, but most of all he wanted her back in his bed.

It was more than three hours later that the message from Nick arrived in Joel's inbox and he still hadn't phoned Sheridan. Now he didn't have time. He picked up the phone and alerted the superintendent who assured him the extra manpower would be allocated in the morning. Swallowing a sigh of frustration, Joel found his partner in the tearoom.

"Fancy putting in some overtime?" he asked.

Ralph grinned. "Sounds good to me."

"Good. The files we've been waiting for have arrived from Craigdon Enterprises. I'd like to get a start on them right away. The extra manpower we've been promised isn't going to show up until the morning."

"Figures."

Ralph followed Joel out of the tearoom, a fresh cup of coffee in hand. Joel forwarded Nick's email to Ralph.

"This is a two-pronged investigation," Joel explained. "We need to check the CCTV footage on the dates that match each of the fifteen transactions. The thing is, we don't know if our perp entered the building early and stayed back late to do his thing, or if he worked his usual hours and then returned sometime later. The access passes only register entry into the lifts."

"So the passes are required to access the floors above the foyer, but not on the way down. Is that right?"

Joel nodded. "Yes. That's right. If a pass has been recorded more than once in the same day, we'll know they left the building at some point and then came back again. Unfortunately, the reports we've been provided with are only raw data. They show in time and date order every time an access pass was used. It means we're going to have to go through each of the fifteen days manually and make a note of when someone's pass was used more than once."

Ralph frowned. "But they could have just gone out for lunch and then returned again."

"True, and no doubt there will be a cluster of re-entries around lunchtime." Joel grimaced. "It's far from an exact science, but I'm hoping that, coupled with the CCTV footage, we'll be able to narrow it down.

"For starters, let's concentrate on Dwight Britton. I'm not ignoring the possibility it might be someone else, but Britton is employed in IT. We already know the hacker used Britton's computer to carry out the transactions. We also know the exact time and date of each transaction. If we can prove Britton was inside the building every time each of the fifteen transactions occurred, we should have enough to arrest him. Let's hope these files contain the evidence we need."

Ralph nodded. "So, do you want me to start on the footage, or the access passes?"

"How about you start on the footage. I'll print out the security paperwork and get a start on that."

As Joel waited for the more than four hundred pages of records to print, impatience coursed through him. It was already late in the afternoon. He didn't kid himself they were going to get through the hours and hours of footage and paper records in one day, but that didn't mean he wasn't going to give it his best shot.

Chapter Eighteen

Joel was back at work the next morning before the sun had made it all the way over the horizon. He'd spent a restless night dreaming about CCTV footage and Dwight Britton and Christopher. He wasn't sure why his half-brother featured so heavily in his dreams, but he did.

By nine o'clock, the squad room was buzzing with Ralph, Brent and the extra manpower promised by their boss. Joel had divided the paper records and the security footage between the team and everyone was busy going through the evidence they had, trying to piece things together.

Joel had already gone through more than half of the security records. To his consternation, Christopher's pass seemed to show up over and over again during the relevant time frame. According to the records, Britton was also at the office every day the transactions had occurred, but so were hundreds of other employees.

Given that each of the fifteen transactions had occurred in the evening, well after most of the staff had gone home, Christopher's after hours' access to Craigdon Enterprises was the most suspicious. The man didn't even work there. Okay, so he was family and he'd always had access to the building, but it was rather odd that he just happened to be there well past closing time on the relevant days.

Was Joel putting too much emphasis on the fact the hacker had used Britton's computer? Was he focused on Britton being the perpetrator because the man was Sheridan's ex-boyfriend? He had to concede, the thought of Britton with his hands all over her, spending night after night with her, filled him with jealousy. Thank God Sheridan had seen sense and ended things with the jerk. But still…

With a determined shake of his head, he pushed all thought of Sheridan aside and concentrated on the final page of records in his hand. One of his colleagues had taken over analysis of the last few dates relevant to the investigation and was working backwards. Once again, Joel discovered it was Christopher's pass that lined up within thirty minutes of the tenth transaction taking place. No one else's pass had been used within two hours of any of the transactions Joel had analyzed.

It has to be Christopher…

Joel's half-brother certainly had motive. He'd been overlooked in his father's billion-dollar estate. He also had means and opportunity, as the access pass indicated. With a sigh, Joel pushed away from his desk and walked over to where his colleague was still bent over a sheaf of papers.

"What did you find out?" Joel asked.

Brent lifted his head. "I'm tracking the last one now. The first four all seem to point toward a Christopher Barrington. It's a bit hard to say, of course, because we can only tell when people entered so it's possible someone was recorded entering the building at half-past eight in the morning and didn't leave until well after knock off time, but Barrington's pass seems to have been used after hours on each of the relevant dates." Brent cocked an eyebrow. "Is that what you were hoping to find?"

Joel blew out his breath. "That's what I've found, too." He grimaced. "Barrington was on my radar, but I really thought the perp was Britton." He sighed again and scrubbed a hand through his hair. "It's not the first time I've been wrong in this investigation."

"Yeah, I heard about Sheridan McClintock's arrest." Brent whistled. "She really is a looker! Is she as hot up close as she looks on TV?"

Joel bit down on a burst of irritation and ignored Brent's question. "I'm going to check in with the guys analyzing the CCTV footage. Now that we've narrowed down the times when Barrington used his pass, we should be able to fast-forward the tapes to that time. We need to double check and make sure it's him."

Joel turned and went to find Ralph and the other two officers who'd been assigned the job of going through the security footage on each of the relevant dates. They were seated at desks in one of the training rooms, their eyes focused on their computer screens where grainy black-and-white footage was displayed.

"Have you found anything?" Joel asked his partner.

Ralph nodded slowly. "Yeah. As a matter of fact, I think we have."

Joel grimaced. "Let me guess: Christopher Barrington."

Ralph frowned. "Who's Christopher Barrington?"

"My half-brother, remember? We ran into him at McClintock one day. He works there."

"Oh, yeah. Now I remember. Tall. Well-built. Dark hair. No, it's not him."

Joel started in surprise. "Are you sure? Christopher's security pass was used on each and every occasion the transactions were made and it was always used after hours."

Ralph turned in his seat to face him. "I'm sure. It's not Christopher. We've checked every hour of the CCTV footage for all fifteen days. The only person who's consistently shown entering the building after hours is Dwight Britton."

Joel frowned in confusion. "But how can that be? The security logs show it's Barrington's pass being used at those times. Unless…"

"Unless what?"

An arc of excitement went through Joel. He always felt this way when he was on the verge of cracking a case wide open. "Unless Christopher gave Britton his pass. It's the only explanation."

Now it was Ralph's turn to frown. "Hang on a minute. Why would Britton borrow someone else's pass? He works at Craigdon. He could just as easily have used his own."

Joel nodded thoughtfully. "You're right. But what if Britton thought he was being smart? Thought he'd throw people off his scent? If we'd only looked at the records of who came into the building, we'd have Christopher in our sights."

Adrenaline surged through him. "Splice all fifteen instances of the footage where you have Britton entering the building. Let's compare each to the date and time stamps on the security records for Barrington's pass. I'll bet a million dollars they match."

Ralph and his team got to work while Joel grabbed the sheets of paper he and Brent had compiled outlining their analysis of the use of Christopher's access pass. The minute Ralph told him they had the footage ready for him, he strode over to their desks.

"Okay, run the first one," he instructed.

He watched the screen as the grainy black-and-white vision showed Dwight Britton entering the building. He went over to the bank of lifts and pressed the "up' button. Within moments, one of the silver doors slid open and Dwight walked inside. The doors closed behind him.

"Pause the tape," Joel ordered.

He checked the time stamp on the access pass records and then looked at the screen. The time stamp, indicating when the pass was used to activate the lifts, was less than twenty seconds after the time Britton stepped inside the lift.

"Okay, let's go to the next one."

The scene was repeated with Britton entering the building in the early evening and stepping inside one of the lifts only moments before Christopher's pass was used. For the sake of thoroughness, they went through all fifteen transactions. It was the same every time.

Dwight Britton had been inside Craigdon Enterprises at each of the times the transactions had occurred and he'd gotten there using someone else's pass.

"The bastard," Joel muttered.

"You're right. He didn't use his own pass," Ralph mused.

Joel smiled grimly. "It's my bet it was a deliberate act on his part. He was trying to point us in another direction. It muddies the water a bit, confuses the jury. Was it him, or was it Christopher? There's no other explanation. He's not stupid, that's for sure. The only thing is, he forgot about the cameras. It's him on the CCTV footage. No matter how much he tried to confuse the evidence, there's no denying he's the one who entered the building each and every time a couple million dollars went missing."

Ralph grinned. "I think we have enough to go and pick up this Britton fellow and bring him back to the station. I'd like to ask him a few questions."

Joel's answering smile was filled with satisfaction. "You bet." He patted Ralph on the back and congratulated the rest of the team for the great result, thanking them all for their efforts.

I have to call Sheridan. I have to let her know before the media get wind of it or she hears it from someone else...

Things had moved from mere speculation to a positive confirmation. Britton was their guy. The next step was to put together an arrest team. Sheridan deserved to be told right away, along with being offered a sincere apology.

With that thought in mind, he returned to his desk and pulled out his phone. He'd still rather give her the news in person, but now they were running out of time. It was possible they'd have Britton in custody by the end of the day. Telling her over the phone was better than not telling her at all.

The phone rang out. He braced himself for leaving a message on her voicemail. To his surprise, she answered on the fifth ring.

"Sheridan McClintock."

"Sheridan, it's Joel."

There was a pause. "I know. You came up in my contacts." Her tone was deadly.

He bit his lip. She was obviously still angry. Fair enough. Still, she'd taken his call. That had to be a good thing.

"Listen, there have been some new developments."

"Oh, really?" she asked in a bored tone. "And is this new development as reliable as the information you used to arrest me? Because if so, I don't want to hear it."

"Please, Sheridan. Is there somewhere we can meet? It's important."

"I'm sorry, Joel. I'm not interested and I don't have the time." Her tone was dismissive.

"But—"

"You've made it quite clear you have no intention of nailing the real culprit. I have no choice but to find him on my own. Good-bye, Joel."

She ended the call before he could get another word in. He immediately phoned her back. The call went through to voicemail.

He cursed under his breath. "Shit!"

And then he had another idea. He wanted to confront Christopher about why he'd handed over his pass to Britton. With a bit of luck, Joel might also be able to swing over and make a visit to Sheridan's office. It was only mid-morning.

Hopefully both of them would be at work. He was willing to take the chance.

Coming to his feet, he reached for his jacket where it hung on the back of his seat. He shrugged into it. Ralph glanced over in his direction. "Off somewhere?"

"Yeah. I'm going over to McClintock. I want to know why my half-brother gave his pass to Britton." He deliberately kept Sheridan out of the conversation. He wasn't about to tell his partner he felt the need to apologize to their earlier suspect. After all, they'd only been doing their job.

"It'll take at least an hour or so to get together an arrest team," he added. "I'll be back long before then."

Ralph nodded. "Okay."

Sheridan thought a visit to the bathroom to splash cool water on her face might help ease her temper, but as she stared into the mirror over the sink and took into account the flush that stained her cheeks, she decided she looked every bit as angry as she had after ending Joel's call.

How *dare* he call her about some so-called new development? The arrogance of the man! Two days earlier, she'd suffered the humiliation of being handcuffed and dragged through her office; taken to a police station; put in a cell. Interrogated, charged, fingerprinted, photographed! And then the final insult, being brought before the court like a common criminal, standing in the dock and being forced to apply for bail. And Detective Joel Craigdon thought she'd give him the time of day when he called! The arrogance of that man!

She reached for some paper towel and patted at the dampness on her cheeks. Pulling out her hairbrush, she swiped it through her waves and then refreshed her lipstick. She was due to meet Dwight at twelve and though she didn't want him to think she'd made any effort for him, neither did she want him to think her life had gone down the toilet since she dumped him—that she no longer cared about her appearance.

Taking another look in the mirror, she was satisfied with what she saw. The fitted, silk jersey sheath dress ended just above her knees and was the exact same shade of blue as her eyes. It was both professional and feminine and the slight stretch in the fabric allowed for ease of movement if she and Dwight actually got around to firing their guns.

With that thought in mind, she tucked her hairbrush and lipstick back into her handbag and slipped the Louis Vuitton over her shoulder. With shoulders back and head held high, she strode from the bathroom.

She cleared her calendar for the day. Then, taking only enough time to tell her EA she was going out and wouldn't be back for four or five hours, Sheridan headed straight for the lifts. The more time she'd had to think about it, the more she was convinced Dwight was the one who'd set her up. It was the only thing that made sense. She'd confront her ex and get him to confess. And then she'd throw the evidence in Detective Craigdon's face. He and his cronies could go to hell. She'd bring Dwight down on her own.

The phone at Christopher's elbow peeled. He finished entering the last few numbers into the spreadsheet open on his computer before reaching over to answer it.

"Christopher Barrington."

"Mr Barrington," the man from the front desk in the foyer of the building said, "I have Detective Joel Craigdon downstairs. He'd like to see you."

Christopher grimaced. *What the hell is Joel doing here again?* Couldn't he just leave them all the hell alone? He'd taken

Sheridan away in handcuffs, surely that was enough? Then again, maybe this wasn't about Sheridan? Maybe Joel had dug far enough to discover what Christopher had been up to after hours?

He should just refuse to see him. But that would only make Joel more suspicious. No, better to brazen it out and pretend he didn't know what the hell his half-brother was on about.

"No problem," he replied. "I'm on my way down."

Christopher spied Joel standing on the other side of the foyer, admiring the Tim Storrier artwork. It was an original and Christopher knew that because he happened to be at the same exhibition when Sheridan had acquired it.

Christopher strode confidently toward his half-brother, his hand outstretched, determined to deflect Joel's suspicions that something was awry. They shook hands.

"Joel. What can I do for you?"

"Is there somewhere we can talk in private?"

The gravity in Joel's tone caused Christopher's belly to somersault with nerves. Though he managed to keep his smile in place, it was an effort. "Yes, of course. I'll take you to my office."

They walked toward the lift. Christopher didn't bother with small talk. He and Joel had never been close. It would have only roused Joel's suspicions if he were to come over too friendly now. After waiting a few minutes in silence for the lift, they were whisked up to Christopher's floor. Once in the corridor, Christopher steered Joel in the direction of the small meeting room used every now and then for visitors.

"I thought we were going to your office?" Joel asked.

Christopher shrugged nonchalantly. He wasn't about to admit to Joel his "office" was no more than a desk partitioned beside ten other similar desks. He hadn't climbed the ranks high enough to warrant a proper office.

"We'll have more privacy in here," was all he said.

Joel didn't comment any further, merely followed Christopher into the well-appointed meeting room. It was a modest space, but no expense had been spared on the long, rectangular table and comfortable chairs. A large smart TV screen hung on one wall and a projector screen was positioned above it. A well-stocked bar was discretely tucked along one side. Christopher didn't bother to offer Joel a drink. This wasn't a social call.

Once again, he plastered a smile on his face. "So, what's this about?"

Joel eyed him solemnly. Christopher's anxiety ratcheted up another notch.

"My team and I have just spent the past couple of days going through CCTV footage."

Christopher felt the color leach from his face. He reached out for the back of the chair closest to him for support. He fought to keep his voice casual. "Really? That sounds… fascinating."

Joel's expression remained grim. "Yes, it was." Joel's gaze narrowed, filled with accusation.

Christopher tried to hold Joel's stare, but it was impossible. Guilt surged through him. He turned away, unable to look at his half-brother a moment longer.

"I can't believe you did it," Joel continued in a voice that was laced with steel. "What do you have to say for yourself, Christopher?"

All of a sudden, Christopher felt overwhelmed. He couldn't continue to deny his involvement when it was obvious Joel had seen everything. Christopher should have realized Zane would have his office under surveillance. It was a stupid mistake and now Christopher would pay for it.

His shoulders slumped on a sigh of defeat. Slowly, he turned to face Joel. "Okay, you're right. I shouldn't have done it. It was stupid and wrong, but I'm not sure why Zane got the police involved. It's not that big a deal. So, I pretended I was the CEO of a billion-dollar company and scored with a few women. So what? There was no harm in it."

Joel frowned. "What the hell are you talking about?"

Christopher stared at his half-brother and saw the confusion in Joel's eyes. He bit his lip. *Hell, is it possible Joel doesn't know about that subterfuge? Have I just put my foot in it and ruined everything?*

Christopher felt his way carefully. "Aren't you talking about me bringing women into McClintock after hours?

Joel shook his head. "No."

Fuck… Christopher mentally kicked himself. "Well what are you talking about then?"

"I'm talking about the CCTV footage I've obtained from Craigdon Enterprises that shows that on at least fifteen separate occasions you gave your security pass to Dwight Britton. We have strong reason to believe Britton went on to transfer millions of dollars into an illegal offshore account on those occasions and you're caught up in the middle of it." Joel's gaze hardened with anger. "Why the hell would you do something like that?"

Christopher gaped in shock. He never imagined Britton's request to use his pass had something to do with this! He told Joel as much.

Joel shot him a dubious look. "Why should I believe you? You've always had a reputation for messing around with the truth. Even now you've just admitted to deceitful behavior, pretending to be Zane Forrest. What other reason would you have to give Britton your pass? He had his own employee pass… How do I know you and Britton weren't in this together? You've been bemoaning the fact you were overlooked in Dad's will. Maybe this was your way of getting back at us, or smearing the good name of Dad's company by getting it caught up in this kind of stuff."

A surge of panic went through Christopher. He might be guilty of a lot of undesirable behavior, but he'd never done anything illegal.

"No, Joel! It wasn't me! I swear, I know nothing about missing millions. Dwight came to me and asked me if he could use my pass. He said he'd lost his and was waiting for security to issue him another one."

Joel continued to regard him with distrust. "Why would he come to you? How did he even know you had a pass to Craigdon Enterprises?"

"I knew him from when he was at McClintock. I didn't work with him, but I knew who he was and that he dated Sheridan. We got talking in the lifts one day and I told him my father was Henry Craigdon. He was amused by the fact I'd chosen to work for the competitor. I told him I had access to Craigdon Enterprises and could come and go as I pleased. I didn't tell him our father and I were estranged."

Christopher shrugged. "When he came to me back in February and asked to use my pass, I didn't see any harm in it. After all, Dad was dead. My days of hanging around Craigdon in the hope that he might notice me were over. I swear, that's the truth."

Joel forced aside the urge to feel sympathetic toward his half-brother. They all knew what it was like to try and win their father's favor, only to fail. Henry Craigdon had been a hard man to impress.

Warding off the depressing memories, Joel shook his head in disgust. "After everything you've done in the past, why should I believe you?"

"Because I'm telling the truth!"

Joel turned away from the pleading look on his half-brother's face. As much as Joel didn't want to admit it,

Christopher's explanation was plausible, if stupid. *Really? Who gives out their security pass?* A lot of people, no doubt. And he sounded distraught enough to be believed.

What was more, though Christopher seemed to go out of his way to antagonize people and stir up trouble, as far as Joel knew his half-brother had never broken the law. Besides, what motive did Christopher have for setting up Sheridan to take the fall? They knew each other as work colleagues but there didn't seem to be anything more going on between them.

Swallowing a sigh, Joel pulled out his phone and called Sheridan. While he was there, he might as well try and sort things out with her. At least apologize. If she refused to accept his apology, that was her prerogative. There was nothing he could do about that.

The phone rang out and then went to voicemail. Joel cursed under his breath. *Is she avoiding me?*

"Something wrong?" Christopher asked.

Joel blinked. For a moment, he'd forgotten his half-brother was still there. And then he remembered Christopher could help him access the floors above.

"Look, I need to speak to Sheridan. She's not answering her phone. Do you think you could get me to her floor?"

Christopher blinked in surprise and then his face broke out into a grin. "Don't tell me you want me to use my pass to activate the lifts?"

Joel shot him a narrow-eyed look. "Will you do it?"

Christopher widened his eyes, his expression a picture of innocence. "Inappropriate use of a security pass is heavily discouraged at McClintock. Don't you know that, Detective?"

Joel gritted his teeth. "Just use the damn pass, Christopher."

Giving a nod of acquiescence, Christopher led the way out of the meeting room and headed toward the lifts. When one arrived, he checked to make sure it was empty and after swiping his pass across the security panel and selecting the number for Sheridan's floor, he stepped back to allow Joel to enter.

"Now we're even," he said, eyeballing Joel.

"It doesn't work that way, Christopher. But thanks, anyway." With that, the doors slid closed.

Nerves danced in Joel's belly as he made his way toward Sheridan's office. Her EA sat behind her desk and looked up as he approached. She eyed him warily. He understood the woman's reticence. The last time he'd been there he'd carted her boss away in handcuffs.

"Hi, I was wondering if I could see Sheridan for a few minutes?" he asked.

Without even consulting the calendar Joel could see opened on the computer screen in front of her, the woman shook her head. "I'm sorry, Detective Craigdon. Sheridan's on an outside appointment."

"Do you know where she went?"

"No, but she said she'd be out for at least four or five hours."

Joel frowned. Either she had a fair distance to travel or she was intending to spend a good deal of time somewhere.

"How long has she been gone?" he asked.

"About half an hour."

Joel compressed his lips on a burst of irritation. *He'd just missed her…* Well, he wasn't going to sit around the McClintock offices for hours waiting for her to show up. He had no way of knowing where she was and though she'd told her EA how long she'd be gone, he could only guess if that were the truth. He'd just have to keep trying her phone and hope she got over her hissy fit enough to pick up and talk to him.

Chapter Nineteen

wight frowned at his computer screen, staring blindly at what was displayed there. He was meant to be working on updating the Craigdon IT systems, but he hadn't been able to keep his mind on the job. He should have already left for his pre-arranged meeting with Sheridan, but he was still trying to work out his plan of attack.

Does she know I'm behind the missing money? Surely she had to suspect him. He'd heard rumors the detectives had made several visits to McClintock over the past couple of weeks and that the last time they'd been there, they'd taken her away in handcuffs. She knew darn well she wasn't behind the transactions. It was only natural after she considered everything, she'd turn her attention to him. He'd be on her radar. He was almost certain that was why she'd called him and arranged to meet. It had nothing to do with forgiveness or wanting them to get back together. He wasn't that stupid.

The police had already interviewed him once and though he'd been able to deflect their suspicions that time, there was no doubt the heat had been turned up. He needed to do something, but he wasn't sure what. The good thing was, apart from them questioning him, the police hadn't yet seemed to make the connection to Craigdon Enterprises.

Then again, the lead detective was Nick Craigdon's

brother. How was that for luck? Dwight had seen the very same detective who'd questioned him head into Nick's office following their "discussion."

Perhaps it had been a friendly visit of a personal nature between brothers and had nothing to do with Dwight, but he had no way of knowing what had been discussed between the two men and he couldn't afford to take any chances the police had finally made the connection between him and what he'd done on Craigdon time.

He needed to get into Nick's office, feel him out for what he might or might not know. And he had to do it quickly. No doubt Sheridan was already on her way to their rendezvous. He didn't want her to give up waiting on him and leave. With that thought in mind, he hurried toward the lifts.

Fortunately he waited no time at all for one to arrive and he was whisked up to the top floor to Nick's office. Luck remained with him when Nick's EA, a dour old woman who'd worked for old Henry, confirmed Nicholas was in.

"I just need a couple of minutes of his time," Dwight murmured, giving her a friendly smile. "It's about the new IT systems."

The old bat regarded him suspiciously, but picked up the phone beside her and spoke into it. A few moments later, she hung up the receiver and looked at him.

"Nicholas has asked me to send you in."

The woman didn't budge from her seat behind the high desk, so Dwight made his way over to the closed door with the newly engraved brass nameplate: *Nicholas Craigdon, Managing Director.*

Dwight knocked brusquely with a burst of confidence he didn't quite feel. Nerves swarmed in his belly, but he deliberately plastered a smile on his face and obeyed the summons to enter that came from inside. Nick sat behind an impressively large red cedar desk. He looked up briefly as

Dwight entered and indicated that he should take a seat. A mess of papers was spread out on the desk before him.

"Dwight. Margaret said you wanted to see me about the new IT systems? What can I do for you?"

Dwight kept his smile firmly in place. "Yes. We've run into a bit of a problem," he lied.

Nick turned a baleful eye in his direction. "Oh?"

Dwight fought against the flush of embarrassment that threatened to explode across his face. He hated the dismissive way Nick treated him. Who the hell did he think he was? It nearly made Dwight wish he'd stolen that money from Craigdon instead.

"Yes," Dwight forced himself to continue. "We've found a bug that's proving hard to eradicate. It's going to take us a little longer to get the new systems in place."

"How long?" Nick asked in a bored tone, barely glancing up from his paperwork.

"Maybe another month, possibly more." Dwight's gaze drifted over the papers scattered across Nick's desk. His eyes snagged on the letterhead used by Craigdon's head of security. Scanning quickly down the page, he realized he was looking at a list of staff security access passes. There were names, times and dates listed beside each entry.

Dwight's heart skipped a beat. *Have the police discovered the link between McClintock's missing millions and Craigdon Enterprises?*

It certainly looked that way. Why else would that kind of printout be lying on the managing director's desk, so soon after a visit from the police? He was filled with a sense of urgency. It was tinged with panic.

I have to get to Sheridan. This is all her fault.

He'd done such a good job of setting her up, even down to "borrowing" her driver's license and passport and using that as identification to set up the offshore account. He'd found her license in her purse that had been casually left hanging over the back of her couch. The passport was in the top drawer of her bedside table. She was so stupid to leave those kinds of important documents lying around for just anyone to access…

"So what do you want me to do about it?"

Dwight blinked at Nick's question. "Excuse me?"

Nick gave him a hard stare. "I said, what do you want me to do about it?"

Dwight thought back to their conversation. *The IT systems. Right.* "Um, nothing. There's nothing you can do. I'll have to work out how to get around the bug that's causing us problems. I just wanted to let you know where we were in the process. That's all."

Nick gave a dismissive nod. "Okay, well thanks."

Dwight pushed away from the desk and stood. "Uh, I'll get back to work now. In fact, I'm going to be out of the office for a few hours. I have some information to follow up on, about this bug. I'll let you know if it pans out."

Nick didn't bother replying. Dwight turned on his heel and fled, his thoughts already on Sheridan and the final steps in his plan.

Sheridan glanced at her watch for the third time. She'd arrived at the firing range late, but there was no sign of Dwight's Range Rover. *Perhaps he's driving something else now?* She looked around the carpark. This time of day, there were only a few vehicles. A couple of SUV's, a BMW, a Toyota 4WD and two Hondas. All of them were empty. Perhaps he'd already headed inside?

With a shrug, she walked into the clubhouse and signed in. Dwight's name wasn't on the register. So he was running late, too. That was fine. As long as he showed. She'd driven all the way out there. She was determined to have things out with him once and for all.

Striding over to the lockers, she fiddled with her combination lock until it opened. Going to the rifle range had been something they'd enjoyed doing together. Sometimes she got there before him and retrieved their guns from the lockers. Other times he got there first and did the honors. It wasn't a big deal that they knew each other's combination, but maybe it was time to change hers.

She pulled out the Smith & Wesson stainless semi-automatic pistol, enjoying the familiar weight of it in her hand. It had belonged to her father and always reminded her of him. Michael McClintock had died from cancer when she was still at university and though Zane and she were close, he could never replace the special place their father held in her heart.

She checked her handbag for the small packet of bullets she'd brought with her and then walked a bit further along the wall of lockers until she came to Dwight's. She turned the dial on his combination, waiting for the familiar click. There was nothing. She tried the combination again. Still, the door remained locked.

He's changed his combination…

The thought filled her head at the same time she heard him call her name.

"Sheridan! There you are!"

She spun around to face him, feeling startled. Heat flooded her cheeks. "S-sorry, I was going to get your gun, but the combination doesn't seem to work."

"I changed it," he said breezily, as if it were of no importance.

"Oh." She nodded to herself. She ought to feel thankful he'd moved on. And she was. She definitely was.

"So, how have you been?" she asked, attempting to make small talk before she went in with her accusations.

"Fine. Of course, nothing's been the same since you dumped me." He stared at her with a hurt expression.

She couldn't tell whether he was genuinely upset, or if it was just a ploy.

Suddenly impatient, she ignored the comment and got straight to the point. "I'm not sure if you heard, but I was arrested for theft the other day. Apparently the police think I've stolen money from my brother's company, to the tune of nearly thirty million dollars." She eyeballed him. "Now, you and I both know I didn't take that money, and I don't have to look far to find the culprit."

She narrowed her gaze on him. He reared back in wide-eyed surprise. "Me? You think it was *me*? Sheridan! I'm shocked!"

She kept her gaze steady on his. "Are you denying you stole the money?"

"Of course I am! My God! Sheridan! You know me better than anyone! Not that long ago, we were in love! We were contemplating a future together. How could you believe me capable of something so heinous?"

"The police told me the perpetrator accessed my computer and login details to transfer the funds. It's obvious someone was trying to set me up. You're the only one I can think of who might have gained access to both." She shrugged. "If you were me, what would you believe?"

"I expect you to believe the man you were in love with couldn't do something like that! How petty do you think I am? I loved you! You were my queen! I would have given you anything! And despite everything, I still love you!"

The earnestness in his expression flooded her with guilt and then she remembered why she'd ended their relationship. She glared at him.

"Have you forgotten, Dwight? You cheated on me! Is that the way you show your undying love? Get real."

Dwight's expression turned contrite. "I'm sorry! It was wrong. But you'd been working late for so many nights.

I was lonely. I didn't mean for it to happen. She paid me attention. I was drunk. You weren't there. Again. It just happened."

Anger flooded through her. "Oh no you don't! Don't go putting this on me! How dare you! This had nothing to do with me! You asshole!"

Like a switch had been flicked, Dwight's demeanor completely changed. The sniveling remorse was replaced with white-hot anger. His eyes burned with a fury she could almost feel as his gaze scorched her. Looking at his features, twisted with hate, she couldn't believe she'd ever found him attractive. How had she not seen him like this before?

He sneered at her. "You want to know the truth? The truth is, I had a lucky escape when you caught me with Diana. She gave me more satisfaction in one night than you had in all the months we were together. Let's face it, Sheridan. You're a dud in bed. There! I said it! That's the truth!" He shuddered. "I can't imagine how I thought I could fake it with you forever."

Sheridan stared at him in shock. Right on the heels of her shock came a blinding hurt and then a furious anger. She knew he was just being malicious, but a tiny part of her couldn't help but wonder if all he said were true. It wasn't like she'd had a whole lot of experience with men. A couple of relationships in college summed up her entire sex life prior to Dwight and he knew it. She had been easy game.

Then she thought of her night with Joel. The sex had been amazing and she was sure he'd felt the same way. She wouldn't believe Joel had been faking it. *Why would he?* As far as he knew, they were never going to see each other again. No one bothered faking it with a stranger. The guy just called it a night and sent the woman home. Didn't they? Of course they did. Dwight was merely trying to hurt her where he knew she was vulnerable. Too bad for him, she'd discovered how amazing sex could be without him.

Suddenly impatient, she sought for a way to end their conversation. All she wanted to do was get out of there. She should have known better than to expect Dwight to confess. She could see his personality and the flaws that came with it, so clearly now. He was a narcissist and would never admit to doing anything wrong.

So, she was no closer to knowing the truth than when she'd arrived, but she'd have to live with that. Before she could bring the meeting to an end, her phone rang, providing a welcome distraction. Digging into her handbag, she pulled it out and glanced at the screen.

Joel.

Great. The last person she wanted to hear from. He'd called her more than half a dozen times since they'd spoken that morning and she'd ignored him every time. Still, if she answered the call it gave her an excuse to bring the conversation with Dwight to an end.

"Sorry, Dwight. I have to take this. Excuse me a minute." She turned her back to him and hit the "accept" button.

"Hello?" she said.

"Sheridan! Thank God! I know you're not feeling kindly toward me and I understand why, but please, hear me out."

"What is it, Joel?"

"I owe you an apology."

"An apology?"

"Yes. There have been some new developments."

From the corner of her eye, she saw Dwight listening avidly to her conversation. Good. Maybe he'd come clean if he knew the police were on his tail.

"So you said, earlier. What kind of new developments?"

"Your computer was hacked."

"Hacked? By who?"

"We believe it was Dwight Britton."

"Dwight? Are you sure?"

"Yes."

The certainty in Joel's tone filled her with satisfaction. She chanced another glance in Dwight's direction. His face had turned white with anger. He looked at her with such malevolence, she felt shaken.

Her hand tightened around her phone. A frisson of unease shivered over her skin. She moved further away and lowered her voice.

"How?"

"He must have had the details of your computer and login. He accessed your server from a computer at Craigdon Enterprises. We have him entering the building after hours around the time of each transaction."

She tried to process the information to reconcile that with her suspicions. Her mind raced. "What's going to happen now?"

"We're putting together an arrest team. Hopefully we'll have him in custody before the end of the day."

"Do you know where he is?" she asked, her heart in her throat.

"No. We'll head over to his workplace first."

"He's... He's not at work," she whispered.

"Sorry, I missed that."

Sheridan glanced again at Dwight. He stood right behind her. She let out a little yelp of surprise.

"Sheridan? Are you all right?"

She heard the note of concern in Joel's voice, but Dwight was glaring at her and making a sign for her to end the call. She wanted to say something else to Joel, to tell him she was there with Dwight, but the look in Dwight's eyes kept her silent.

"Um, Joel? I... I have to go. I'll talk to you later."

Listening to Sheridan's conversation with the detective, Dwight had grown increasingly irate. He hadn't expected the police to connect the dots so quickly. No doubt Sheridan had helped with that. He should have known she'd point the finger at him. She wanted to hurt him like he'd hurt her.

He didn't give a shit if he hurt her. He'd only sucked up to her to further his career and financial ambitions. He intended to marry her and get her pregnant and take over her position in the company. Maybe not as head of finance right away. Head of IT would have been a start. He'd have found some way to maneuver himself into a position of power. He figured Sheridan would have been too busy changing dirty diapers to worry about what was going on at McClintock.

Then she'd found the photos of his night of passion with Diana on his phone and his plans had turned to shit. He thought he could talk her around, but she took the high ground and completely refused to listen. Then she got her brother involved. Zane Forrest was built like a bear. He was one guy Dwight didn't want to take on. Zane made it clear Dwight was to pack up his stuff and move on. With Zane breathing down his neck, and a severance package that would tide him over for years, he didn't argue.

The memory of Sheridan's brother standing over him, glaring at him like he was a piece of shit, still filled him with anger and humiliation. He stared at Sheridan and saw red. His vision blurred, his breath came fast. He tasted the hatred he felt.

I'm going to kill her…

The thought popped into his consciousness and immediately made itself at home. They were at a gun range. She still held her gun. He could easily make it look like an accident…

No, there were too many cameras. But maybe he could make it look like suicide?

He watched as she tossed her phone back into her handbag, her gun still in her other hand.

"I'm sorry, Dwight. Something's come up. I have to leave."

Dwight knew exactly what was going on in her head. Before she'd even arrived there she'd already drawn her own conclusions. Whatever the detective had told her had only reinforced her belief in Dwight's guilt. Now she couldn't get away from him quickly enough.

No problem. He wouldn't kill her here. That was okay. He liked the suicide idea. He was sure he could make it work. It wouldn't take him long to come up with another plan. But he needed her gun.

He gave her a fake smile "Of course. You're always so busy. Go."

She turned on her heel and took three steps forward before pulling up short. "Oh, my pistol."

He moved toward her. "I'll take it and lock it up for you. Same combination?"

She hesitated, but then nodded distractedly. "Thanks." She handed him her gun and then turned away and strode quickly toward the carpark.

Dwight watched her leave. When her car disappeared from sight, he went over to her locker and went through the motions of returning her gun. Carefully, he turned his back on the CCTV camera fixed to the wall behind him and tucked the pistol into the waistband of his pants. With casual nonchalance, he made his way out of the clubhouse and smiled.

Chapter Twenty

Sheridan glanced in her rearview mirror, feeling apprehensive. It was possible Dwight might not realize how close the police were to closing in on him, but she didn't want to risk having him follow her, just in case. A shiver overtook her as she recalled the way he'd morphed into some angry stranger… He'd looked at her with such hate she'd been afraid he'd hurt her. The thought that her mild-mannered, heartbroken ex-boyfriend could behave in such a way was baffling and so totally out of character. It gave her pause. Had he always been that person, concealing his true personality behind a submissive manner and passive smile? To fool her…

She marveled that he could have sustained such a front for so long. She thought she knew him and knew him well. Catching him cheating had thrown her world into a spin. She hadn't seen it coming. A bit like the man she'd just left behind at the range.

It probably hadn't been wise to hand over her gun and rely on him to lock it away safely, but at the time all she could think of was getting away from him. Not arousing his suspicions.

She'd already accused him of being the thief and now Joel had confirmed it. Which meant Dwight must be feeling the heat. He wasn't stupid. If she'd managed to work it out, he'd have to know the police wouldn't be far behind…and that could make him desperate. Desperate men were capable of anything and now he was likely armed… She needed to call Zane and warn him, just in case Dwight decided to pay her brother a visit.

He'd been furious when Zane had leaned on him to pack his things and get the hell out of McClintock. She couldn't bear that her connection to Britton might get her brother hurt.

Pulling over to the side of the road, she dug in her handbag for her phone. Zane was always on her back to upgrade her old Honda to a newer vehicle with Bluetooth, but she loved her little car. She'd bought it with the money she'd saved from her first job. It was as much of a part of her as Zane. Despite the fact it didn't have the latest technology, she didn't see the need for an upgrade.

She dialed Zane's number and waited for him to answer. She was grateful when he did. "Oh, Zane. It's Sheridan."

"Yes, I know. Your name came up on my screen," he said dryly.

"Yes, okay. Listen. I've just come from the gun range at Condell Park. I met Dwight there."

"I thought we agreed you'd meet with him in public? There's hardly ever anyone there this time of day."

"Yes, well anyway. The thing is, I'm now absolutely certain he's our thief."

"But the transactions occurred after he left. Do you think he got access somehow after hours?"

"Up until now, I didn't know how he'd gone about it."

"So how did you figure it out?"

"Not me. The detective. Joel Craigdon. He called me a few moments ago. He told me they've got Dwight on CCTV footage. He hacked into my server from a computer at Craigdon Enterprises. With my computer and login details at hand, it was pretty easy for him to initiate each of the transfers from a distance and make it look like it came from me."

Zane swore under his breath. "The asshole. I'm going to kill him."

"Don't say things like that," she admonished. "Listen," she continued, "Joel said they were putting together an arrest team. They're expecting to find Dwight at work. But he's not there. I just left him at the gun range. I'm not sure where he's headed from there."

"Joel, is it? So you're on first name basis with the detective now," Zane said dryly.

Sheridan made a sound of exasperation. "Zane! Build a bridge! This isn't about me and Joel or you and Joel or Dad and Henry Craigdon. The police are closing in on Dwight and he's getting nervous. You know how he feels about you. Just watch out and call Joel and let him know about Dwight."

"Okay! Okay! No need to get your knickers in a knot. I'll call him and pass on the information."

"Good. Thank you. Oh, and one other thing," she added. "It's possible Dwight might be armed."

She explained how she'd wanted to hightail it away from there and he'd offered to lock up her gun. "I left before he'd done it, so I can't be sure he locked it away like he said or whether he has it with him. I want you to know in case he turns up at McClintock looking for you. After I confronted him about the theft, he got angry. He scared me. Turned into someone I didn't even recognize. I don't want anyone to get hurt."

"It's fine, Sheridan. Don't worry about it. That little prick isn't going to lay a hand on me." Zane's tone was grim and filled with certainty. It gave Sheridan a modicum of comfort to know her brother had been alerted and could take care of himself.

"Where are you now?" Zane asked.

"I'm on my way back to the office. I'm probably an hour and a half away."

"All right. Well, drive safely."

"Thanks, Zane. I will. I'll see you soon." With that, she ended the call and tossed her phone back in her handbag. Checking her rearview mirror, she flipped on her indicator and merged back into the traffic.

Joel was in the process of bringing the arrest team up to speed when his phone rang. Excusing himself, he turned away, pulled the phone out of his pocket and checked the screen.

No Caller ID.

He cursed and answered the call. In his line of work, he couldn't afford to ignore phone calls, especially anonymous ones. Some of the best tips came from callers who didn't want to be identified.

"Detective Craigdon."

"Detective, this is Zane Forrest."

Joel's eyebrows rose in surprise. "Mr Forrest. What can I do for you?"

"Look, we might have gotten off on the wrong foot, but I need you to listen. I just spoke to Sheridan. She told me what you've discovered about Dwight Britton."

Joel compressed his lips. "Yeah. In fact, we're putting together an arrest team as we speak."

"My sister said you were headed to Craigdon Enterprises to find him, but he was just at the gun range out at Condell Park. With Sheridan."

Joel frowned, incredulous. "Why would she be with him at a gun range?"

"She asked him to meet her. She hoped to get him to confess to the theft and to setting her up."

Joel's jaw dropped open in shock. "*What?* Is she crazy? This guy's dangerous! If he has any idea she suspects him, there's no telling what he might do."

"That's the thing," Zane replied, his voice grim. "She confronted him about it. He denied it, of course, but he didn't react well to her accusations."

"What the hell was she *thinking?*" Joel's words exploded into the conversation, concern for her safety igniting his temper.

"Exactly," Zane agreed. "Thank goodness she's on her way back to the office. But it gets worse. She thinks Britton might be armed. She gave him her pistol to lock away at the gun range. She didn't hang around to make sure he did it. I just thought you ought to know."

Joel made a sound of frustration in the back of his throat, still trying to get his head around Sheridan's stupidity. "Thanks," he muttered. "I appreciate the heads up."

"It's fine. Just…be careful, okay?"

As soon as Joel ended the call with Zane he dialed Sheridan's number. Now he understood why she'd sounded so weird and why she'd brought their call to such an abrupt end. Britton had been nearby. Maybe even close enough to hear their conversation… If that were so, and Britton knew how close they were to arresting him, he might panic and do something stupid. Things could quickly get out of control. On top of that, there was now a real possibility he was armed.

Zane had told him Sheridan was on her way back to the office. The news gave him a modicum of comfort, but he still wanted to talk to her and make sure. The phone continued to ring out until it finally went through to voicemail. He swallowed a curse and left a message for her to call him.

With nothing else to do, he shoved his phone back in his pocket and continued going over the details with the arrest team. This time, he added the information that their suspect could be armed. He also changed their plan of attack. It appeared the suspect might not be at his place of work. Instead, there was a chance he was headed for McClintock Properties. It was decided they'd start their search for him there.

Privately, Joel was no more certain that Britton would turn up at McClintock than he was that the man might just make a run for it, but with Sheridan headed back to her office, he wanted to make sure she arrived there safely—without Britton in tow.

Joel made a mental note to put a call into the airport security offices and alert them Britton might be looking to book himself a ticket to distant shores. Joel would make sure the man was apprehended long before he made it to the boarding line.

Dwight threw his Range Rover into gear and headed away from the gun range. On the seat beside him was Sheridan's pistol. He'd grabbed a spare box of bullets he'd found in her locker and once he was in his car had filled each of the chambers. She'd been stupid to trust him with the thing, especially after she'd just finished telling him how she suspected he was the thief.

How did she think I'd react? Did she think I'd congratulate her for being so clever, for working it all out? Not likely. Especially not now she had the police on his tail.

Anger flooded through him. He should have just shot her there and then, but it would have been messy and difficult to explain. The whole thing would have been captured on camera and he wouldn't stand a chance claiming self-defense. No, it was better for him to take a few moments to calm down and come up with a better plan.

The suicide option still appealed to him. He could force her at gunpoint to write a note explaining how she'd stolen the money and now couldn't live with herself. After all, he'd gone to pains to ensure the evidence all pointed to her. She'd use her own gun, one she'd removed from her locker at the gun range, and took back to her office.

He was sure that's where she was headed. She'd always been devoted to her work. It was one of the reasons his eye had wandered. He'd been tired of her always telling him she was too busy to go out. Honestly, he'd been tired of her, period.

He thought once he'd gotten her into his bed it would be a small thing to get her to move in. Granted, his cramped apartment couldn't compare to the plush pad she had in the Eastern Suburbs, but it wasn't too shabby.

The trouble was, she resisted his attempts to cajole her into taking their relationship to the next level and she seemed to be quite happy to maintain the status quo where they could go out with each other and otherwise maintain their own space. The delay in progressing things to the point it would appear the natural thing for him to propose, had chaffed him no end. It had been all he could do to keep the pretense of a loving boyfriend in place when all he wanted to do was strangle her.

But he'd spent far too much time cultivating her favor to throw everything away over a little bump in the road. He'd double his efforts to impress her with his devotion and meanwhile he'd relieved his frustrations in other ways.

His diversion with Diana hadn't been the first time he'd been unfaithful. Even now he couldn't believe he'd been stupid enough to leave the evidence on his phone. Usually he uploaded any images to his account in the cloud, where he could scroll through them at leisure, reliving each experience without fear of being caught.

But Sheridan had found the photos before he'd deleted them and then the shit had hit the fan. His carefully laid plans were blown apart and he was left to pick up the pieces. He was sure he could have persuaded her to forgive him and take him back if her caveman brother hadn't interfered…

Once again, his anger rushed to the fore. The very thought of Zane Forrest sent Dwight's blood boiling.

Perhaps I can kill both of them and make it look like a murder/suicide? Perhaps Sheridan's note could explain how her brother had discovered her treachery and threatened to turn her in to the police? She killed him in a panic and then turned the gun on herself…

It was plausible, but it was also going to be difficult to execute. Zane was a big man. Well over six feet. On top of that he was built like a boxer—all broad shoulders, wide chest, a wall of muscle. The man had fists like dinner plates. There was no way Dwight could best him in a fight. No, he had to come up with some other way to get both Sheridan and her brother to do his bidding.

His glance fell on the pistol. No one messed with a loaded gun, no matter how strong they were. Sheridan and Zane had grown up around firearms. They knew better than most how dangerous and unpredictable a weapon could be when handled by a person with evil intent.

Dwight chuckled. Yes, that's how he'd do it. He'd cajole someone to let him go up to see Sheridan. Maybe he could convince Christopher Barrington to loan him his pass again. It had worked well enough in the past. Only this time, he needed the pass to give him access to McClintock Properties. Once inside the premises, he'd overpower Sheridan in her office, tie her up and gag her so she couldn't alert anyone to what was going on. Then he'd take a photo and send it to Zane's phone. He'd make sure he had the gun pointing to Sheridan's head.

It would be followed with a clear warning. If Zane did anything stupid, like calling the police, Sheridan would be dead at the first hint of a siren. Zane would be wise to meet Dwight quietly in Sheridan's office. Then, with both of them at his mercy, the fun would really begin.

Sheridan joined the throng of traffic headed toward the city. It was mid-afternoon. Almost time for school pickup. The burgeoning traffic was testament to that. She tapped her steering wheel, impatient to get back to the office, far away from Dwight where she could finally feel safe.

Every now and then she glanced in her rearview mirror, checking for his Range Rover, but so far she hadn't seen any sign of him. Either he wasn't tailing her or he was keeping well back and following her from a distance, gaining on her slowly, like she was his prey.

That unsettling thought sent shivers of foreboding down her spine. She forced her mind away from Dwight and focused on someone who evoked something quite different.

Joel.

She prayed Zane had been able to reach him and warn him about the possibility Dwight might be armed. Even if he'd locked her gun away as he promised, there was always the chance he'd signed his own gun out. She couldn't bear the thought of anything happening to her brother...or to Joel.

Joel.

The anger had dissipated when he told her he'd continued working on the case. Had dug deeper though all the evidence pointed to her. Now, feeling tremendous relief to be off the hook, and away from Dwight she thought of Joel and her heart soared.

Was there ever a sexier, sweeter, kinder man on Earth? She didn't think so. Somewhere along the way, she'd come to care for him. He was everything she hadn't realized she wanted in a man. When all this was over, she hoped their relationship could be salvaged. Otherwise, it would be a real shame.

She wasn't the kind of woman who fell in love easily and she wasn't at that point with Joel yet, but she could be. If she allowed herself to forget about their past disagreements and accept he was merely doing his job. If she concentrated on everything that was good and wonderful between them…

Heat centered in her core and she squirmed on the seat. Just the memory of his touch on her skin filled her with need. He ignited feelings inside her that were foreign, but now she knew how good it felt to be wanted completely, without reservation… To have a man gaze at her with eyes filled with desire…and more. And to feel the same about him. It was a heady combination, more addictive than any drug. She wanted more of it. Much more. And she wanted it for all time.

She didn't know how Joel felt about commitment. He'd lived with MJ for five years and hadn't taken it any further. It told her he was prepared to commit to some extent, but it still left her with a lot of questions.

She suddenly yearned for the investigation to be over. For anxiety and questions to be eased. For her and Joel to be able to spend time together without the specter of criminal conduct and police involvement hanging over their heads. Now that they finally had the evidence they needed to prove Dwight was their guy, hopefully Joel could close the case and let the courts take over.

And then they could see if the spark they acknowledged was between them could turn into a fire that could burn now and long into the future…

Over the noise of the traffic, she heard the faint sound of her phone ringing. She glanced at her handbag. It was way out of reach. She was hemmed in on either side, with a truck on her left and an SUV on her right. There was no way she could pull over to the side. She had no choice but to let it go through to voicemail.

Despite everything, she smiled. She could almost hear Zane saying that if she had Bluetooth, she could just answer the phone without having to worry about it. She need never miss a call again. Oh, well. Maybe he was right. Maybe it was time to think about upgrading…

Maybe she'd talk to Joel about it, seek out his advice. He seemed like the kind of man who knew a lot about things like that. Yes, that's what she'd do. As soon as this thing with Dwight and the theft had been resolved, she'd call Joel and ask him out on the pretext that she needed advice on what kind of car she should buy. Men loved to be asked for their opinion and it meant she got to spend time with him without having to swallow her pride. It was a perfect solution.

Completely unaware of the dark-colored Range Rover that had slipped right up behind her, she smiled.

Chapter Twenty One

Joel activated his flashing lights and siren and went speeding through the streets. Ralph was in the seat beside him.

"Did we get an APB out on Britton's navy-blue Ranger Rover?"

Ralph nodded. "Yep. Dispatch has already received a report from one of the other units. It's been spotted near Parramatta heading toward the city."

Joel's gut swirled with dread. Both companies had their offices in the city. He couldn't be sure whether Britton was headed for Craigdon Enterprises or McClintock Properties, but he wasn't taking any chances. Sheridan's safety was paramount. With that thought in mind, he dialed her number again. It rang out, like it had the last three times he'd called her. Eventually it went to voicemail.

He thumped the steering wheel. "Damn! Why doesn't she pick up? Surely she can hear her phone, even over the traffic. Where is she? God, if he's taken her…"

He refused to finish the thought. With a quick glance over his shoulder, he changed lanes and stepped on the accelerator.

Dwight's heart thumped with anticipation and his adrenaline ran high. Up ahead of him, he watched as Sheridan's indicator blinked on and she pulled her car to the curb. Given the late hour of the day, he surmised she'd chosen to park outside her building rather than in her usual spot in the underground staff carpark. Fortunately, there was another empty space nearby. He pulled over, killed his ignition and waited until she'd climbed out of her car.

With casual movements, as if she didn't have a worry in the world, she swung her handbag over her shoulder, flipped her hair and began to walk in the direction of her office. It seemed she'd already dismissed their encounter from her mind.

How dare she set him aside so easily? Did she have any idea how dangerous he was? How he skated on a razor's edge between rational thinking and throwing it all to hell? She ought to fear him, show him more respect! Maybe she needed to be taught a lesson?

All at once, his control snapped and he was overcome with fury. A red haze clouded his vision. He leaped out of his vehicle and stormed toward her. Whipping out the pistol from the waistband of his pants, his heart lurched with anticipation. Blood thundered in his veins.

His carefully laid plans of only moments ago were blown to a million pieces. Through that haze he realized Sheridan had to die and she had to die now. He'd ambush her right on the street—to hell with the consequences. With a spine-tingling war cry and filled with bloodlust, he charged toward her.

Sheridan heard a chilling cry and turned to see Dwight running toward her. In his right hand, he held her pistol and he swung it wildly in the air. People around her screamed, scattered in all directions.

Sheridan's heart stood still. She willed her feet to move, but they were frozen to the spot. Dwight closed in on her, so close she saw the madness in his eyes. The world stood still for a millisecond and then everything moved in slow motion. The screaming of the onlookers, the noise of the traffic, the rabid shouting coming from Dwight's mouth…all of it disintegrated into nothing but a muted buzzing sound.

And then Dwight came to a complete halt and stared her in the eye. He was less than five yards away from her. His chest rose and fell. Spittle clung to the side of his mouth. He raised his arm and took aim. Time hung suspended. Sheridan stiffened and stared death in the face…

Joel's car screeched to a halt and he dived out of the police vehicle, Ralph not far behind him. From a distance he saw Dwight running toward Sheridan, gun in hand. Joel's blood ran cold.

Please, no. Please, no. Please, no…

The silent mantra echoed in his head. At the same time, his training kicked in and he went straight into police mode.

"Stop! Police! Drop the weapon!" he shouted. Ralph had also drawn his weapon. Both of them had their guns aimed at Dwight.

"Drop the weapon! Put your hands in the air!" Joel shouted again.

Dwight shot a frantic look in their direction. Catching sight of the lunacy in the man's gaze, Joel's heart plummeted. Britton had snapped. There was no sign of sanity in his eyes and that was so very dangerous.

Joel caught Ralph's eye and motioned for him to move to the left of Britton. Joel slowly closed in on the right. Britton shot them another panicked look and trained the gun back on Sheridan.

Joel didn't dare look at her. He focused all of his attention on the man who threatened her life.

"Put the gun down, Dwight," he said in a quieter tone. "Take it easy, nice and easy. Drop the gun, Dwight."

Dwight's arm wavered, dropped a bit. Joel held his breath. With his gun still trained on the madman, he calmly tried again.

"We have you surrounded, Dwight. There's no way you're getting away with this. Don't make it worse than it is. Put the gun down and step away with your hands up."

Dwight shot them another desperate glance and Joel eased out a breath. Thank God the man seemed to be listening…

Then a shot rang out and Sheridan screamed. Grabbing her shoulder, she stared in horror at the blood that seeped through her fingers. As if in slow motion, her eyes rolled back and she collapsed in a heap on the concrete.

A scream of denial tore from Joel's throat. A moment later all hell broke loose. He took aim and fired at Dwight. The man fell soundlessly to the ground. Joel shouted at Ralph who ran to Dwight and started CPR. Joel raced over to Sheridan and frantically checked her vitals. Her pulse was fast and irregular, but she was breathing. Blood continued to seep through her blouse, but thank God the bullet had missed the artery.

Sirens blared in the distance. People cried out in alarm. Heedless of the gathering crowd of first responders and curious bystanders, Joel pulled her into his embrace. Her eyes fluttered open and some of the color returned to her pale cheeks.

"Joel?" she murmured, her eyes clouded with confusion and pain.

Bending his head he gently kissed her and sent up a silent prayer of gratitude. "Thank God, you're going to be all right," he whispered, his voice hoarse with emotion.

And then her eyes closed again and she lost consciousness.

He yelled for an ambulance, refusing to move from her side until the paramedics had strapped her on the gurney. With lights and sirens blazing, the ambulance took off toward the hospital, Joel in fast pursuit behind them.

Sheridan's shoulder was on fire. She'd never been in so much pain. The ambulance hit a bump in the road and despite the medication the paramedics had already administered, she cried out.

"It's all right, Sheridan. We're almost there." The voice of one of the paramedics who rode in the back with her, soothed her in a calm voice.

Sheridan bit her lip and nodded. Tears formed in the corners of her eyes. Everything was still a blur of movement and noise and excruciating pain. She tried to come to terms with what had happened. She'd been heading back to the office when Dwight appeared from nowhere. He had yelled and shouted and waved her gun around like a crazy man.

And then the police had arrived—Joel and his partner— and she'd been giddy with relief. But then Dwight fired at her. She'd felt the pain in her upper arm before the sound of the gun's blast reached her. The world had tilted. A flash of Joel's stricken expression appeared as she lost consciousness and slid to the ground.

Joel.

When she'd opened her eyes and found him looking down at her with such a devastated expression, she was sure she must be dying. Dwight had shot her and now her lifeblood was slowly pouring out of her as Joel held her in his arms…

Thankfully the paramedics reassured her the bullet had entered the muscle in her upper arm and had exited cleanly out the other side. They'd stemmed the flow of blood and were now taking her to the hospital for treatment.

As the pain meds finally kicked in, her recollections turned hazy. Joel hadn't been allowed with her in the ambulance, but he'd assured her he was following close behind and that he'd be there when she woke up.

Joel.

She smiled. Despite everything they'd been through, he was the only man she wanted by her side. She knew he'd be there for her, through thick and thin, and that theirs was a special kind of love. She couldn't believe that earlier in the day she would have denied she was in love with him. It was funny how a kiss with death had brought into focus the things that were really important. Joel might not have told her he loved her, but even through her pain, she'd seen it in his eyes. He'd been terrified by the thought he could have lost her and she knew exactly how that felt.

Her eyelids grew heavier. She struggled to stay awake, but it was too much effort. Her last thought before she drifted off was of Joel.

The next time Sheridan awoke she was in a hospital bed. The light in the room was dim. In the distance, she heard the murmur of voices, the intermittent beep of a monitor, the occasional squeak of a rubber-soled shoe, even a burst of laughter. She blinked and made out the silhouette of someone slumped in the seat beside her bed. Dark, shiny hair, thick beard, a weary gaze. Joel came into focus. With an effort, she gathered the strength required to reach toward him.

At her touch, he gasped. "Sheridan!" Relief flooded his features. "Thank God you're awake!"

She tried to give him a reassuring smile, but the effort was beyond her. Instead, she touched him again. He took her hand and brought it to his lips, pressing a soft kiss against it. Tears filled her eyes.

He immediately looked distraught. "Oh, Sheridan! Babe, please don't cry. You're going to be okay. The doctor said the bullet passed through cleanly and there shouldn't be any long-lasting effects. She prescribed adequate doses of pain meds, but if you need more, you're to let me know."

He looked so concerned she would have laughed if it didn't hurt so much. She tried to lift her injured arm and winced. She might be on pain meds, but they hadn't removed all feeling. Her arm was bandaged from her shoulder all the way to her elbow. Still, it could have been far worse.

As if reading her mind, Joel's expression darkened. "I can't believe that bastard shot you. If I hadn't yelled out at him right at that moment… If the shot had been true…" His voice trailed off and he shuddered. "I can't believe how close I came to losing you."

The raw emotion in his voice was reflected in his eyes. Despite the painful wound, tears of gratitude and love filled Sheridan's eyes.

"It wasn't your fault," she whispered. "In fact, if you hadn't shown up when you did, he might have remained calm enough to take proper aim. I'm sure seeing you and Ralph and hearing the sirens sent him into a panic. He's an excellent shot. He must have pulled the trigger without thinking."

Joel's lips tightened. "Don't cut him any slack. He shot you! He could have killed you!"

Sheridan gently squeezed his hand. "Yes. But he didn't. And we can be thankful for that."

"Oh, I'm thankful all right." His gaze filled with an intensity that stole Sheridan's breath. "You might think this is a reaction to nearly losing you, but the truth is, I've fallen in love with you, Sheridan. I had even before this." He gave her a lopsided smile. "I just hadn't gotten around to telling you. I hope you believe me."

She nodded and fresh tears of joy filled her eyes. "Of course I believe you! I feel the same way."

He looked at her in disbelief. "You do?"

"Yes!" And then she was laughing and crying and it hurt so much, but it was also good. Her heart was full to bursting.

Joel Craigdon loves me! And I love him! Does life get any sweeter?

And then he leaned over and gently kissed her on the mouth. She melted under his touch. He kissed her softly, his lips lingering, and she felt all the love he had inside. When he eventually lifted his head, she sighed.

"That was so good."

His eyes darkened with emotion. "That was just the start. Just wait until you get out of hospital and I can love you properly…"

Her belly somersaulted at the promise in his eyes. "I love you, Joel."

He held her gaze, his blue eyes luminous with the shimmer of tears. "I love you, too."

Joel left her to get some rest and promised to return in the morning. The next day he walked into her room dressed in his usual work clothes of a tailored suit and tasteful tie and almost hidden behind an enormous display of flowers he carried in his arms.

"Joel! You shouldn't have!" she exclaimed, grinning widely.

He smiled back and after setting the flowers on a side table, leaned over and kissed her. "You're looking a lot better today."

"I feel better, too. Not quite like I've been run over by a Mack truck." She shot him a cheeky look. "More like a scooter."

"I'm glad to hear it."

She sobered. "What's happening with Dwight?" she asked softly.

Joel propped a hip against her bed. "He'll be fine. Lucky for him, Ralph's CPR efforts at the scene were successful. The bullet hit him in the chest, but missed his heart. Not so lucky for him is that when he recovers he'll face a string of charges, not the least being attempted murder."

"What about the theft? Has he confessed?"

"Surprisingly, yes. I think he sees it as the lesser evil. Kind of using it as a bargaining tool."

She felt a frisson of unease. "Will it work?"

Noticing her expression, he hurried to reassure her. "Now that he's been charged, the matter's out of our hands. The prosecutor's office takes over from here. But even if he pleads guilty to a lesser charge, he'll be facing considerable jail time. You don't have to worry about him. He'll be out of your life for good."

"Did he explain why he took the money?"

"He said it was an act of revenge because you dumped him. He wanted to cause trouble for you and thought that was a good way to do it. He had access to your computer and login details and knew how to hack into the server from afar. He'd also swiped your driver's license and passport when you weren't looking and took copies. He used them to open the offshore account. He said he had no intention of keeping the money for himself. In fact, he claims he was the one who tipped off the police."

Sheridan looked at Joel in surprise. "Do you believe him?"

"I guess it makes sense in a weird way. We haven't found any evidence that he acted in cohort with anyone else. It looks like he came up with the idea all by himself and put it into action. He claims he knew the missing money would eventually be noticed by someone at McClintock and then an investigation would begin."

"So why did he bother with the tip-off?"

"He says he got impatient. He'd been siphoning off money for months and no one had cottoned on. He decided to help things along."

"What's happened to the money?"

"It's been returned to McClintock accounts."

Sheridan smiled. "Zane will be pleased about that."

Joel grinned. "You bet."

A knock on the door snagged their attention. Both of them looked toward the half-open door. A young woman with glossy blond hair and bright red lipstick, wearing a white lab coat and a stethoscope draped around her neck appeared in the opening. She took the time to close the door behind her before turning to face the bed. Spying Joel, her face broke into a smile.

"Joel! Fancying seeing you here!" She stepped forward and gave him a hug. He grinned and hugged her back.

A shaft of jealousy arced through Sheridan. Who was this woman who touched the man she loved with such casual intimacy?

As if reading her thoughts, the woman turned toward her and smiled. "I'm Doctor Isabella Craigdon. I was on duty when you were brought in. I assisted during your surgery."

Sheridan barely heard what the woman said. Her mind had stumbled on the word "Craigdon."

"Craigdon? Are you and Joel related?" she asked in a carefully casual tone.

The glamorous woman, who looked like she'd stepped from the pages of a fashion shoot, winked.

"You could say that." She glanced over her shoulder. "Tell her Joel."

Joel sighed and rolled his eyes. "She's my sister." He looked at Isabella. "Isabella, this is Sheridan. Sheridan, meet Isabella."

Now that Sheridan knew the woman was no competition for Joel's heart, she relaxed against the sheets. "You assisted in my surgery?"

"Yes. Lucky for you, I have specialist training in bullet wounds. Fortunately, we don't get too many of them in Sydney, but I'm in demand when we do."

"What kind of surgery did I need?" Sheridan asked, curious. She'd been regularly checked over by nurses, but no one had actually explained to her what procedure was done.

"We had to check that the bullet wasn't still in there. You were lucky. It passed through the muscle and out the other side. Didn't even so much as nick a bone. We manipulated your arm a bit at the shoulder, cleaned the wound thoroughly and stitched you up. You'll likely have a sore shoulder and arm for a bit, and couple of small scars to remind you of the experience, but otherwise you should recover well."

Sheridan felt a renewed sense of relief and a wave of gratitude for Isabella and the rest of her medical team.

"Thank you," she said somberly. "I'm sure if I hadn't received such excellent treatment, I might not be feeling so well today."

Isabella accepted her comment graciously and then picked up the chart that hung on the end of Sheridan's bed. She checked over the entries and nodded her approval. "It looks like you're doing great. Keep up the good work. Once you're eating and drinking normally, we'll remove the IV. If your pain remains under control, you should be free to go home tomorrow or the next day."

Sheridan glanced at Joel and then smiled at Isabella. "That sounds great."

The sound of someone arguing outside interrupted them. All three of them turned toward the door just as it swung open and an older woman, tall and trim and elegant, and with a headful of thick, perfectly coiffed white hair strode into the room.

Joel stared at the woman in shock. "Mom! What are *you* doing here?"

Chapter Twenty Two

"I'm sorry for barging in like this, Joel, but I was scared to death. I saw the breaking news on TV. They said shots were fired. Someone caught the whole thing on their phone. It's all over the Internet. I recognized you right away and had to make sure you were all right." Without drawing breath, the woman turned her laser-sharp gaze on Sheridan.

"Hello, I'm Elizabeth Craigdon. Joel's mother."

"And mine," Isabella added dryly.

Sheridan looked from one to the other and included Isabella in her bemused gaze. Joel came to her rescue.

"Mom, this is Sheridan McClintock."

Elizabeth frowned. "McClintock? Are you any relation of Michael McClintock?"

Sheridan nodded. "Yes. He was my father."

Elizabeth's perfectly groomed eyebrows rose. "Your father? I see."

Once again, Joel ran interference. "Yes, Mom. We both know he was Dad's fiercest competitor. But give the man's children a break. He's been dead for quite some years."

"Yes, of course," Elizabeth replied, as if it were of no consequence. "And heaven knows, your father was no saint, especially when it came to business." She pinned Sheridan with her gaze once more. "When you're feeling better, you must come over for brunch. I can't wait to hear all about you."

Isabella regarded Sheridan quizzically. "Am I missing something?"

Joel blushed adorably. Sheridan waited for him to speak, curious about what he might say.

"Issy, the thing is… Sheridan and I… That is, Sheridan and I have known each other for a while now. Long before"—he indicated the hospital bed with his hands—"all this happened. And, the thing is, we're…we're in love. I'm sure my heart stopped beating for a few moments when I realized she'd been shot."

The look he gave Sheridan was so full of love and relief, she couldn't help but smile back.

"It's true," she said softly. "Joel and I are in love."

"Well!" Isabella exclaimed. "I see." She rounded on Joel. "I thought you were here on police business. You could have told me she was your girlfriend!"

Joel blushed again. Sheridan thought that was adorable… and incredibly sexy. Before she could say anything more, the half-open door was pushed open so hard it slammed against the wall.

Joel tensed at the unexpected intrusion and instinctively reached for his gun. "What the—"

MJ burst into the room. Looking around at the people gathered in front of her, she appeared momentarily startled. Like the day had gotten even stranger.

"Mary-Jane? What the hell are *you* doing here?" Joel asked.

As if he'd startled her out of a daze, she blinked rapidly and then rounded on him, shrieking like a banshee.

"I *knew* you wouldn't call me! You told me you would, but you didn't! You lied to me! And you're avoiding me, Joel.

And if there's one thing you should have learned in all the years we were together, it's that *I will not be ignored!*"

The room fell into a shocked silence. Identical expressions of astonishment and confusion flooded everyone's faces in turn. Joel ducked his head, embarrassed beyond imagining, that the woman who stood before them screaming so shrilly had once been his long-term girlfriend.

On a burst of irritation, he stepped toward her. "For God's sake, MJ! You only called me yesterday afternoon! I've been busy! Didn't you see the news? There was a shooting. Does any of this matter to you?"

She sneered. "Oh, I saw it all right. How do you think I knew you were here? I guessed you'd be at the hospital, with your lover." She glared at Sheridan who looked more bewildered than anyone. MJ looked back at Joel and her lip curled up in disgust. "Don't try and deny it. I saw the way you held her, even kissed her for the cameras. You were all over her."

Joel shook his head, his temper starting to rise. Sheridan and his family shouldn't be subject to this nonsense. Sheridan was recovering from a bullet wound, for God's sake! He'd deal with MJ and her histrionics some other time. With that thought in mind, he took her firmly by the elbow and led her toward the door.

"You need to leave, MJ. This isn't the time or the place. I said I'd call you and I will. We'll discuss whatever it is, later," he said in a no-nonsense tone.

MJ wrenched away. "No! Not until I show you *this!*" She reached into her handbag and pulled something out.

Joel frowned. "What is it?"

"It looks like an ultrasound picture," Isabella mused.

MJ turned to face his sister with a self-satisfied grin. "Go to the top of the class, Doctor Isabella."

Joel's gut filled with a sudden sense of foreboding. "What the hell are you doing with an ultrasound picture?"

MJ's grin widened. She laid her hand against her slightly protruding belly. "It's my baby. *Our* baby."

Joel reeled back in shock. "What the hell? No way! I've been overseas for months! How far along are you?"

He snuck a look at Sheridan. She'd gone as white as the sheet. MJ sidled up to him and stroked him on the arm.

"Don't you remember that night, right before you broke up with me?"

Joel wrenched his arm away from her touch and moved to the other side of the room, all the while shaking his head in denial.

"No, I don't believe you." He looked at Sheridan again and begged her to understand. "It's not mine. I swear, Sheridan, the baby is not mine."

Sheridan looked at him, her expression aghast and confused. Isabella stepped toward MJ and snatched the ultrasound picture out of MJ's fingers. Lifting it up to the light, Isabella studied the miniature x-ray closely. She shook her head, her expression grim.

"Relax, Joel. This ultrasound isn't authentic to MJ. There's no name, no date, no patient ID. It's just a picture. There's no way it's legitimate."

"Of course it is!" MJ protested.

Isabella gave the woman a hard look. "No, MJ. It's not. I've seen plenty of these. This isn't the real deal. You've gotten hold of this from somewhere and had it digitally altered, removed the name of the actual patient and the date of the screening. It's nothing more than an anonymous fetus. A forgery, in fact."

Joel stared at his ex-girlfriend in disbelief. He couldn't believe she'd stooped so low as to try to trap him this way. The thing was, he knew she wasn't bright enough to pull this off on her own. "Who put you up to this, MJ?"

A panicked look filled her eyes. "No! You have it all wrong!

It's your baby! You're going to be a daddy!"

Joel gave her his deadly cop stare. "MJ, tell me the truth." After a tense minute, she crumbled.

"It's all Christopher's fault!" she wailed, throwing up her hands in an over-the-top show of dramatics. "Christopher made me do it! He was the one who came up with the idea. He got the ultrasound picture from someone and gave it to me."

Joel stared at her in disbelief. It would never cease to amaze him the depths some people would go to deceive others to get their way…

He shook his head. MJ took one more look at him and left the room, sobbing.

Elizabeth looked as shocked as any of them. "I can't believe Christopher would do something like that," she said, dazed. "How could he be so vindictive? That poor boy!"

Joel scowled. "Don't go feeling sorry for him, Mom. He knew exactly what he was doing. He seems to enjoy going out of his way to make other people miserable. Have you forgotten what he did to Grace?"

Elizabeth sighed, but continued to look distressed. "Of course I haven't forgotten. What he did was terrible. It's just lucky it didn't affect her the way he intended. Oh, Christopher! What will become of you? I worry for you…"

Joel turned away from his mother, filled with impatience. She was far better than he to be able to feel sympathy for his half-brother. Right now Joel wanted nothing more than to punch Christopher in the face. Hard. With an effort, he controlled his temper and took a deep breath and when he eased it out he let go some of his tension. He moved over to Sheridan's side.

"I'm sorry about that. Please forgive me. My family is…a little unconventional."

Instead of questions and accusations, she reached up and

tenderly cupped his cheek with her hand and smiled. "Aren't they all?"

Joel headed out of the hospital and crossed the road over to the visitor carpark, feeling better than he had for a long time. Sheridan was going to be fine. The case was closed. She loved him and he loved her. Life was, and would be, good.

Glancing to his right before crossing the road, he spied Zane Forrest heading toward the hospital entrance carrying a bouquet of flowers. Slowing his steps, Joel came to a halt and waited for Zane to see him. Joel could tell the exact instant Sheridan's brother recognized him. The man's progress halted and his shoulders tensed.

Joel closed the distance between them and stuck out his hand in greeting. Zane hesitated and then shook the proffered hand.

"I owe you an apology and I want to thank you for saving my sister's life," Zane told him.

Joel accepted the apology with a casual shrug. "We all handle things in our own way. You were close to your late father and he never got on with mine. I understand your loyalty to your father and your need to honor his memory by standing with him against the Craigdons."

"It's not quite like that, but—"

"It's okay," Joel assured him. "Like I said, I understand. If I'd been close to my dad, I'd probably feel the same way. Although I'm a little perplexed why you're still so angry about it. Surely my father didn't do anything to you personally?"

Zane eyed him solemnly. "No, not to me. To my sister."

Joel tensed in shock. "My father knew Sheridan?"

"Yes."

Knowing what his father was capable of, Joel hardly dared to ask the question, but he needed to know what had put Zane so far off side. "What happened?"

Zane sighed. "Sheridan would probably disapprove of me telling you, but if you really want to understand my animosity, it's important that you know."

Joel felt a frisson of unease. He braced himself for what was to come.

"It was a few years ago," Zane continued. "At a business awards night. Your father was there holding court with his cronies. He'd had way too much to drink. Still, that's no excuse. I was there with Sheridan. She went to the bar for a drink and ran into your father. He made a pass at her, said some unflattering things about what he'd like to do with her and then got aggrieved when she told him off."

Joel shook his head in disbelief. "That's terrible. No wonder you're so pissed at us."

Zane's expression remained grave. "That's not the worst of it."

Joel closed his eyes, almost unable to bear it. "Please don't tell me he—"

"No, at least, not with Sheridan. He had an affair with our mother."

Joel didn't know why he was shocked. It wasn't like he hadn't known his father had been unfaithful and with many different women.

"Tell me about it," he urged.

Zane sighed again. "I don't know how long it had been going on. All I remember was coming home from school one day and finding them in bed together. They must have lost track of time. Mom was shocked to see me. Henry seemed to take it in his stride. He offered me a hundred dollars and urged me to forget about what I'd seen."

"The prick," Joel muttered. A wave of anger washed over him at his father's arrogance.

Zane cleared his throat and continued. "I told him where to shove his money and went and called my dad. He and Mom had a massive argument. That night, she died of a stroke. I was fifteen. The doctors told us there was nothing we could have done. Mom had been a walking time bomb. A blood clot in her brain had dislodged and caused the stroke. It could have happened at any time."

He looked at Joel and his expression was bleak. His eyes were filled with tears. "Try telling that to a kid. In my mind, it was your father's fault. And partly mine. I never forgave him."

Joel shook his head again, not knowing what to say. What could he say? It was a horrible story of tragedy and pain and again, his father was at the heart of it.

Oh, Dad! You were so selfish! You destroyed so many lives. Not the least some of your family. I hope you're at peace because the rest of us sure as hell aren't.

"I want you to know I don't hold a grudge against you or your family anymore," Zane said quietly. "Yesterday, you saved my sister's life. As far as I'm concerned, the slate's been wiped clean."

"I love her," Joel said simply.

"You make sure you take care of her, or you'll have me to answer to."

Joel stared at him. "You have my word. Now and for the rest of our lives."

The late afternoon sun blazed through the floor-to-ceiling glass of Joel's harborside apartment, creating warm shards of light across the living room floor. A light, salty breeze drifted in through the open sliding door that led out to the balcony. Sheridan stood, cuddling Roxy in one arm and Gypsy in the other, and stared out at the magnificent view. The harbor was gloriously blue, dotted with whitecaps and a myriad of watercraft. It had been a perfect, clear, crisp winter day.

Ten days before, Sheridan had been released from the hospital and though her shoulder and arm were still sore, the wound was healing well. She'd always bear the scars to remind her how close she'd come to dying, but that was a small price to pay. She was just grateful no one else had been hurt by Dwight.

Even now, she felt disbelief that a man she thought she'd known well, had known intimately, had been secretly harboring so many troubled thoughts. It shook her confidence in her ability to gauge people through their words and actions. After all, her take on Dwight had been so wrong.

As if able to read her thoughts, Joel came up behind her and slid his arms around her waist. He pressed a soft kiss against her temple.

"Whatever you're thinking, you're wrong," he murmured against her skin.

She turned slightly and looked at him. "What makes you think that?"

"Oh, something about the way your body's as stiff as a board. Even the dogs can feel it. Then there's the frown." He traced a fingertip across her forehead, smoothing out the lines.

She smiled. "Okay, you're right. I was thinking about Dwight."

Joel turned her in his arms until she faced him. He took the dogs from her, set them on the floor and regarded her soberly.

"I can't say I'm sorry I shot him, Sheridan. To tell you the truth, I wish my aim had been true so this was over once and for all. When I saw him shoot you, my heart stopped. Then my training kicked in. I acted instinctively. It was imperative I stop him from getting off a second shot. It was you or him. I chose you and I'd do it again in an instant."

The intensity in his gaze filled her with warmth. Here was a man she could depend upon to protect her and keep her safe. A man she'd never imagined would come into her life, but someone she loved with all her heart. He'd shot the man who'd been determined to kill her. As a result, Joel was under investigation for discharging his weapon. He'd acted without hesitation to save her life and would do so again.

A surge of love flooded through her. Draping her good arm around his neck, she pulled his head down to hers and kissed him. His lips were firm and full and welcoming. His soft beard tickled her skin. With a groan, he pulled her hard against him. She felt the unmistakable evidence of his desire against her stomach and it sent an answering need shooting through her.

The kiss deepened. Tongues touched, became entwined. Joel's hand came around and cupped her ass, pressing her even closer. And then he bent and lifted her in his arms and carried her down the hallway to his bedroom.

The drapes were still open and the same magical view she'd enjoyed from the living room was on display. Joel set her down gently on the bed and then followed her. Careful of her bandaged arm, he covered her body with his. With unerring precision, he found her lips again.

She could kiss him forever…

Though Sheridan wasn't as experienced as some women when it came to men, she'd had her fair share of kisses. It had become clear to her from the very first moment her lips touched Joel's that not all men were created equal when it came to kissing. His lips were full and soft and sensual. Like the priceless artworks that decorated the walls and shelves of his apartment, he put his heart and soul into it, taking his time, savoring each sensation, never in a rush. He'd elevated kissing to an art form.

In her other relationships, kissing had always been a prelude to the main event; a means to an end. But with Joel it was completely different. *He* was completely different. He was like no man she'd ever known. Even during their first encounter, as hot and heavy as it had been, he'd taken his time kissing her and had been first and foremost concerned about her pleasure. That was a heady feeling and one she'd crave for the rest of her life.

And then he was tugging at her T-shirt and pulling it over her head, taking care to lift it free of her bandage without causing her pain. Her bra went the same way as her shirt and then he buried his face between her breasts.

Inhaling her skin, he kissed his way over to her nipple and then suckled. Her back arched in response to the exquisite feelings he evoked in her as his hot mouth devoured her. He switched his attention to her other breast and treated her nipple to the same loving attention. Heat swirled in her center. She moved restlessly against him, but he wasn't going to be rushed. Instead, he moved lower, kissing his way across her ribcage and down her stomach before he moved even lower and started loving the most sensitive part of her with his mouth.

His magical tongue stroked and laved and slid through her moist warmth. With his hands holding her hips fast, he loved her until she was nearly mad with need.

"Please," she begged.

He merely smiled. "Please, what?"

"Fuck me."

His eyes flashed with emotion and he growled low in his throat. Reaching over to the bedside drawer, he pulled out a condom and sheathed himself. Nudging her thighs open, he positioned himself so that with the slightest movement of his hips, his cock pressed against her entrance. She rocked her hips upward, encouraging him and with a hard thrust of his hips, he plunged inside her.

Clinging to his shoulders, she rode the wild thrusts as he plunged in and out of her with increasing frenzy. Tension built up inside her, almost unbearable, an agony and an ecstasy combined. She strained forward, close, so close to the crest, yearning for fulfillment.

And then she was there, crying out in relief, crashing over the other side. Her inner muscles tightened around Joel and her breath came loud and fast. With a shout of triumph, he reached his own climax and momentarily collapsed against her.

"Ouch," she said, moving her arm out of the way.

"Sorry, babe," he mumbled against her neck, exhausted. A few moments later, he rolled to his side and gently gathered her against him.

He pressed a kiss against her hair. "I love you."

She tenderly cupped her hand around his bearded cheek. "I love you, too."

It was some time later when Joel managed to stir himself enough to think about getting something to eat. Sheridan lay quietly against him. He could tell from her breathing she'd come awake. The sun had long ago set and night brought with it a special kind of beauty outside his window. The harbor reflected hundreds of twinkling lights. He was cocooned in warmth and comfort, with his arms wrapped around the woman he loved. Life didn't get any better.

"What are you thinking?" Sheridan murmured, stroking her finger idly through his beard.

He reached for the lamp on the table beside him and switched it on. A soft glow filled the room. He turned on his side and looked at her.

"Just that my life is perfect. I have the woman I love beside me. A family I care about and who cares about me. Enough money to be incredibly comfortable and a bed that can't be beaten anywhere in the world."

She smiled. "It *is* a pretty terrific bed."

He kissed her on the nose. "Actually, I think it's because of the woman I'm sharing it with."

She smiled and kissed him softly on the mouth and then

rested her head on his chest. Her fingers threaded through his chest hair, stroking lightly. "I had no idea Christopher was your half-brother," she murmured.

"Yep. We shared the same father."

"So why isn't he a Craigdon?"

Joel sighed. "It's not a pretty story. Christopher's mother used to work for Dad. Or at least, they worked in the same office. She was a secretary. Dad was an accountant. I can't remember the exact details."

Sheridan's eyebrows rose in surprise. "An accountant? So he wasn't always a property developer?"

"No. He studied accountancy at university and his first job after he graduated was with Doherty and Associates. It was an accounting firm started by my maternal grandfather."

"Is that where your parents met?"

"Yes. Mom worked at the same firm. But they didn't meet until after Dad's fling with Christopher's mother."

"Okay. Keep going."

"Anyway, Evelyn Baker was young and pretty and caught my father's eye. I think she was twenty. Dad was twenty-five. According to Dad, it was a mutual decision to have a fling. It was never meant to be serious. Then Evelyn fell pregnant."

Joel grimaced. "This is where it gets ugly. Apparently when she told Dad she was having a baby, Dad refused to have anything to do with her."

Sheridan looked at him, aghast. "Don't tell me he denied he was the father?"

"Yes. She was forced to have a DNA test to prove his paternity. Even then, Dad wasn't interested in taking responsibility. For him this had been a bit of fun, but he'd never taken it seriously. When Evelyn became pregnant, she basically ruined everything. Dad was young and ambitious. The last thing he wanted was to be saddled with a wife and child. So he ditched her and left her to raise their son on her own."

Sheridan shook her head in disbelief. "That poor woman! Did he give her any financial support?"

"Not near enough and you need to remember, the system wasn't quite as good as it is these days in making recalcitrant fathers pay. From what I've heard through Christopher, he and his mom struggled financially for a good part of his childhood. It wasn't until Evelyn met and married Frank Barrington that life looked up for them."

Sheridan frowned. "Frank Barrington? Of mining fame?"

Joel nodded. "Yes. Evelyn was forced to leave Doherty Accounting and apparently went to work for Barrington Mining Group. At some point she and Frank fell in love and married. Frank legally adopted Christopher when he was twelve."

Another frown marred the smooth skin of Sheridan's forehead. "So if Christopher is the adopted son of Frank Barrington, why doesn't he work for Barrington Mining? I'm sure his skills in the contracts office would come in handy there."

Joel shrugged. "I'm not sure. Frank and Evelyn went on to have a heap of kids themselves. Maybe Christopher feels like he doesn't quite fit in there. Kind of like how he feels about being a Craigdon."

Sheridan snuggled against him and sighed. "I kind of understand now why he wanted to cause trouble for you with MJ. It sounds like he's felt unwanted and awkward for all of his life. It must be tough belonging to two families but not *really* belonging to either of them."

"Don't go feeling too sorry for him," Joel said dryly. "Christopher has a habit of going out of his way to be nasty. I can't believe the stunt he pulled with MJ. Of course, he seems to be happiest when he's making his Craigdon siblings miserable."

He told her about Grace Gunning, the woman who was

soon to be his brother Callum's wife, and how cruel Christopher had been.

"At a time when Grace's life was falling apart," Joel explained, "She's a recovering alcoholic. Christopher went out of his way to tempt her with alcohol with the hope he might push her over the edge, all in the name of some misguided loyalty to Grace's late husband's parents."

"That's terrible!" Sheridan cried, her expression appalled.

"Yeah. But that's Christopher. I just wish he'd grow up. He's forty years of age, for goodness sake! I understand how he's always felt robbed of his birthright and ever since Dad left him out of the will… But hell… I wish to God he'd get over this grudge he's been carrying for so long and leave the rest of us alone."

Sheridan giggled. "You know he asked me out?"

Joel's gut tightened in anger. "How dare he?"

"It's okay," she laughed. "I turned him down."

"If he comes anywhere near you…"

Sheridan kissed him. "Do you want me to ask Zane to fire him?"

Joel sighed and shook his head. "No, I don't want to be vindictive. I'm sure his personality flaws don't get in the way of his work."

Sheridan fell silent. The sound of a ferry horn blasted in the distance. Joel looked at her and then frowned at the expression on her face. She looked like she wanted to say something, but wasn't sure how to go about it.

"What is it, Sheridan?"

She compressed her lips and glanced away and then finally looked at him again. The uncertainty in her gaze startled him.

"Sheridan? What is it, babe?"

"I was just thinking back to when I was in the hospital and your ex-girlfriend came bursting in. You looked kind of horrified when she showed you that ultrasound. Do you… Do you *want* to have kids some day?"

He hurried to reassure her. "Yes, of course. I've always wanted kids. I've been waiting all this time to meet their mother. And now I have."

He moved toward her, intent on kissing her. She tilted her face up to meet his. When their lips met, the love they felt for each other made this the sweetest kiss there was.

When at last Joel pulled slowly away, he looked down at her and grinned. "The only thing is, I'm an old-fashioned guy. I'd like to get married first. Is that okay with you?"

Sheridan's answering smile illuminated the love that shone from her eyes. She leaned up and kissed him again. "That's more than okay with me."

Note to Readers

I do hope you have enjoyed reading Joel and Sheridan's story. If you've enjoyed this book, I would really appreciate it if you could leave a review at Goodreads and your favorite digital retailer. Every review increases visibility and helps other readers to find books they enjoy.

Receive a free book when you sign up for my newsletter if you like to receive news on upcoming stories, release dates, book launches and other snippets. I love to receive feedback from my readers. Please feel free to contact me at chris@christaylorauthor.com.au.

Isabella is the next book in the Craigdon Family Dynasty series.

Keep reading below for a sneak peek at Isabella:

Chapter One

Seated at her dressing table with the bright, Hollywood-style lightbulbs bordering the mirror, Isabella Craigdon put the finishing touches to her makeup. Heavily-shadowed eyelids, lined dramatically with black pencil gave her an exotic, mysterious look. Three coats of bright red, kiss-proof lipstick covered her full shapely lips. A slash of blush highlighted her cheekbones and two coats of black mascara lengthened her already-long eyelashes by a quarter of an inch. She sat back in her chair and surveyed her appearance, satisfied with the results. Now for her hair.

She twisted the long blond strands into a bun and pinned it low on her neck. Reaching for one of the hairnets she kept hidden in the top drawer of her dressing table, she pulled it over her head. Next came the wig. She stood and crossed the room to her walk-in robe.

Opening one of the many doors that concealed her vast and expensive wardrobe, she scanned the wigs that hung on foam heads and filled several of the shelves. After only a moment's hesitation, she selected the long, dark-red wig. Her new client hadn't requested a specific hair color, but she felt the red would be perfect.

Like she always did before a first meeting, she'd done some research on Raine Fairfax. After all, it paid to be prepared.

Knowing a bit about her client meant she'd be able to engage him in conversation, flatter him with her knowledge of his interests, his life. Plus, it was a way to ensure her safety, something she never took for granted as an escort.

Of course, the agency she worked for assured her they did background checks on all of her clients, but it didn't hurt to do a little checking of her own. She hadn't found a single red flag when it came to Raine Fairfax. In fact, he seemed too good to be true.

The Internet had provided her with several images of the thirty-year-old CEO of Fairfax Investments. Each time she'd gazed upon another image, her heart had raced. Raine's thick, auburn-colored hair framed an unbelievably handsome face. Blue eyes, square jaw, chiseled cheekbones. She was sure the professional headshot on his company's website must have been airbrushed. No one could look that good.

There must be some hidden flaws, something that had escaped media attention. A shrewish ex-wife. An illegitimate child. A drug habit. Or perhaps he was a gambler?

Not that any of that mattered. She'd been hired to escort him to dinner and afterwards…who knew? The five thousand dollars he'd paid upfront for her services meant she was his for the night.

A shiver of excitement rippled over her skin. Her nipples tightened in response. The thought of kissing those firm lips, running her finger across that chiseled jaw. Though she hadn't found any pictures of him shirtless, anyone could see he wore his clothes well. Broad shoulders were emphasized by a well-cut tuxedo. From what she could see, his waist was narrow, his stomach looked taut and flat. She could only imagine what he looked like naked. Perhaps by the end of the night she'd find out…

The thought sent another shiver of anticipation through her. There were many perks to being an escort, but this was one of the best. She didn't think of herself as promiscuous. Her clients didn't always share her body, but she wouldn't deny she enjoyed a robust sex life. She couldn't imagine limiting her passions to one man. That had been the main reason she'd broken things off with Luke.

Part of the terms she'd struck with her agency meant that she had full control over the men she agreed to escort and the decision as to whether she had sex with them. She always took care to research them prior to meeting and would wait until they met face to face before deciding how the night would end.

Moving back to the dressing table, she used the mirror to ensure the long wig sat securely in place. She took care to ensure her clients never guessed she concealed most of herself beneath heavy makeup and a wig. While she enjoyed pretending to be someone other than a surgeon and the daughter of a wealthy mogul, neither did she want to be recognized. It wouldn't do if her little secret got out.

She was the daughter of Henry Craigdon, property developer extraordinaire and highly respected businessman. She also had four brothers who would have been appalled to learn of her secret life. She could do without the scrutiny and the judgement. She knew they'd disapprove. Just like her father would have done.

Fortunately, Henry had gone to his grave none the wiser about the way his little girl often spent her nights. Though she wasn't ashamed of how she chose to spend her leisure time, neither did she wish to hurt the people she loved.

The truth was, she missed her father. She'd been closer to him than any of his six children. Seven, counting her half-brother Christopher Barrington. She was glad he hadn't discovered her secret life. Still, even knowing how he would have disapproved hadn't been enough for her to stop.

Perversely it had been her father's flagrant philandering

and her mother's apparent acceptance of it that had set Isabella on her rebellious path. She was self aware enough to recognize why she'd started. But it had become addictive.

She liked the thrill of living life on the edge and the glowing warmth and admiration in the eyes of her clients was always good for her ego. She liked the feeling of power that came with being in control, granting them the favor of her presence, or even a kiss. Sometimes they got to have her all night, but it was always on her terms. No matter how much money had changed hands, her agency made it clear to her clients she was the one who called the shots. She'd never experienced that kind of power and control. It was a heady feeling, intoxicating. It was what made it so hard to stop.

The knowledge of her parents' outrage if they knew her secret was also tantalizing despite the fact she'd never tell. After all, she was good at keeping secrets.

Applying a final coat of clear gloss over her ruby-red lips, she sprayed herself with perfume and then smiled at her reflection. She was pleased with what she saw. Gone were her trademark blond tresses. Instead, her eyes looked even greener against the dark red of her wig.

Turning to the side, she smoothed her hands over the black cocktail dress with the beaded bodice that fit her like a glove. The glass beads sparkled under the overhead lights. Satisfied, she bent and slipped her feet into a pair of black stilettos. She collected her evening bag containing the essentials off her bed and tossed in the tube of gloss.

Finally, she picked up her phone from the dresser and took a selfie. It was important she record the persona she used for this client. She'd learned early to keep a record so that she didn't get the characters she played mixed up, especially when it came to her regulars.

Harold like brunettes. Jimmy liked short black hair. Russell preferred blondes. Jeremy liked curls. They were all different and she always aimed to please. It was one of the reasons they kept coming back.

Satisfied with the selfie, she tossed her phone into her evening bag. She closed the clasp with a snap. Giving herself a final once-over in the mirror, she headed for the door.

Raine Fairfax took another sip from his beer and silently surveyed the room. The two-story Circular Quay restaurant boasted a magnificent view of Sydney Harbour that looked its glittering best on this balmy August evening. He'd arrived just ahead of the appointed time and was already seated at a table.

Though the night was still early, the place teemed with patrons. Despite the number of people, the conversation was muted. This wasn't the kind of place for robustness. Subtle music came from a young Japanese pianist seated at a baby grand.

Raine glanced at his watch and did his best to stem his impatience. His date was only a couple of minutes late. Nothing in the scheme of things. Especially if she'd had to battle the Friday night traffic. Still, he prided himself on his punctuality and demanded the same kind of attention from his work colleagues and friends. Even his dates weren't excluded.

As the CEO of a Fortune 500 company, Raine knew the value of his time. He also had regard for others. He'd flown into Sydney from Brisbane only a couple of hours earlier. He had important meetings in the morning. He thought he'd take the evening to relax and unwind and there was nothing like the company of a beautiful, anonymous woman to make that happen.

He liked the freedom and ease of using an escort agency to supply him with the companionship he needed, especially when visiting interstate. He had nothing against commitment, but he didn't have the time required to put into a serious relationship and he preferred not to pick up his bedpartners on the fly.

The other problem was the publicity. Everyone carried a phone. Almost as many people wanted their five seconds of fame. If a woman he took home recognized him, he took the risk that their romantic encounter might end up doing the rounds of the Internet. So far he'd been lucky, but there was always the chance his luck would run out.

The escort agency prided itself on the wit and beauty of the women it employed and had assured him of the utmost discretion. This was the first time he'd used this agency and he hoped his faith in the promises made wasn't misplaced.

A movement at the front of the restaurant caught his attention and he looked across in time to see a stunning redhead walk up to the maitre'd. He was too far away to hear their conversation, but he saw the man nod toward the woman and then turn and head in his direction. Raine's gut clenched in anticipation. *Was this beauty his date....?*

As she followed the maitre'd to his table, Raine took the time to catalogue her features. Tall and slim and busty, she was curvy in all the right places. She wore a tight-fitting black dress that ended high on her thighs. The overhead lights caught the beadwork on her dress. They sparkled like diamonds, holding him entranced. They matched the sparkles on her purse, clutched in a slender hand. If pressed, he would have admitted to a weakness for leggy blondes, but this woman with the fiery hair and lipstick was one of the most beautiful women he'd ever seen.

The maitre'd came to a halt at his table and acknowledged Raine with the slightest inclination of his head. As the waiter pulled out the chair for Raine's date, he saw the gleam of admiration and the faintest hint of envy in the other man's gaze.

Raine dismissed the man with a brief nod and then turned his attention to the woman seated across from him.

"Good evening. I'm Raine Fairfax. Thank you for meeting me for dinner."

The woman regarded him with a lazy smile. Her sultry air of confidence made his heart race. Blood rushed to his groin, hardening his cock. He cleared his throat and shifted in his seat. The way they were going, he might not make it through dinner. She'd dressed up in her finery for him. Feeding her was the least he could do.

And then she reached out toward him, offering her hand. "I'm Chloe. It's nice to meet you."

He shook her hand and tried not to notice the softness of her skin. As if sensing his reaction, she shot him a knowing grin. It annoyed him that he was so transparent, but no doubt she was used to men reacting like that. Not only her clients, but any man.

Their waiter appeared and took their drinks order. Raine ordered another beer. He looked across at Chloe.

"What are you drinking?"

"I'll have a glass of Shiraz."

"Let's get a bottle," Raine suggested, scanning the wine list. He gave his selection to the waiter who promised to return soon.

"So, Raine. What brings you to town?" she asked.

"Business. I have a couple of meetings in the morning."

"I understand you invest in resources. Tell me about it. It sounds fascinating."

He blinked in surprise. He hadn't expected her to know anything about him. It refreshing that his dinner companion had taken the time to get to know him, or at least what he was about.

"Yes, that's correct. I'm always on the lookout for a good deal. Mostly oil and gas and iron ore, but I've recently taken an interest in coal."

Her perfectly groomed eyebrows rose in surprise. "Coal? I thought coal was on the way out."

He laughed. "Don't believe everything you hear. The fact is, until we have a viable alternative, coal is here to stay."

"What's your position on nuclear? Surely it's time for this country to reverse the ban and enter into open and frank discussions about the use of nuclear energy? After all, it's the cleanest energy there is."

Once again she'd surprised him. Keen intelligence shone from her green eyes. Not only was she beautiful, she was smarter than his average date.

"You're right," he agreed. "I'm all for nuclear energy. We have the largest uranium deposits in the world. Why aren't we using them?"

She smiled and there was a grudging admiration in her eyes. Perhaps he'd surprised her, too?

"The cost of infrastructure has always been a deterrent to governments, hasn't it?" she asked,

Once again, he was impressed. "Of course, but we need to start somewhere."

"Does this mean you're looking to invest in uranium mining?" she asked.

He shrugged. "It's definitely on my radar. I think nuclear energy is the way of our future."

The waiter arrived with their drinks. Raine sampled the bottle of wine and gave it his approval. The waiter filled Chloe's glass and handed Raine another beer before stepping slightly back.

"Are you ready to order?" the waiter asked.

Raine looked at Chloe. She laughed apologetically and shook her head. The infectious sound of it was pleasant on his ears and made him want to smile.

"I haven't had a chance to look at the menu," she said.

Raine turned to the waiter. "Could you please give us a few more minutes?"

"Of course," he agreed and moved quietly away.

Raine watched Chloe study the menu. Her expression turned somber. A slight frown marred the smooth skin of her forehead. He chuckled at the look of concentration on her face.

"Something wrong?" he asked.

She glanced up at him. "No. Just trying to decide between the pan seared sirloin with mashed potato and asparagus in a red wine jus or the skillet fried chicken breast with mushrooms, steamed green beans and avocado."

He smiled in surprise. "I like a woman with a healthy appetite."

She looked up and grinned. "You bet. I hope you have a healthy limit on your credit card. This isn't going to be cheap."

He gave her a lazy grin. She was like no other woman he'd ever dated. She intrigued him, she interested him, he wanted to get to know her better. "I thought the five thousand dollars I put up for your company tonight might have convinced you I don't do things on the cheap."

Her eyes flared with an indefinable emotion. His gut somersaulted on a surge of desire. When her tongue stole out and traced the outline of her lips, his cock rose in response. And then she looked him directly in the face, her expression bold and sassy.

"From the moment I saw you I knew I was in for a memorable night."

For Raine, the rest of the meal passed in a haze of sexual desire. They traded quips, heavy with innuendo. Desire-fueled lingering looks and light touches heightened his senses to the point where staying in control was becoming an increasing battle. He wanted to fuck her madly. After paying the bill, he guided

Chloe out of the restaurant with his arm casually around her waist, noting again the envy on the waiter's face.

Once outside the restaurant, he steered her in the direction of his hotel.

"Where are we going?" she asked.

He tightened his grip around her waist and pulled her in close against him. "Back to my room for a nightcap."

The slow and sexy smile she gave him in response stole his breath. His heart somersaulted and then took off at a rush. The erection he'd nursed all evening hardened almost painfully. He lengthened his stride. To his relief, she did the same. His hotel room seemed an impossible distance away.

"I take it we're in a hurry," she murmured, nuzzling the side of his neck.

"Oh, yeah, baby. We're in a hurry all right. Lucky for us, my hotel is right around the corner."

He made it right to the double front doors of the hotel before his control snapped. Taking her into his arms, he kissed her. The feel of her luscious lips against his was like nothing he'd ever experienced. He pressed his tongue against their seam, seeking entry and she opened her mouth and obliged.

His tongue swept inside and met hers. They sparred and tangled and tasted. Pressed hard against him, her breasts crushed against his chest, his blood pumped wildly with desire. It felt like any moment he might disgrace himself. He needed to get upstairs and fast.

Breaking off the kiss, he took her hand and half-dragged her into the hotel. She tripped in her high heels and almost fell on the top steps and then laughed exuberantly when he caught her in his arms. Holding her close against him, they made their way over to the lifts. He released her only long enough to press the "up" button and then pulled her in close again. She leaned her head on his shoulder and he realized with a start he liked the feel of it there. He didn't usually feel so comfortable with a woman he'd paid to be by his side and he'd never gone for clingy.

He enjoyed the company of beautiful women and was happy to pay for that companionship when he was away from home. He preferred to dine out in company than dine alone. The same went for the comfortable bed he'd paid for. It was way better to share it with a desirable woman than to spend the night on his own.

Especially a woman like Chloe.

The *ding* of the lift snagged his attention and as soon as the doors slid open, he led Chloe inside. He touched the sensor pad with his room card and selected his floor. The lift whisked them upwards and in a matter of seconds, he'd ushered her into the corridor and into his room.

The door hadn't even closed behind them when she stepped into his arms. Her hands came up and clasped behind his neck. Her lips unerringly found his. Her kiss was every bit as passionate as it had been outside the hotel. With his hands on either side of her hips, he held her tightly against him. His erection raged. It was all he could do not to tear off her clothes and bury himself inside her. From the urgency behind her kisses, it seemed she felt the same.

And then she reached back and undid her zipper and shimmied out of her dress. He stared at the sight of her standing before him in nothing more than black, sheer lace underwear.

Chapter Two

Isabella stood tall and proud and almost naked before Raine. She'd been blessed with an enviable figure and was confident in her own skin. Many men before Raine had looked at her with the same kind of heated desire, their cheeks flushed with need, but this was the first time she felt something more than mere physical attraction toward the man she was about to sleep with.

She hadn't expected Raine Fairfax to be quite so engaging. His easy wit, intelligence and ability to appear interested in her opinions was refreshing. Then there was his physical appearance. The images she'd found online hadn't done him justice. No picture could capture the essence of his humor and the sparkle of amusement that often filled his eyes. Their deep blue color was mesmerizing and reminded her of the waters of Sydney Harbour—expressive and dark with hidden depths she wanted to discover.

Her reaction to him was foreign. During her work as an escort, she'd spent the night with only a select handful of her clients and had walked away from each encounter feeling satisfied, but this was different. Raine was different. *She* felt different. He intrigued her. He made her curious. She wanted to know more about him and that was bad.

Sometimes she only saw a client for one night. She had a few regulars who always looked her up when they were in town on business, but the majority of her clients were in the "occasional hookups" category. And that was fine with her. She was in it for the thrill. She wasn't looking for a boyfriend and nor were her clients looking for anything more.

For two years, she'd tried her best to be someone's girlfriend. It hadn't worked out. Luke was cute and funny and smart. Like her, he was a busy surgeon. But the spark between them had fizzled long before she'd expected. It had taken her another six months of trying even harder to make things work before she'd finally called it quits.

Her decision had also been helped along by the fact Luke wanted to settle down and have children. His need to take their relationship to a more permanent level of commitment had given her the impetus she needed to break things off. It had been difficult and emotional, mainly for him, but she'd never regretted her decision. She wasn't the marrying kind.

"God, you're sexy."

The husky words snapped her out of her reverie. She smiled and moved closer, reaching out toward him. With slow and deliberate movements, her fingers slid his silk tie from its knot. Without taking her eyes off him, she tossed it to the floor. Then she started on the buttons of his fine linen shirt. She could feel the quality of the fabric beneath her fingers. She'd expect nothing but the finest from the CEO of a Fortune 500 company.

Releasing the last button, she spread the shirt wide. He wore a white singlet against his skin. She tugged at the hem and pulled it loose from his suit pants. She slipped her hands beneath the singlet and scraped her nails against the warmth of his skin.

Just as she imagined, he was all hard muscle. His belly was flat and taut. Her fingers walked higher until she found his nipples. They were hard little nubs of excitement. With her gaze still on his, she lightly pinched them, enjoying his quick intake of breath. She flattened her hands against his pectorals, relishing the feel of hard muscle against her skin.

He moved as if to pull off his shirt, but she stopped him. "Uh, uh. All in good time. There's no rush. I'm all yours for the night."

His breathing quickened. Desire darkened his eyes. Slowly, deliberately, she pushed the shirt off his shoulders and then pulled it off his body. The singlet came next. She eased it over his head, making sure the fabric scraped across his sensitive nipples. She heard his little hiss of breath and smiled.

"Nice?" she asked.

He nodded, his gaze fixed on hers. "Nice."

With his naked chest now exposed to her gaze, she took her time looking her fill. He was perfectly formed with a broad, muscular chest and a washboard stomach. The lightest sprinkling of brown hair covered his pectorals and a fine line of hair snaked from below his belly button and disappeared inside his pants. Heat exploded inside her at the thought of what was to come. He was a fine specimen of a man. There was no doubt about that.

Unable to stop herself from touching him, she reached out and flattened her palm against his chest. His heart thumped beneath her hand. She slid her palm lower, slowly inching toward his pants.

His belt momentarily stopped her progress. He tried to brush her hands aside, intent on removing the obstacle himself, but she was having none of it.

"Uh, uh. Hands by your side. I don't need your help."

With quiet efficiency, she pulled the belt from its loops and dropped it to the floor. Next came the button and zipper on his pants. Releasing both, he pushed his pants down over his hips, taking his underwear with it.

His cock sprang up out of a dark nest of curls, thick and hard and glistening. Another wave of heat centered in her core. Without conscious thought, she licked her lips in anticipation. She couldn't wait to taste him.

He moved toward her, but once again she put him off. Dropping to her knees in front of him, she fitted her hand around his impressive shaft and took him in her mouth. His groan of pleasure mirrored hers. She opened her mouth wide, to take as much of him as she could. Her tongue stroked and teased. With her other hand, she reached between his legs and cupped his balls. They were full and tight.

Running her tongue along the length of his shaft, she then swirled it across his tip. She tasted the evidence of his desire and grinned. He wasn't the only one desperate for release. Taking him once again in her mouth, she sucked in rhythmic pressure, her other hand keeping a hold on his balls. He groaned again.

"I'm gonna come if you keep that up."

She turned her face up toward him and grinned. "You're paying. Do whatever you like."

With a muffled curse, he pulled her to her feet. He reached around behind her and undid the clasp on her bra. Her breasts sprang free. His gaze zeroed in on her nipples, hard and puckered with need.

"God, you're so beautiful," he muttered and then bent his head to one of her breasts.

His breath was hot on her skin. The tug of his teeth on her sensitive flesh sent a spiral of desire ricocheting through her and centering between her legs. He kneaded her other breast with his hand and then his fingers stole down lower.

Dipping under the waistband of her lacy underwear, his fingers slipped over her mound and then caressed her slit. She was already dripping with need.

"You're so wet."

"I've been wanting to fuck you all night," she replied.

He growled low in his throat. Without warning, he slipped two fingers roughly inside her. She gasped. Another wave of hot need swept through her.

"You like that?" he asked.

She stared into his eyes that glittered with desire. "Yes. I like that very much."

He smiled lazily. "I thought you might."

With that, he reached for her panties and pulled them down her hips. She stepped out of them and then turned her back on him and bent over to undo the strap of her stilettos. His finger traced the seam of her buttocks before slapping her lightly on one cheek. She jumped and he laughed. A moment later, he scooped her up in his arms and deposited her on the wide bed. He picked up his pants and withdrew his wallet and pulled out a condom. Sheathing himself, he returned to the bed.

The drapes were closed and the only light came from a lamp that stood on the bedside table. It bathed them both in a yellow glow, increasing the intimacy of the moment. He followed her down and covered her body with his before kissing her deeply once again.

His erection was a hard brand against her thigh. She moved restlessly against him, wanting him inside her. With her breasts full and heavy with need and a fire raging between her thighs, she rolled until she straddled him.

He laughed. "You're a confident one. I'll give you that."

She gave him a nonchalant shrug. "I know what I want. It's as simple as that."

He regarded her from half-closed lids. "And what do you want?"

"I want this." With that, she impaled herself on his cock.

They both gasped from the impact. His cock was hard and thick and stretched her inner muscles. She lifted her hips until just the tip of his shaft was inside her and then pushed herself down again. Over and over she rode him until her need built to fever pitch.

She glanced down at him. His hands held her hips fast. His eyes were closed. A frown of concentration marred the smooth skin of his forehead. And then he rolled them over, keeping them joined, until he was bent over her, a look of satisfaction on his face.

"My turn," he said.

His thrusts became more urgent. His frown turned darker. She clung to his shoulders, loving the feel of him inside her. She was almost at the peak. And then on a guttural groan he climaxed and it was enough to send her over the edge. He cried out and so did she. He collapsed against her, breathing hard. It was a long time later before both of them had caught their breath. As if only just becoming aware of his weight on her, he rolled off her with a muttered apology and lay on his back. Isabella took a moment to collect her thoughts.

Not only was he smart and funny, he was also a superb lover. She felt a twinge of disappointment that she might not see him again. That was usually the way these things worked. She decided to sound him out.

"So, do you come to Sydney often?"

He threw her a lazy glance. A smile tugged at his lips. "No. But maybe I need to change that?"

His words gave her a jolt of excitement. "Any reason in particular?"

"Well, we've just fucked almost to the point of exhaustion and yet I want to fuck you again. It's not usually that way with me. What I do know is that I'd like to see you again. Is that okay with you?"

She grinned. "How long are you in town?"

"Longer than I expected. I'll call my office in the morning and reschedule my appointments for the rest of the week. How does that sound?"

Her grin widened. She reached out and scraped her fingernails across his chest. "That sounds pretty darn good to me."

Raine chuckled and drew her to him. They came together, limbs entwined, in another passionate kiss.

Isabella approached the patient in the bed and smiled. "Good morning, Mr Whitehouse. How are you feeling?"

The elderly man attempted a smile, but it came out looking more like a grimace. "Better than I was yesterday."

"That's good to hear. You gave your wife a scare when you fell off that roof." She glanced at the woman seated beside the bed.

"You sure did," his wife answered with a shudder. "When I looked out the kitchen window and saw you on the ground, I was sure you were dead."

Isabella's patient offered another strained smile. "I thought I was dead, too," he replied. "Only that it hurt so much I knew I wasn't on the way up to heaven."

"Well, you're on the mend, now," Isabella soothed. "Although you're going to be sore for awhile. You ruptured your spleen and broke a couple of ribs. Fortunately, there was no damage to any of your other internal organs. All I can recommend now is regular pain medication and rest. Using a score from one to ten, with one being next to no pain and ten being unbearable, how is the pain right now?"

"It's about a six," the patient responded.

Isabella checked the chart that hung from the end of the man's bed. "It looks like you're due for some more pain killers within the hour. Can you hold on until then?"

"Yes, Doctor. I can wait that long."

"Good. Is there anything else you need?"

"No," he replied. "But I want to thank you for what you did. When I fell off that roof, I thought I was a gonna for sure."

She smiled. "There's no need for thanks. I'm just glad you're okay."

The man's elderly wife reached out and took Isabella's hand. "Thank you for everything, Doctor. I mean it. When I think about how far Keith fell, it could have been so much worse."

Isabella shot Keith a smile. "Well, you take care, Mr Whitehouse. And no more climbing on the roof. Leave that to the experts."

He had the grace to look embarrassed. She turned and headed for the door. "I'll call in and see you again this evening. If you need anything, don't hesitate to call the nurse."

She left to another chorus of thank yous and closed the door quietly behind her. Checking her patient list, she headed for the next room. Charlie McDermott was young and good looking with a cheeky look in his eyes. He was a laborer on a building site and had slipped with a band saw. He'd sliced a decent chunk out of his left arm, cutting through ligaments, tendons and bone. She'd assisted in the surgery, along with doctors who specialized in orthopedics and plastics. Despite the pain he was no doubt in, he greeted her with a cheery smile.

"Hi, Doc. It's good to see you."

"And you, too Charlie. How's the arm this morning?"

He lifted the arm in question. It was stabilized by a splint and covered in bandages. A plaster cast wouldn't be applied until after the swelling went down.

"It feels pretty good, considering."

She smiled. "Yeah, you did a pretty good job of trying to get rid of it."

He grinned. "Well, I am right-handed. I must have thought I didn't need the left one."

She laughed and shook her head. At the same time, she reached for his chart on the end of the bed. She checked over the entries for his vital signs, including the administration of his pain medication. Everything looked in order.

"How's the pain this morning?" she asked.

"Probably a three," he replied.

"That's good. I've charted plenty of pain meds. Don't forget to let the nurses know if you need something."

"Thanks, Doc. Listen, when do you think I can get out of here?"

She frowned. "Charlie, you were only operated on yesterday. You're going to be in here at least a couple more days, depending on how things go. Is there someplace you need to be?"

He looked chagrinned. "Yeah, you could say that."

She looked at him with a raised eyebrow. He blushed. "I'm supposed to be getting married on Saturday."

She closed her eyes briefly and shook her head. "Oh, Charlie!"

"Yeah," he continued, embarrassed. "My fiancé's going ape at the thought I might not make it to the wedding. She's been planning this all year. We're going to lose a shitload of money if I don't show."

Isabella regarded him sympathetically. "I'm sorry, Charlie. I really am. But you've suffered a serious injury. Apart from the pain, there's always a risk of infection. I can't promise you'll be out of here in time to make the wedding.

His shoulders slumped in disappointment. The look on his face tugged at Isabella's heart. She wasn't at all interested in marriage herself, but that didn't mean she didn't understand its importance for others. After all, her oldest brother, Jett had been happily married for years and two of her other brothers had recently found the love of their lives. Not everyone felt as jaded about love and marriage as she did.

"Let's see how it goes, Charlie. We have two more days before Saturday. You never know. You might surprise us all and be well enough to leave by then."

His expression immediately brightened. She urged him to keep on top of his pain with regular doses of medication and told him she'd be back to see him later that afternoon. As the door to his room closed behind her, she couldn't help but think about Raine.

She'd left him in the early hours of the next morning, sleeping off another enthusiastic bout of sex. She'd been tired, but strangely full of anticipation at the thought of seeing him again. She'd never felt that way before. Not even with Luke. And definitely not with a client. Though she had a few regulars and a handful of other men she chose to see every now and then, none of them filled her with this strange sense of excitement and nervousness. She was eager to see him again. He'd rearranged his schedule to stay in Sydney for the rest of the week.

Of course, it had also meant she'd had to juggle a couple of her shifts. Raine knew nothing of her day job and that's the way it would stay. It was one thing to enjoy the company of handsome strangers, but there was no way she'd let her hobby cross over into her real life. The woman Raine had met was a fantasy. She didn't exist in real life. She was a fun character Isabella liked to play. Chloe, the sexy redhead. Nothing more.

Still, it would be fun while it lasted. Raine was here for a few more days. He was smart and sexy and entertaining. He knew how to drive her wild. Isabella was determined to make the most of it.

Chapter Three

Raine tried to concentrate on the presentation being delivered by two senior executives of a reputable coal seam gas mining exploration company. Hoffmans Mining was a company he'd been watching for some time with a view to investing and he'd flown down to Sydney for the express purpose of hearing their proposal. The information they'd presented so far had been riveting, but Raine had barely been able to keep his mind from wandering.

Of course, his lack of focus had everything to do with the woman he'd met two nights earlier. She'd been incredible. Not only in bed, although the sex had been sensational, but also over dinner. She'd been interesting, engaging and enthusiastic. Her insights had shown a keen intelligence. No doubt she'd researched his background in order to flatter him, but the strange thing was, it had worked. He couldn't wait to see her again.

Unable to wait another minute, he abruptly excused himself and left the boardroom. The executive stopped mid-sentence, staring after him in surprise, but he was already out the door. As soon as he was out of earshot, he pulled out his phone and dialed the number of Chloe's escort agency. To his disappointment, the call went through to voicemail. He almost hung up, but then decided to leave a message.

"It's Raine Fairfax. I'd like to see Chloe tonight. Please have her call me."

With that, he ended the call and feeling less than satisfied, forced himself to return to the boardroom.

The prepaid mobile phone Isabella used for her escort work buzzed in the pocket of her lab coat, indicating an incoming call. Checking there was no one in hearing range, she pulled out the phone and answered it.

"Hello?"

"Isabella, it's Melody."

"Hi," Isabella responded to the woman who owned the escort agency.

"Listen, I've had a call from Harold Rodenstock. He wants to see you."

Isabella smiled. Harold was one of her regulars. She'd been spending time with him on and off ever since she'd moved back to Sydney. It had been a month since she'd seen him last. The thought had actually occurred to her that he might have been unwell, or worse. After all, he was in his seventies.

"Of course," she now responded. "Harold's a sweetie. When does he want to meet?"

"Tonight. Are you free?"

Isabella thought briefly of Raine. He'd told her he was in town for the next few days, but she hadn't heard from him. Perhaps he'd changed his mind? Oh, well. That was his loss. There were plenty of other men out there who sought her company. Men like Harold.

"Yes," she said. "I'm free. Tell him I'll meet him at seven."

"He wants to go to dinner at Antonio's and then to a show at the State Theater. Are you okay with that?"

"Of course."

"Great. I'll let him know right away. Have a good night."

Isabella ended the call and dropped the phone back in her pocket. She still had a couple of more patients to see before she finished her ward round. She was also due in the operating theater by eleven. She needed to put thoughts of Raine Fairfax out of her mind and get on with her work.

With that in mind, she turned and headed toward the bank of lifts at the end of the corridor. Her remaining two patients were on the ward above her. She pressed the "up" button and waited. Then the phone in her pocket buzzed again.

She checked the screen. It was the escort agency. "Hi, Melody. Did you forget something?"

"No. Sorry, Chloe. I just checked my messages. The call must have come in while I was on the phone to you earlier. It's a message from Raine Fairfax. The man you met with the other night."

Images of the two of them rolling around on his hotel bed immediately bombarded her. With an effort, she kept her voice casual. "I remember him."

"Well, it seems he wants to see you again. Tonight, in fact."

"But—"

"Yes. And I've already confirmed the booking with Harold. He's beyond excited. He's really looking forward to seeing you again."

Isabella bit her lip. As much as she wanted to see Raine again, she'd already made a commitment to Harold and even though the night wouldn't end in sex, she didn't want to let him down.

"It's all right. Tell Raine I can't meet him for dinner, but I might be able to meet him for a drink after I've finished with Harold. What time does the show end?"

"I think he said it would be over by ten."

"Good. Tell Raine I can meet him at half-past ten in the city."

"Okay, will do. If he's happy to do that, I'll text you the details."

"Thanks, Melody."

Once again, Isabella ended the call and dropped the phone into the pocket of her lab coat. She had an early shift the next morning. She'd better not be up too late with Raine. Her job as a surgeon in the busy Sydney Harbour hospital was demanding. She needed to be on top of her game. She never knew when she'd be called in to assist during an emergency surgery and she wouldn't jeopardize the health of her patients by pulling an all-nighter, no matter how tempting the man was.

Isabella had finished up with her final patient when her phone beeped, indicating an incoming text. She pulled the phone out of her pocket and checked the screen.

Drinks at the Marble Bar at 10.30pm. Have fun! Melody

Despite herself, Isabella's heart leaped in anticipation. The Marble Bar was situated inside the same building that housed the Hilton Hotel. Two nights ago, Raine had been staying in a hotel down near Circular Quay. Had he switched hotels, or did he have a fondness for the Marble Bar?

Isabella could understand its attraction. Dimly lit and with an elegance and sophistication not found in many of the bars in the city, it was a place favored by older professionals who wanted to get away from the noise and rambunctiousness of a younger crowd. Not that Raine was old. In fact, he didn't look much older than she was. But if she was honest, she preferred the quieter, more sophisticated drinking establishments. She looked forward to their meeting.

But first she had to get through a day in the operating theater and then dinner and a show with Harold. He was such a sweetie. He treated her like a favored granddaughter rather than a companion he'd paid for the night. He'd made it quite clear at the outset he wasn't looking for sex and she'd been relieved about that. She refused to sleep with clients she didn't find attractive and as much as she had a healthy libido, it didn't stretch to sleeping with men old enough to be her grandfather.

Raine took a sip from his latté and stared out at the wide expanse of Sydney Harbour. Seated at an outdoor table at one of a number of cafés that lined the wharf on Circular Quay, he took the time to enjoy the cloudless blue sky and warm, late winter sunshine. Seagulls and pigeons squawked around his feet, moving in and around the tables, fighting over scraps. He was tempted to throw them a bit of his blueberry muffin, but there were signs everyone advising patrons not to feed the birds.

He hadn't expected to have this extra time in Sydney. In fact, he should already be on a plane. His plan had been to meet with the mining company and look over their prospectus and then head straight back home to Brisbane. But then he hadn't factored in his reaction to Chloe. His plans were awry.

He didn't want to leave without seeing her again, at least once. He needed to satisfy himself that his initial reaction had been a one-off. After all, it had been a few weeks since he'd had sex. Surely she couldn't possibly affect him to the same extent a second time. For his own sanity, he needed to meet with her again and reassure himself she was just another woman—albeit a beautiful one.

His phone beeped indicating a new text. Pulling it out of his pocket, he checked the screen. Despite himself, his heart jumped in anticipation. The text was from the escort agency confirming his upcoming meeting with Chloe. *Half-past ten at the Marble Bar.* He would have preferred they meet earlier for dinner, but apparently Chloe had a previous engagement. The thought of her meeting with another client filled him with an unfamiliar feeling—and irrational surge of jealousy.

His reaction came as a surprise. He barely knew the

woman. And right from the outset he'd known she was an escort. He'd paid to spend time with her, just like her other clients. Still, even knowing the reality of how she chose to make a living and that they'd never have met if she wasn't an escort didn't make him feel better. He wondered how much it would cost to have her all to himself.

How long would it take for him to tire of her? A week? A month? Six months? It was hard to tell. He'd never been in a serious relationship. Not because he had a phobia about commitment. It was merely that he'd spent much of his twenties working ninety-hour weeks building his business. A business he'd started from scratch and was immensely proud of.

He'd had the odd girlfriend over the years, but nothing serious. It was why he preferred to avail himself of escort services. Everyone knew where they stood. Raine got to spend time in the company of a beautiful woman and the woman was well paid. There were no expectations of any kind of relationship developing and no feelings to be taken into account. It was a mutually beneficial business arrangement. Nothing more, nothing less.

That's how it was meant to be with Chloe. Raine had researched the agency before making contact with them. They had plenty of five star reviews. Encouraged, he'd requested a beautiful, lively and engaging companion for the evening.

She'd lived up to his expectations. In fact, she'd surpassed them. What was more, she could actually hold a decent conversation. And as for the sex… It was mind blowing. He wanted more. Much more. He recognized his infatuation. But how long would it last?

It was just that she'd surprised him, with her beauty and her brains. And yes, the amazing sex. Maybe it was because it had been three months since he'd been with a woman. Maybe the sex with Chloe was amazing because he hadn't had any in a while.

No, that wasn't fair. He'd had plenty of sex in his thirty years on the planet. The sex with Chloe had been better, wilder, more incredible than any previous experience. He was eager to repeat it.

He took another sip of his coffee. A wind had blown up, turning the waves into low whitecaps. The honk of a ferry startled him. He watched the large vessel approach the wharf as the captain negotiated the mooring. There was no room for error. The ferry docked smoothly against the wharf and the passengers began to alight. Raine silently admired the captain's skill.

Raine had been a rower back in high school. His team had made it to the nationals. He knew what it was like to pit himself against the water and the importance of fitness, stamina, courage and teamwork. They were skills that had held him in good stead in his business and helped him ensure he remained in good shape.

The sound of his phone ringing interrupted his musings. He pulled it out and checked the screen.

Brock.

"Hi, bro. How are you?" he asked.

"What's this I hear you're not coming back until tomorrow? You were meant to be back in the office today."

"Good morning to you, too," he responded dryly.

"Yeah, well. Good morning. I just spoke to Yvonne. She said you called to let her know you've been delayed."

Raine drew in a breath and eased it out. He and his brother had worked together almost from the start. Together they were Fairfax Investments. Raine trusted Brock with his business and with his life, but that didn't mean he had to explain every decision to Brock. Especially when the reason for his delay had nothing to do with business.

"Yes. Something's come up."

"I see. What's her name?"

Heat crept up Raine's neck. He should have known his brother would guess his change of plans had something to do with a woman.

He feigned confusion. "What the hell are you talking about?"

"Come on, Raine. You went down there for a meeting that should have been done and dusted within a few hours. I'll concede that you might have had to go back the next day to seek clarification, but by the time you get back to the office you'll have been away four days. You hate being away from the office. You haven't taken a vacation in years. Now you're suddenly caught up in Sydney for four days? I'm not buying it. Something else is going on."

Raine cast around for an excuse and came up with nothing. Trying to bullshit Brock was an exercise in futility. He and his brother were close. They knew each other better than anyone. No matter what excuse he gave Brock, his brother would sense it wasn't true.

"Okay, you're right," he conceded. "I've met someone."

"Hell, she must be pretty special for you to delay your trip home."

Raine thought of Chloe and smiled. "She's special enough. But nothing serious. I met her the night before last. We had dinner. I'm meeting her again tonight. That's it."

"You make it sound so casual," Brock commented. "But I'm not buying it. Raine Fairfax does not miss a day in the office for any woman, let alone one who means nothing."

"I didn't say she didn't mean anything," he protested. "Merely that she's just a woman I enjoyed spending time with and I'd like to see her again before I leave. Is that a crime?"

"Not at all, bro. You have me intrigued. I'd like to meet the woman who's managed to keep my brother from his work."

"Not a chance. In fact, after tonight we probably won't

see each other again." The thought filled Raine with disappointment. He was immediately annoyed by his reaction.

"Why do you say that? You're only a flight away."

"It's…complicated."

"I see. She's married."

"No! I mean, I don't think so. No, I'm sure she would have told me."

"Did you ask?"

"No, of course not. But—"

"Then how do you know?"

"If she was married, why would she have accepted an invitation out to dinner?"

"Oh, Raine. You've lived a sheltered life."

A surge of irritation went through him. "Fuck off, Brock. I know enough to know this woman isn't married. She isn't that kind of girl."

"What kind of girl is that?"

"Deceitful. Dishonest. She isn't like that."

"Okay, well, I believe you. After all, you're the one who's met her for dinner."

"Thank you. Don't forget, I'm a good judge of character."

"Yeah, yeah, yeah. Surely we don't need to go over this again?" Brock's tone was edged with exasperation.

"Hey, I'm not the one who thought their ex-girlfriend was a brain surgeon living in a spiffy apartment on the Brisbane River."

"That's not fair!" Brock protested. "How was I to know Cecilia was so full of shit? The sad thing was, I really liked her. Not for who she was or where she lived, but she seemed like such a nice person. I still don't know why she pretended she was someone she wasn't. As if I cared about what she did or what kind of apartment she owned."

"I guess she thought she wouldn't stand a chance with you if you'd known the truth," Raine said quietly.

"Am I really that shallow?"

Raine heard the hurt behind his brother's voice. He hurried to reassure him. "Of course not. But look at it from an outsider's point of view. You're a good-looking, successful, self-made millionaire. You're also one of the city's most eligible bachelors. You constantly show up in the social pages with a beautiful woman on your arm. Most women probably think they don't stand a chance with you. I can understand why Cecelia felt the need to fabricate a life that had nothing to do with the reality of who she was and what she did for a living. She wanted to impress you. I guess you ought to be flattered she went to so much trouble. I mean, using all of her savings to rent that riverside apartment for the few months you were together, getting a pager that she had friends message pretending to be from the hospital. Even leaving a white lab coat on the back seat of her car."

"Yeah, the Audi. That was rented, too."

Raine sighed. "Anyway, bro. Forget about it. Forget about her. There are plenty of other women out there. Not all of them lie and deceive to get what they want. I'm sure Chloe isn't like that."

Brock pounced. "*Chloe?*"

Raine cursed under his breath. He hadn't meant to reveal anything about his mystery woman, especially not to his brother. But there was nothing he could do about it now.

"Yes, her name is Chloe."

"Nice."

"Yes, she is. But like I said, it's nothing serious."

"So what do you have planned for tonight?" Brock teased. "Wining and dining in one of Sydney's finest restaurants and then some horizontal dancing on the sheets?"

Raine grimaced. "She's busy. We're meeting for drinks later tonight."

"Oh, drinks? Well, I guess it's better than nothing. She

sounds interesting, this Chloe. I mean, what kind of girl is too busy for the great Raine Fairfax?"

Raine tamped down his irritation. He was also a bit put out that Chloe hadn't been available for dinner. It seemed she wasn't as impressed with him as he'd been with her. Either that, or she was actually busy.

"Knock it off, Brock. You know I never use my position to get what I want."

"Maybe you should? You want Chloe, don't you?"

At Brock's words, the memory of his night with Chloe flooded Raine's mind. Her lips… The way she'd kissed him… The way she'd taken him in her mouth… And then afterwards… They'd exhausted themselves.

Tiring of the conversation, Raine brought it to an end. "Look, there's nothing more to say. I'll be in Sydney tonight and then back in the office tomorrow. See you then."

"Sure, bro. Whatever you say. Don't do anything I wouldn't do."

Raine ended the call to the sound of Brock's laughter. He tossed the phone down on the table and sighed.

ISABELLA is available for preorder at all of the digital retailers.
It will be released on 31 October, 2020.

About the Author

Chris Taylor grew up on a farm in north-west New South Wales, Australia. She always had a thirst for stories and recalls writing her first book at the ripe old age of eight. Always a lover of romance and happily-ever-afters, a career in criminal law sparked her interest in intrigue and suspense. For Chris to be able to combine romance with suspense in her books is a dream come true.

Chris is married to Linden and is the mother of five children. If not behind her computer, you can find her doing the school run, taxiing children to swimming lessons, football, ballet and cricket. In her spare time, Chris loves to read her favorite authors who include Richard North Patterson, Sandra Brown, Kathleen E Woodiwiss and Jude Devereaux.

You can find out more about Chris and sign up for her newsletter at her website:

http://www.christaylorauthor.com.au